Advance Praise for

THE INNOCENTS

"A gripping and credible page-turner about children surviving in the wilderness, but more than that: this Adam and Eve struggle to make sense of a world that's somewhere between Eden and Hell. Michael Crummey writes like an avenging angel, never putting a word wrong."
—Emma Donoghue, author of *Room*

"*The Innocents* is a dazzling and myriad achievement. Set against the unforgiving Newfoundland frontier, this harrowing tale of two siblings eking out a teetering existence is difficult to witness and impossible to put to down. But what makes this story timeless is Crummey's rich depiction of the human heart in extremis, the unflagging beat of life in a world that is too much to bear. Set aside whatever you're reading and pick this up—*The Innocents* is a masterpiece." —Smith Henderson, author of *Fourth of July Creek*

"*The Innocents* is a fantastic read. Written in graceful and evocative prose, Ada and Evered's story blurs the boundary between the quotidian and the strange until it becomes a meditation on the curious fact of existence itself. A wonderfully provocative and insightful book." —Kevin Powers, author of *The Yellow Birds*

"Few novels have cast their spell on me as deeply as *The Innocents*. I am reminded of Dickens, not just the nineteenth-century setting and the imperiled children, but the artfulness: brilliant plot, unforgettable minor characters, perfect pacing. Yet Michael Crummey's poetic voice and landscape are his own. *The Innocents* is brilliant." —Ron Rash, author of *Serena*

"Michael Crummey is a writer of enormous talent. . . . Crummey writes like an old pro, and, not so incidentally, also like an old soul, who has borne witness to tragic tendencies of humans for generations, and views them with awe and sadness and a clear-eyed compassion."
—*Ottawa Citizen*

"Crummey's powers of storytelling and evocation are considerable."
—*Vancouver Sun*

"Crummey forges unforgettable characters and fashions spectacular, riveting stories. . . . He reminds us our stories, rather than being an entertaining diversion, actually reveal to us who we are." —*Winnipeg Free Press*

"Crummey knows how to write, period." —*The Telegram* (St. John's)

"Michael Crummey's move to the forefront of contemporary Canadian literature has been swift. . . . Crummey is a master at weaving past and present, the particular and the universal. . . . Crummey examines themes that are too often reduced to black and white, with disastrous consequences. In contrast, he creates powerful fiction through multiple shades of grey that produce a shocking spectrum of colour." —*Guelph Mercury*

"[Crummey] skillfully capture[s] the unique feel and voices of Canada's rugged east coast." —*TIME*

"When you've found an author with the kind of power Crummey has, one of the first things to do is to head back to the bookstore looking for more." —*Atlantic Books Today*

The Innocents

A NOVEL

MICHAEL CRUMMEY

DOUBLEDAY CANADA

Doubleday Canada and colophon are registered trademarks of
Penguin Random House Canada Limited.

Library and Archives Canada Cataloguing in Publication

Title: The innocents : a novel / Michael Crummey.
Names: Crummey, Michael, 1965- author.
Identifiers: Canadiana (print) 20190051620 | Canadiana (ebook)
20190051639 | ISBN 9780385685412
(hardcover) | ISBN 9780385685429 (EPUB)
Classification: LCC PS8555.R84 I55 2019 | DDC C813/.54—dc23

This book is a work of fiction. Names, characters, places and incidents are
products of the author's imagination or are used fictitiously. Any resemblance
to actual events or locales or persons, living or dead, is entirely coincidental.

Jacket design by Emily Mahon
Jacket painting: Banded Gneiss, Hopedale, Labrador by Diana Dabinett

Printed and bound in Canada

Published in Canada by Doubleday Canada,
a division of Penguin Random House Canada Limited

www.penguinrandomhouse.ca

10 9 8 7 6 5 4 3 2 1

Penguin
Random House
DOUBLEDAY CANADA

for
Martha Kanya-Forstner

There are forty or fifty knots; less than twenty are in regular use. None has been invented at any known time, in any known place, by any known person. All are of immemorial antiquity.

R. G. COLLINGWOOD, *The New Leviathan*

THE INNOCENTS

The Driven Snow.

They were still youngsters that winter. They lost their baby sister before the first snowfall. Their mother laid the infant in a shallow trough beside the only other grave in the cove and she sang the lullaby she'd sung all her children to sleep with, which was as much as they had to offer of ceremony. The woman was deathly sick herself by then, coughing up clots of blood into her hands.

The ground was frozen solid when she died and even if their father had been well enough to shovel there was no digging a grave for her. He and Evered shifted the covering of reeds and alders away from the overturned boat and hauled it down to the landwash before they carried the corpse from the house. They set it in the boat along with half a dozen stones scavenged along the shore. Their father slumped against the gunwale to catch his breath.

"Will I come out with you?" Evered asked.

He shook his head. "You stay with your sister," he said.

The two youngsters watched him row away from shore and out beyond the shoal water with his dead wife. They saw him leaning below the gunwales for what seemed a long time, his head and shoulders bobbing up now and then. He was working at something awkward and unpleasant it seemed though neither could guess what it was. They watched him wrestling the weight of the corpse with his back to the shore. He was far enough off they couldn't see that their mother was naked when she was tipped into the black of the winter ocean.

Their father tried to hand the clothes to his daughter when he rowed in but Ada held her hands behind her back and shook her head fiercely.

"You'll have need of these," their father said. "Now the once."

Evered took them, folding the limp fabric against his stomach. The sour smell of a long illness and of his mother which he couldn't separate in his head. "I'll set them by for her," he said.

Their father nodded. He was too exhausted to climb from the boat and he sat there a long while. A dwy of snow had blown in across the bay and it turned the hair of his bowed head white as they waited.

Their father died in his bed before the new year.

Without speaking of it they acted as if he was only asleep and they left him lying there for the better part of a week. Hoping he might wake up coughing in the middle of the night, complaining about the cold or asking after a drink of water. During the day they dawdled about in the store and spent as much time outside as they could stand, cleaving and stacking wood or hauling buckets of water from the brook, picking along the landwash for gull feathers and mussel shells and wish rocks to add to Ada's collection. Inside they tended the fireplace and drank their bare-legged tea and spoke in whispers so as not to disturb the man.

On the fifth night of the vigil Ada woke from a dream of her parents. They were standing back on, holding hands and looking at her over their shoulders. Her mother was naked and soaking wet, her hair streaming water.

"What is it you're bawling over, Sister?" Evered asked.

"He can't stay," she whispered.

"Don't be talking foolishness."

"He can't stay there like that, Brother."

And he set to bawling with her then, the two helpless youngsters holding on to one another in the pitch.

Before it was properly light he pulled back the one ragged blanket and hauled his father's body to the floor. The heels smacking like mallets against the frozen ground. His sister moved to pick up her father's legs but Evered wouldn't allow it. The man of the house suddenly. "You sit there," he said. "Until I gets back."

He gripped the shoulders of his father's shirt. He expected it to feel like hauling a seine of fish but there was a rigidness to the corpse that made it surprisingly easy to drag through the doorway. Only once on the way down to the water was he forced to stop to catch his breath and shake the numbness from his hands.

He rowed out to the deeps beyond the shoal grounds, as close to the same spot as he could guess judging by his distance from the shore. Their parents might be together down there was his thought or within sight of one another at least, though he knew nothing below the ocean surface sat still for long. He tried to strip off the man's clothes for practical reasons but his father's eyes were half-open and he lost his nerve for meddling.

Before pushing off the beach he'd gathered a length of old netting and enough stones to keep the body under and he tied that improvised anchor around his father's waist. The day was still and cold, the ocean flat calm. He did not want to watch once the body slapped into the water and the rocks were hefted over the gunwale to take it down. But he couldn't make himself look away from that descent until long after his father had passed out of sight and into the black.

He stared out at the spot where the man sank from view as he rowed in through the skerries. His teeth chattering helplessly, his mind swimming. Even after the keel brought up in the shallows he kept rowing at the water like a headless chicken strutting around the chopping block. He didn't stop until Ada called his name behind him.

"I told you to wait where you was till I come back," he said, trying to set the oars and find his feet.

"I was watching for you heading in," she said.

He stumbled as he climbed over the gunwale, his face like chalk. "I needs to lie down for a bit," he said.

Ada did her best to haul the boat out of reach of the tide, calling after her brother as he staggered up the path to the tilt. By the time she came into the room he was already asleep in their bed. He slept so long and in such a stillness that Ada considered he might have died on her as well. She sat across the room until dark and then climbed into her parents' bed where she lay whispering to her dead sister to keep herself company.

Evered didn't wake until late the following morning. He sat bolt upright in the bed and seemed not to know where he was before he caught sight of her. She stared at him a long time without speaking.

"What is it, Sister?" he said.

She pointed then and he reached up to touch his crown.

"Your hair," she said.

She thought of their father's bowed head in the boat after he had committed their mother to the ocean's deep, the drift that had settled on it like a veil.

"What about me hair?"

"It's gone all white," she said.

As the driven snow, their mother would have said of it.

They were left together in the cove then with its dirt-floored stud tilt, with its garden of root vegetables and its scatter of outbuildings, with its looming circle of hills and rattling brook and its view of the ocean's grey expanse beyond the harbour skerries. The cove was the heart and sum of all creation in their eyes and they were alone there with the little knowledge of the world passed on haphazard and gleaned by chance.

—The ocean and the firmament and the sum of God's
  stars were created in seven days.
—Sun hounds prophesy coarse weather.
—The death of a horse is the life of a crow.
—You were never to sleep before the fire was douted.
—The winter's flour and salt pork had to last till the
  first seals came in on the ice in March month.
—The dead reside in heaven and heaven sits among the
  stars.

—Nothing below the ocean's surface lies still.

—Idleness is the root of all troubles.

—Their baby sister died an innocent and sits at God's right hand and hears their prayers.

—Any creature on the earth or in the sea could be killed and eaten.

—A body must bear what can't be helped.

Mary Oram. Her Utensils.

For weeks after their father died the youngsters did little but sleep, lying in bed all hours for the warmth, for the comfort of the other's breathing beside them. The days were short and the one glassless window was shuttered against the weather and their time passed in cold twilight and bottomless dark.

Every day Evered put in a fire after the sun was up. Once it had taken off the sharpest edge of the cold he lifted Ada out of bed as he did when she was but a piss-ass maid of two or three, sitting her on the slop pail and standing close enough she could lean shivering against his leg. She wasn't far off his height but thin as the rames, still a child in every respect but for her hands which had been put to adult work years since and looked like the asperous hands of a crone. She clutched a doll she'd made of rags for their baby sister and clung to now as a relic of a blessed time irrevocably lost. She leaned her head against her brother's thigh until she was done, then he carried her back to bed where they held one another against the smothering silence.

Neither child had an appetite to speak of or the heart to make a proper meal. Evered each day rewarmed a scurfy pot of pea soup and offered a bowl to Ada but he couldn't convince her to eat it. She subsisted solely on cakes of hardtack that she gnawed to a paste as she lay in bed. They barely spoke. Evered sometimes woke in the dark to the sound of Ada whispering aloud but he was never able to decipher what she was saying or to who and he was afraid to ask.

He ventured outside to empty the slops or haul up water from the brook or to split an armful of firewood. The woodpile closest to the tilt diminished steadily and he felt something in him waning at the same irremediable pace. He was lightheaded and unsteady from lack of food and lying in bed for so long and from a pooling sense of dread he could not shake. It sent him looking for his father's flintlock, a rifle he'd never loaded or fired and had been sitting so long unused in the store that the iron works shone with rust. He set the derelict weapon in a corner near the hearth as if its presence alone might offer some protection or comfort.

He stoked up the fire before he crawled back into bed, Ada lifting the covers to the heat underneath, tucking her arms around him. Every day it was harder to leave that cocoon. It struck him one evening as the light was failing that they might die there in each other's arms and he said, "Do you think it might be we ought to shift over to Mockbeggar?"

They'd never left the cove where they were born and neither could say if Mockbeggar was fit to eat. They knew Cornelius Strapp's schooner sailed from Mockbeggar to anchor off the harbour spring and fall to drop supplies and load in their season's catch of fish. They knew their father rowed over to fetch Mary Oram when their mother was near her time. Beyond that it might have been located in the Holy Lands or on the moon.

"I don't know," Ada said. "You think we might bunk in with Mary Oram?"

Just the mention of the woman was enough to put a misgiving in Evered's mind. "I doubt she'd bother with the likes of we," he said.

"You think Mary Oram's some kind of witch," Ada whispered.

"No more than you do," he said. He regretted bringing the subject up at all. "I figures we can muck it out here we puts our mind to it," he said. And a moment later he said, "I idn't afraid of her."

Ada shook her head against his chest, "You're an awful liar, Brother."

He pulled her into his neck. "Go to sleep out of it," he said.

Mary Oram was the only person not related to them by blood they'd ever kept company with. This was during the last stages of their mother's pregnancy when she was just able to get around the property, following behind her swollen belly like a cart awkwardly hauled about by a goat. She could barely reach around the bulk of it to set the kettle over the fire, she was out of breath taking the slop pail to the landwash in the mornings. She couldn't sit or lie in any position for more than a few minutes at a time. A month before Cornelius Strapp's schooner was due with the spring's supplies their mother woke with cramps that made her keen.

"It's your time," their father said.

Another contraction ripped through her and she shook her head as if she was trying to clear her mind of some flash recalled from a nightmare. "It's nothing," she said.

"I'll have to go for Mary Oram," he told her.

"There's no cause to be bothering Mary Oram," she said through her teeth. "You can manage if it comes to that, Sennet."

"God's nails," he said. "What good am I going to be lying a cold junk on the floor? You'd have perished in the bed if Mary Oram wouldn't here to look out to you last time."

"It's nothing," she said again.

Their father turned away from her to gather up his coat, pocketing three cakes of hardtack for a lunch.

"If you goes off in that boat today, Sennet Best, I swear to God," she said.

Evered followed his father down to the landwash. "Should I come with you?" he asked.

"You watch after those two," his father said as he set the oars and pulled away from the shoreline. He glanced over his shoulder toward open water where an easterly breeze was blowing up chop. "It'll be a bit of a haul if the wind don't shift," he shouted. "I'll be back late tomorrow or next day, God willing."

Evered watched his father lean into the steady cross-handed stroke. "I don't know what to do," he called. "What do I do?"

"You stay with them," his father said. And he said a few things more that Evered couldn't hear over the wind and the rut of the surf against the shoreline.

Their father made it back to them before dark the following day. He'd refused even to lay his head for an hour before starting the return leg and rowed through the night and he ran up from the shoreline ahead of Mary Oram, half expecting to find his wife or the new child dead. But she was sitting calmly next the fire with a mug of tea resting on the plateau of her stomach. He turned in a circle as if a full view of the little stud tilt might help him make sense of things.

"Hello, Sarah Best," Mary Oram said behind him. She had come in the door unnoticed and everyone turned to look at her. She was an imp of a figure, no taller than Ada, dressed in clothes made of calico and wool and a colourful knitted hat on her bald head, a leather satchel over one shoulder. Her eyebrows and eyelashes were so blonde and sparse her face seemed bald as well. She had the air of a badly made doll stuffed with sawdust that had suddenly come to life. Her hands were delicate and colourless and without fingernails. She nodded toward the youngsters sitting together on the edge of their bed. "You two is both mine," she said and they were too terrified by the sight of her to ask what she meant. It occurred to Ada to wonder if everyone in Mockbeggar looked and moved and talked like Mary Oram.

"I told him it wouldn't me time," Sarah Best said.

The contractions had forced their mother from her bed after their father left them. She paced the length of the tiny hovel a hundred times and then she had Ada kneel to put on her shoes so she could walk outside. Within an hour the cramping had subsided enough she was able to eat. By the afternoon it was clear nothing would come of it and she spent the rest of the day hauling seaweed from the landwash to the farm garden on the Downs.

Mary Oram crossed the room and slipped a hand under their mother's clothes to prod at the baby. "Do you know how far along?"

"Last September month," their mother said. "That was the last time I had my visitor," she said in a whisper.

Their father walked past them and fell into his bed, covering his head with a blanket.

"You're not far off your time," Mary Oram said. "No more than a fortnight, I'd say, unless this youngster has other ideas."

"I'll be cutting it out with a fish knife if I has to carry it much longer."

Their father was already snoring under the blanket. Mary Oram said, "It's just as well I stays on now I'm here. Spare the man another night's rowing."

"Yes, maid," their mother said. "You'll share a bunk with the youngsters till we gets this thing settled."

"I can sleep up to the store," Evered said and Ada dug her nails into his wrist.

"Sure I don't take up no room," Mary Oram said. "You won't even know I'm here."

For the next five nights the woman slept next them in their single bunk, Ada against the wall lying head to tail beside Evered and he head to tail beside the midwife. She wore her knitted cap and her shoes and she lay still as a corpse to morning.

Those periods of dead sleep seemed to be the only time Mary Oram was quiet. Evered spent the days helping his father raise the fishing stage where the cod would be cleaned and salted the coming season, up to his bawbles in the bitter cold of the Atlantic setting footings for the platform where the cutting table and salt shack would stand, holding the poles in place as his father worked above. And still he chose it over hearing

Mary Oram prattle on about the proper cure for chilblains or how a good fright to a pregnant woman left a permanent sign on the baby, listing the dozens of birthmarks and disfigurements she'd encountered alongside their likely causes.

She could talk the bark off a tree, their father said, a note of awed disbelief in his voice.

It made Evered think of how little his parents spoke of anything other than the work at hand or the vagaries of the weather. He'd assumed that was the way of adults and there was a suffocating weight on his chest in Mary Oram's presence. It felt as if half the world had mobbed into the tilt in her wake and he was being trampled beneath that seething occupation.

Ada avoided Mary Oram as well, sitting up on a thwart of the boat to watch her father and brother work, fetching them tools or holding longers in place as they were nailed down. There was something eerie about a figure that was in every particular a match for her own size and shape though the face and demeanour belonged to another creature altogether. She couldn't avoid thinking she might suffer a similar fate, to grow old in her child's body. She kept clear of Mary Oram for fear it was a condition that was catching, insisted Evered sleep between them.

Down on the landwash Ada asked how long Mary Oram would be staying in the cove.

"Till the baby comes," her father said.

She nodded over that non-answer a minute. "What if the baby don't come?"

He laughed. "Then she'll be here till the world ends won't she."

She didn't know if her father was being serious but it was a novel notion to her, that the world they knew might not be constant and everlasting but something creaturely, something perishable. Ada glanced at Evered to see if this was news to him as well. But he was bothered by something else altogether.

"Could the baby not come?" he said. He was thinking of his mother up and pacing the length of the tilt when they crawled from their bunks to start the day, heaving massive sighs and chewing viciously at her bottom lip, one hand supporting the girth of her belly. He was thinking of her threat to take a knife to herself if the child delayed its arrival. "Why would the baby not come?"

"God's reeving nails," their father said, "can we just get on with putting the stage in shape?"

He looked past his children suddenly, squinting up the rise, and they both turned to see Mary Oram outside the tilt. "It's time," she called down to them.

"All right," their father said.

"Send up the young one," Mary Oram said before she disappeared back into the house. And an unfamiliar voice reached them in the stillness, a sucking guttural complaint that seemed not quite human.

"What is that?" Evered asked.

"I imagine that's your mother," their father said. "Go on now, Daughter," he said.

"What do Mary Oram want me for?"

"Whatever it is needs doing up there I expect."

Ada looked to Evered but he wouldn't hold her eye.

"Go on," her father repeated and she turned to make her way up toward the tortured sound of her mother's voice.

———

The door was propped wide as was the single window's wooden shutter but the daylight barely touched the permanent dusk at the back of the tilt. Mary Oram had water on to boil in the fireplace and had lit the lamp and set it near where her mother was lying with her skirts lifted high around her thighs. The dirt floor was covered in a layer of dry sand and Ada could see where Sarah Best had used a stick to draw a pattern near the fireplace, an elaborate series of interconnecting circles at the hearth's edge.

"Come hold the lamp close," Mary Oram said when she caught sight of Ada in the doorway.

Ada had never seen her mother's bare legs or the black patch of hair between them or the pulpy slash of flesh where it looked for all the world like the woman was coming apart.

"Closer now," Mary Oram snapped. "There's nothing here will hurt you."

Ada stepped nearer with the light though the reassurance offered no comfort. She tried to look over the massive belly but her mother's face was beyond the lamp's reach.

"Did you know you was having a sister?" Mary Oram asked.

Ada gaped at her. She had forgotten for a moment there was a child at the centre of the bizarre state of affairs. She shook her head.

"Well then," Mary Oram said. "A sister you'll have. I knew it the minute I come through the door and seen your mother sitting there. Please God this one don't take her time like yourself now."

"Me?"

"Two days we was strapped up in here like this, waiting on you. Me with only your father for help. And he fainted dead away in the midst of it all." She reached out to guide the lamp in Ada's hand to one side where she had laid out her utensils. A straight razor, Ada saw there. Mary Oram said, "I allow this one is some terrible size though." She took up a needle and held it to the lamp to pass a length of thread through the eye. "Sarah Best," she said, "next time you wants to have a youngster, have a youngster. Not a bloody cow."

Her mother came up on her elbows, rising out of a pool of darkness into the lamp's dark light. Her face was half-hidden by her hair which lay plastered to the skin with sweat. "Shut up, Mary Oram," she said. "For the love of God just be quiet." And she descended into the black again. The look of the woman so wild and unfamiliar that it seemed to Ada a stranger was lying there in the approximate shape and form of her mother.

"That's just the baby talking," Mary Oram said quietly. "She said some cruel things to your father the last time she was in the throes of it."

Her mother shouted out something wordless and profane, then set into keening again. Mary Oram laid the needle and thread back on the bed and when the contraction passed she forced the nailless fingers of one childsize hand inside Sarah Best's body, her face turned to the ceiling as she rooted blindly.

"You're coming along, Missus," Mary Oram said.

"Is it almost over," Ada whispered.

"She's coming along," she said again.

But nothing apparent happened for the rest of the morning and into the afternoon, the recurring contractions like knots in an endless string unwinding through the day. They ate nothing and Evered and their father didn't venture inside to check on them or to look for something to eat themselves.

Mary Oram periodically sent the girl to throw out a basin of dirty water and refill it from the pot kept hot in the fireplace and Ada leaned in over the bunk with a cloth to wipe her mother's tormented face.

It was coming on to dark when some stay shifted and the day went sudden, Ada's mother leaning into the weight of the unborn creature with a new resolve and Mary Oram calling for the light to be brought closer as the crown of the child's head appeared, a sliver of pink skin and slick dark hair. Ada had guessed at the absurd truth of what was meant to happen hours earlier though it seemed a physical impossibility still. She felt a pressure on her bladder, acute and rising, but the urgency in the events at hand forced her to stay at her post.

"We're going to have to help it along some," Mary Oram announced and she reached for the razor. The horror of what the blade was meant for passed through Ada's body like a burning coal and she pissed onto the dirt floor, the liquid running down her legs and soaking her bare feet. But she did not cry and she managed to stand her ground as Mary Oram went about the awful business.

After it crowned the baby came in a rush of blood and fluid and Mary Oram knelt at the bedside to catch the slippery infant in her lap. Ada staring at the ugly thing cabled to her mother, the eyes clenched tight against the new light, against the room's chill. It looked like something not halfways completed, the tuberous head three sizes too large for the body. Mary Oram reached a finger into the tiny mouth to root out a plug of yellow mucus and lifted the child by the ankles to slap her behind. She set the bawling youngster on her mother's stomach, then took up the straight razor to cut the umbilical cord and she knotted it off.

"We wants a fresh pan of water," Mary Oram said.

Ada was afraid she would fall if she moved. Mary Oram glanced at her and turned to take the lamp from her hands.

"You done fine," she said. "Go get us some clean water."

Ada carried in the pan on her quivering legs, her feet wet with cold urine and the floor of the tilt a mess of blood and afterbirth, and she was careful not to spill a drop as she went as if some additional calamity would befall them if she did. She set the water on the bed beside her mother who was murmuring to the infant on her chest, then she sat on the opposite bunk listening to her sister bawl while Mary Oram carried on with her ministrations, lifting each of the baby's limbs in turn, counting to make sure she had all her fingers and toes.

Ada had no idea what she'd just witnessed. It didn't seem possible what her mother had suffered was the normal course of things and not a drawn-out catastrophic accident from which she would likely never recover.

"Bring in the light," Mary Oram said over her shoulder and Ada got up to hold the lamp close to her mother's traumatized flesh. Mary Oram took up the needle and thread and for a moment Ada thought she planned to stitch her from stem to stern.

"Is it always like this?" she whispered.

"Like what, child?"

Ada gestured with the lamp as Mary Oram made three tidy stitches then tied off and broke the thread. "Like this," she said.

Mary Oram got to her feet and smiled across at the girl. "No, my love," she said. She rinsed her hands in the pan of water and wiped them in the filthy skirt of her apron. "Sometimes it don't go well at all."

———

Evered and his father kept clear of the tilt all that day, an agreement they came to without a word of discussion. For a while he tried to guess from his father's face whether he should worry but there was nothing in the man's expression to tell him. And as long as they were at work he managed almost to ignore what they were busy ignoring.

It was a surprise to him that Ada had been called upon though she was still not much above a child. Whenever he happened to glance up at the tilt the bewildering enormity of what his sister was witnessing first-hand caught him unawares, like taking a gale of wind broadside to the boat as it cleared a point of land. Each time he had to fight to turn nose-on to that weather and ride it out. But he did his level best to mirror his father's apparent indifference, going at the work with a steady mechanical rhythm that had its own numbing effect.

Once they had finished setting the last of the longers on the stagehead his father collected shovels and brin bags from the store and they walked to the west end of the harbour, the only stretch where there was sand enough to shovel. They filled the bags with wooden spades hand-milled in Mockbeggar half a lifetime past, the hewn troughs worked smooth by the grain of steady use. They carted the sand back to the clearing below the tilt and left it there, walking out to the brook to be far enough from the woman's distress that the wind covered most of the turmoil, though not quite all. They tried to satisfy their hunger by drinking water from their cupped hands, then they lit a fire and sat close to the heat and waited.

"How much longer till they're done?" Evered asked.

His father shook his head. "We might have to sleep down here yet."

"What did you want with the sand?"

"I expect we'll have to dredge the tilt clear," his father said. "Lay down a fresh cover."

It was a ways to dark still but Sennet Best lay out by the fire and flung an arm over his face and slept. Evered wandered down to the landwash and hunted for a crab shell or piece of driftwood to add to Ada's collection. She kept a shelf full of scavenged bric-a-brac over their bed, a tableau that she arranged and rearranged until the individual pieces were laid out to her satisfaction. It was always strangely satisfying to look at, as if there was a logic to where some shell or stone sat in relation to the whole. He'd tried to do the same himself on occasion but had no knack for it, the end result looking exactly like the pile of detritus it was.

The tide was out and he clambered over the rocks, searching the crevices aimlessly, killing time. Now and again he stopped where he was to wonder what could be happening in the tilt that would require clearing every bit of sand off the floor when it was over.

After the ugly work was done Mary Oram washed and swaddled the baby and that was enough to bring the child into the realm of the room and its inhabitants, to make her seem human.

"She's the spit of you, she is, Sarah Best," the midwife said.

Ada could see there was something of her mother in the shape of the infant's nose and the cleft of her chin. And the face that had seemed alien and grotesque when it first appeared was completely changed by that recognition.

"What is her name?" Ada asked.

Sarah Best was half-asleep with her mouth to the newborn's downy crown and she glanced across at Ada without raising her head. "I don't know," she said. "What should we call her?"

It hadn't occurred to Ada that a name was bestowed on a person and not something you were born with. The lack made the infant seem almost as naked and pitiable as when she first landed in Mary Oram's lap.

The list of Christian names Ada knew was short and all were gleaned from the handful of wayward Bible stories her mother had misremembered from her earliest years without church or priest to correct them. There was Ruth who was daughter- or sister-in-law to Naomi who lost her husband and two sons and the two women moved to a country called Boaz in the Holy Lands. There was Rachel who killed her sister Leah to marry her sister's husband and died giving birth to a child. There was Mary who soaked her feet in the dew out picking berries one fall and so fell pregnant with Jesus.

Mary Oram had already taken the name of Jesus's mother. And Ada thought the stories of Ruth and Naomi and Rachel and Leah were too dark to shadow her sister all her life. But there was Martha, sister to Lazarus, who roused her brother from the tomb as if he was being woken from a nap.

"You should go fetch the men," Mary Oram said. She was stoking up the fire to set about making a meal in the gloom. "They're like to be starved by now."

Ada reached to touch her sister's cheeks, the perfect swirl of the ears so translucent that the dull lamplight shone through them. It hardly seemed possible such a delicate thing could have been at the centre of the appalling storm that had just passed over them. There was something dreamlike about the episode, behind them now and losing its immediacy already. One of the baby's hands was curled into a fist and circled gently like some inanimate thing in a field stirred by the wind.

"What about Martha?" she said.

Sarah Best nodded. "Martha sounds fine," she said. "Go on and get your father."

Outside Ada could see the low simmering light of the fire over toward the brook. Evered was wandering on the landwash directly below, a small dark figure against the darkening ocean. He straightened from the rocks when he saw her and raised a hand. But she hesitated before heading down. It was the first time in her life she knew something of real import that Evered and her father did not. They had been biding hours for the news she carried and keeping it to herself was unexpectedly pleasurable.

She watched Evered watching her until he called up the rise and she started toward him then, trying to sort her news into a manageable list. She was within arm's length before she could make out his face and even then she couldn't read his expression for certain. He looked like he had done something to disappoint her.

He held a hand out to her. "I found you this," he said.

She brought it up close to see it, a seabird's skull picked clean and weathered to a white that almost seemed to glow in the dim. The bone so delicately fluted it looked to be carved by hand and so much like the whorls of her sister's ears that Ada could hardly speak for the lump rising in her throat.

"Mary Oram is cooking supper," she said.

"Father's over to the brook," Evered said. "I'll fetch him home."

She nodded and started toward the tilt, cradling the skull in one hand. It hadn't gone the way she'd thought it would at all. She turned back and called across to her brother in the rapidly closing darkness.

"Her name is Martha," she said.

Evered turned toward his sister's voice.

"I give it to her," Ada said. "Her name."

They stood that way a minute, not able to see more than the vaguest outline of one another.

"We'll be up the once," Evered said.

Mary Oram stayed on awhile to keep an eye on the infant and their mother. She lay beside Ada and Evered with her freakish hands folded over her chest, as still as the dead even when Martha woke crying to be fed. It felt to Ada like a blessed time, the winter behind them and the summer supplies aboard *The Hope* no more than a few weeks off, the infant healthy and mostly content. Though on occasion she woke to a low stifled sobbing across the room, a sound that was meant to be kept private and could only have been her mother.

A week after the birth Ada was conscripted to hold the lamp again while Mary Oram took out her mother's stitches, snipping and tweezering the thread clear.

"There now," Mary Oram said. "Good as new you are."

Her mother threw her skirts down over her legs. "God help me, I don't feel like new," she said.

"You'll have more youngsters running around here yet," Mary Oram said.

And Sarah Best surprised them both then, hiding her face and crying behind her hands. Martha was lying on the bed beside her mother and she started bawling as well. Mary Oram picked up the baby and handed her to Ada.

"I swear," her mother said in a whisper. "I won't go through this again."

"Hush now," Mary Oram whispered. "It's just the shock of it. You felt the same after young Ada was borned."

"And how many did I lose between times?" her mother said. She seemed oblivious to her two daughters sitting across the room. "There's been three since Ada."

Ada was trying to quiet her sister but she was watching her mother's face. For the second time in the space of a week it looked as if a stranger peered out of those familiar features.

"There's something can be done," her mother said. "You must know something to do."

Mary Oram shook her head. "A body must bear what can't be helped," she said.

"I swear to God," Sarah Best said. "I'll drown myself in the cove."

"Hush now," Mary Oram said again. She turned to Ada. "It's just the shock of it," she said. "You go on now, take the little one up to see your father."

Ada left the two women and walked to the store where Sennet Best and Evered had been hand-milling lumber with an eye to adding a room to the tilt. There was no one about and she sat inside with the inconsolable infant. She felt helpless to quiet her and it was all she could do not to join in. Thinking of her mother's threat to abandon them.

Evered poked his head in the door. "Some set of lungs on her," he said.

"I can't make her stop," Ada said.

He lifted Martha out of his sister's lap and settled the infant
against his arm. He circled her open mouth with his pinky until
she latched on to the tip. He smiled at Ada as the youngster
quieted. "You was the same way," he said. "When you was a
piss-ass maid."

She said, "We can't ever leave her, Brother."

"Who? The little one?"

"Promise me," she said.

Evered held his smile but without the same certainty. Nodded
to say all right.

The family's farm garden was on a plateau toward the west end
of the cove. It was set at the edge of a peat bog they called the
Downs and was the only bit of ground within walking distance
deep enough to plant. The earth was wet and black and barely
arable but for the seaweed and caplin hauled up from the beach
and turned into the soil each spring to feed the potatoes and
turnip and cabbage and beets they set there.

The garden was the women's preserve, trenching and weed-
ing the plot while Evered and his father were off in the boat
after the fish. But as his mother was lying in and Ada occupied
with Martha, Evered was sent up to turn the rotting seaweed
into the soil. He was lost in that work when he heard his name
spoken aloud behind him. He threw down the shovel and
jumped across three furrows, his heart pounding in his throat.

"Give you a scare," Mary Oram said.

"No," Evered said. "I'm best kind."

She nodded and stood watching him. She'd lost her garru-
lous nature in the time she'd been with them as if the quiet in

the cove had rubbed off on her. And the new reticence made the woman more mystifying and formidable. Evered walked back to the spade and picked it up as casually as he could manage.

"I come to pay my respects," Mary Oram said.

She walked past the furrowed ground to where the bog began in earnest. The black earth there deep enough to harrow something close to six feet down. The plot was barely discernible, a small rectangular depression bordered with beach stones. There was no marker to say who lay there. Evered kept at the work but couldn't help glancing up to where Mary Oram stood.

"You don't mind being up here alone?" she said.

He shrugged, turned another spadeful of soil. He was thinking he preferred being alone, that it was Mary Oram staring down at the dead that was making his skin crawl. He didn't know why she felt the need to offer her respects to the stranger or how she knew he was there, a fellow who'd washed up on the beach in the first years his father was fishing from the cove. The two eyes eaten out by sea lice his father had told him and as Evered was picturing the empty sockets of that ruined face Sennet Best added, "Don't you be talking any of this old mash to your mother now, she don't need none of that in her head."

Mary Oram turned from the grave and Evered stood straight, leaning on the handle. "That was all before your time," she said.

"First when Father come out here," Evered said before he realized it wasn't a question but a statement the woman was making. She watched him with an otherworldy stare that made him think she was hearing the words in his head before he spoke and hearing words he didn't intend to speak aloud besides. "The little one seems to be doing fine," she said finally. "I expect I'll be heading back to Mockbeggar come morning."

He nodded, hoping not to show how welcome this bit of news was to him.

"I'll leave you to it," she said.

He tried not to watch her go, leaning into the work. But he snuck a last glance as she went down the rise. And without knowing for certain what it meant he made the sign of the cross at her back three times, the way his mother would at the sight of crows.

They were up before light the next morning. The youngsters followed their father down to the landwash while Mary Oram took a final look at the baby and at Sarah Best. It was clear and very cold. Ada sat on a patch of snow still clinging to shadow in a rock crevice on the beach, watching her father and Evered haul the freshly tarred boat into the shallows and tying it off at the stage rails.

When her father saw her there he said, "You shouldn't pitch on the snow like that."

"Why not?"

"The cold will go right up through you," he said. "It idn't good for your girl parts."

Evered said, "What girl parts?"

"Never you mind," their father said.

"What girl parts?" Ada said.

"We're about set here," their father said. "Go on and fetch Mary Oram."

She walked up the rise, her head swimming. She had no idea what the man was warning her against. She pictured her mother lying back with her legs spread and the infant splitting her wide. The story of Mary from the Bible came to mind, how she soaked her feet out picking berries and so fell pregnant with Jesus. She wondered if it was some exposure to the cold that caused babies to take hold in there.

She was still picking her way through that conjecture when she stepped inside. The two women interrupted in the midst of some whispered deliberation as they turned to her.

"Father's ready," Ada said.

Sarah Best was nursing the baby and Mary Oram waved at her to stay in her seat. She went to Ada at the door but stopped there, turning back to the room. She rooted in her leather bag of utensils and came up with a hank of twine. She walked back to Sarah Best and knelt on the floor beside her, placed the string across the woman's belly.

"You're certain," Mary Oram said.

Ada's mother nodded.

"All right," Mary Oram whispered. She knotted the string three times and put her hand over top of it on Sarah Best's stomach. She said, "May earth bear on you with all its might and main." And she carried on repeating that line often enough that the words started to lose their meaning in Ada's ears. When Mary Oram finally got to her feet she tucked the string into a pocket at the front of Sarah Best's dress.

"Is that it then?" her mother asked.

"God willing," Mary Oram said, "that's it." She turned to Ada and shooed her out the door ahead of her.

Ada and Evered lay side by side that night and resumed their interrupted ritual of talking quietly to one another before falling asleep and whenever they happened to stir awake.

They spoke of their father's warning about Ada's girl parts and they couldn't but see Mary Oram's influence on the bizarre concern. Ada felt herself unequal to the nightmarish details of their sister's birth and even the removal of the stitches was too intimate and unaccountable to describe. But she told Evered about their mother's demented spell when she threatened to drown herself in the cove, about the string Mary Oram had knotted three times and the strange incantation she'd repeated over their mother's belly before she left. Evered told her about his encounter with Mary Oram at the farm garden, she standing silent at the stranger's gravesite, and the sense he had of the woman looking into his head to see his thoughts before he spoke them. All these incidents they ran through the gauntlet of childish awe and speculation that created their shared vision of the world, that made the youngsters feel as close as rind on a tree.

At the stagehead that morning their father had picked the woman up and lifted her down into the boat like a hogshead of flour, then rowed her through the skerries into open water. Ada and Evered ran out the eastern arm of the cove and stood on the farthest point to watch as her figure receded. They stayed there until the boat and its occupants disappeared completely, to be certain she was gone.

Pack Ice. A Whitecoat.

They holed up at the stud tilt in a grey limbo for the better part of two months, without desire or interest beyond the other's mute company. Though as the days began to lengthen they felt a vague sense of expectation steal over them, both waiting without knowing what they were waiting for until the pack ice drifted down from the Labrador sea at the beginning of March and the youngsters woke one morning to the sound of it gouging at the shoreline.

The little harbour was barred by rocks and skerries drawing just a fathom of water at low tide and no vessel larger than a bully boat could sail into the cove. But that frozen armada choked the bay come spring. Their father had always taken down the stage in the fall to save it from the weight grinding against the beach. Pans raftered up on the landwash as the miles of pack behind it muscled in on the current, the leading edge buckling under that pressure. An intermittent round of concussions echoing in the air as if a brigade of freebooters was trying to break through the stone foundation of a fortress.

The ice marked the start of a season beyond winter in the

cove and the racket of its arrival filled Ada and Evered with a jittery energy that made it impossible to lie still. They went down to the beach where the ice field stretched as far as they could see, rising and falling on the ocean swell. They could feel the cold razoring off the frigid surface through the little clothes they wore and Ada shivered against it. The white was tinged blue and pink as the early light rose and the quiver running up her spine was almost a pleasure. She had come down to the shore without her sister's ragdoll and she reached for her brother's hand.

"There'll be seals coming in on that," Evered said.

For the first time since their mother died at the start of the winter they both felt ravenously, painfully hungry.

Every day for the next two weeks Evered left in the early light to beat his way to the farthest point on the harbour. It was an easy stroll out the beach come summer but rough walking with the shore overrun by slabs and crags of ice. He had to pick his way in through the alder and tuck before breaking out onto the stretch of open rock at the point where he had a view to the horizon east and west of the cove.

The point lay open to the weather which passed through spells of snow and cold rain and sleet and bouts of blinding arctic sunlight that offered not the barest hint of warmth. He owned only a single pair of breeches—every day he regretted not stripping his father's trousers before tipping his body into the ocean—but he had the man's leather red jacks and he wrapped his calves in strips of canvas against the rough ice and the salt water. He wore a worsted wool cap that he fortified with a length of cloth tied around his head, he had cuffs and sealskin mitts. Every hour or so he walked back and forth to the scrub trees to bring a hint of feeling into his frozen feet.

Occasionally he caught sight of Ada moving about the property at the foot of the cove. He knew she was watching for him when she was outside the tilt, raising a hand to the point. It was the only moment of pleasure in those bitter uneventful vigils as the pack ice slow-wheeled on the currents.

Evered was bound and determined to have a seal though for the first time in their young lives there was no real lack of food in the house come March month, their parents too ill through much of the fall to eat their share of the winter store. They still had dried peas and flour, they had salt fish and salt pork and a barrel of last summer's vegetables in the root cellar. But every night he and Ada talked themselves to sleep with speculation about when the seals might come close enough to shore and how the fresh meat would taste and what use a tanned skin could be put to. It was life's persistence those conversations hinted at, the world carrying on though their parents and sister were no longer in it.

Every day Evered saw seals, featureless black dots in the distance. He had been his father's eyes out there in springs past, the man myopic and turning one ear to the icy expanse, listening to their dog-barks drift in on the wind. "I'm hearing seven or eight," he'd say. "Are they close enough to go after?"

If the seals drifted handy to shore, Evered lead his father out over the swaying white field after them. But the ocean was a shifting jigsaw of pans and open leads and pressure ridges and his father wouldn't set foot upon it if the animals were more than a few hundred yards off.

Evered wasn't willing to chance going any further himself now. A body could be caught out there for days if the wind tacked offshore. He might never make it back to solid ground. The cove sometimes emptied of pans in the space of an hour, the ice edge moving steadily out to sea as if some vessel beyond the horizon had hooked a line and towed it. And two hours on or the following morning the harbour was blocked again.

It was a raw disappointment to him to give up the watch and begin the trudge back every day. His legs so wooden he had trouble keeping his feet, using the gaff as a walking stick. Ada went down to meet him on the landwash if she saw him coming. Putting an arm around his waist to help him up the rise.

She had the fire built high and the kettle boiling and she sat him in front of the heat with a mug of tea. She knelt in the sand to unwind the stiff canvas around his shins and haul off the leather boots and she held his feet in her lap, rubbing blood back into the skin. The pain as feeling returned to his toes so exquisite that Evered had to chew on the inside of his mouth to hold off the tears. The cloth wrapped around his head was frozen to his woollen cap and his cap was frozen to his white hair. Ada waited until he'd finished his tea to work them off and hang them on the line above the fire to dry.

Every day he said, "There was two or three almost in close enough." He was wanting to keep her spirits up. "I was half a mind to go out after them," he said.

"Tomorrow," she said. "Tomorrow they'll come in."

"Please God and the weather," he said.

Those two weeks were Ada's first experience of solitary time. She had never in her life been more than a good shout from someone's ear, never further than the width of the burn-over in the berry hills or the few minutes' walk from the Downs to company. She watched Evered make his way to the point each morning, following his slow progress along the beach. She called luck to him along his route and he shouted back until he was out of earshot. The isolation she felt then was so unfamiliar she took it for a physical ailment that worsened when she sat idle.

There was no shortage of work to distract her. She baked bread and hung out the stale bedclothes and boiled wood ash to make soap, she cut splits and filled the woodbox and fetched pots of snow to melt over the fire. She took any excuse to wander around the property or down to the landwash, keeping an eye for Evered. Each time she stepped outside she was afraid he wouldn't be where she expected him, gone down onto the ice beyond the rocks. Part of her hoped the seals would never come close enough to tempt him off the point.

When the wind forced him to coopy down in a cleft he was almost invisible. She stood a long time watching for the white flash of his face turning toward the bottom of the cove. Raising her hand when it finally appeared and waiting for a wave in return.

When she was working inside she talked aloud to her dead sister as she had when Martha was alive, narrating her activities or offering up rhetorical questions to the child who sucked her fist and stared patiently. Her father had taken to calling Ada *Young Mary Oram*.

"If Young Mary Oram stops talking long enough to spoon

up some food," he'd say. "If you can edge a word in around Young Mary Oram there."

Ada felt Martha listening now with the same forbearance. She never doubted she was being heard. Alone in the tilt or waking in the dead of night she felt her sister's constant silent attention. That the infant might have been granted some sway in the universe as their mother suggested seemed a small compensation for her fate. Ada prayed to Martha to bring the seals in to shore or to keep them out to sea depending on whether desire or fear was ascendant in her heart. She prayed Evered would be kept safe. And her connection to the dead child felt more vital and sustaining the longer she was alone with her.

By the middle of the month the ice field moved offshore and stayed out there, miles into open sea. Evered thought the ice was nearly done for the season which likely meant he'd missed his chance at the seals. He couldn't avoid reading the failure as a judgement on their prospects in the cove, and the rekindled doubts made him reconsider shifting across to Mockbeggar. But Ada carried a red coal of guilt even to have entertained the suggestion weeks earlier and she refused outright.

"We can't leave Martha alone here," she said.

He sat with that notion awhile.

"We promised we'd stay with her," Ada said.

Evered had a vague recollection of some such commitment being made in the long-ago before the sickness overtook the cove. He couldn't see how it applied to their new circumstances but he didn't have the acumen or the heart to argue it. If they were going to stay, he told her, he'd have to launch the boat to try for a seal as he and his father did when the ice was lying offshore or slobby enough to push through, rowing and poling and hauling their way to the seals on larger pans at the ice edge. But Ada knew it was a fool's errand to take the boat out to the ice alone.

"We got food to eat," she said.

"It idn't that," he said though he couldn't explain what it was even to himself and that frustration made him more insistent on the venture. Ada wouldn't hear of it unless he agreed to take her along.

They were both surprised to be arguing. Their mother and father never bickered in their presence. They set to the daily round of work with the rigid single-mindedness required to keep body and soul together and the youngsters had adopted the same pliable way with one another. Their disagreements had been shallow and easily settled. And all the same it came naturally to them now to take up opposite ends of the rope and pull all they were worth. It felt as if they had discovered something new in the world, something exhilarating and unpleasant in equal measure. They lay awake in the dark a long time, only their shoulders touching, stewing in their separate pots.

"If I don't take the boat out there'll be no seals here the spring," Evered said.

"The boat don't go in the water but I'll be in it," Ada said.

He guessed by her tone there was nothing he could say to shift her on the issue and he turned to face the wall, too furious to sleep. A little awed by her spine.

"Perhaps the ice will come in tomorrow," she said, "if the wind shifts."

"It don't seem one bit likely," he said.

Twice during the night Ada woke and knew by his breathing Evered was awake beside her. Any other time she would have spoken to him to make the dark more hospitable and they would have chatted aimlessly until they drifted off again. But a fear kept her quiet, a sense she had that he might choose not to answer her and pretend to be asleep instead.

When he made a move to climb from the bed she tried to talk Evered out of the vigil. The wind was up and they both knew from how it struck the tilt it was blowing offshore. But Evered crawled over her into the bitter chill and she followed after him, lighting the fire to heat their breakfast as he hauled on the buskins and wrapped his calves.

She tried to draw him out with their usual talk as she worked over the fire, asking how he had slept and what he had dreamt through the night and what he thought the chances were of landing a seal. Evered answered with shrugs and grunts and wouldn't meet her eye. The unfamiliar distance between them made her anxious to stay close and she suggested she might spend the day on the point with him.

"We'd be coming back to a cold house," Evered said. "I'd be happier there was a fire and a mug of tea when I gets in."

Ada recognized the truth of that. But it felt no less an evasion all the same.

Evered left before it was fairly light. The cove was free of ice but the beach was still strewn with blocks pushed onto the rocks at high tide and stranded there. Ada watched him until he settled in his customary lookout on the rocks and when she saw the flash of his face turning back to the cove she raised her hand. Evered looked away out to the ocean and didn't wave first or last. She stood there waiting until a drift of sleet drove her inside to the fire.

All morning she turned it over in her mind. She'd gotten her way about taking the boat out to the ice and felt she was in the right. It was a riddle to see a person could get what they wanted and regret it, could even regret wanting it in the first place.

She was so confounded by that strife the length of the morning that she didn't give a moment's thought to her sister until she heard the dead child crying outside. Ada stopped still in the tilt, her head cocked to one side, her heart hammering.

Nothing, nothing.

She was ready to dismiss it as the wind in the trees when it came again, a youngster bawling helplessly, the cry a long way off but unmistakable. She tore out of the tilt and stopped at the top of the rise, listening again. She had missed the wind coming around onshore. Miles-long stretches of pack were floating beyond the harbour skerries and the cove was slushed full with pans. She heard the crying youngster again, the voice coming up from directly below her. From the ice in the cove.

Ada cupped her hands to her mouth and called. She was crying herself now as she bawled her sister's name. The pans rose and fell on the swell, a long curved vein of slob in the heart of the cove circling with the tide's pull. She ran headlong down the rise to the landwash, trying to pinpoint the voice though there was nothing to see out there but white, white, white.

"Martha!" she shouted into the wind.

———

But for that first glance Evered didn't turn his head to the bottom of the cove all morning. He knew Ada was watching for him after he settled on the point, he knew she would wave to him when he looked her way. And he hadn't waved back for spite. He sat alone in the cold then, the bitter seeping deeper every hour. He wouldn't turn to look for her or make the short trek to the trees and back to warm himself for fear he'd catch sight of her and, against his own desire, refuse to return her raised hand a second time.

He tucked into his food mid-morning, eating against the cold, against a faceless centreless disgust with himself. Before he'd finished the last morsel the wind had swung around and blew onshore for the first time in days. Evered shook his head at the sudden shift, torn between anticipating another chance at seals close to shore and a childish irritation to see the world at large siding with Ada.

He hadn't slept more than an hour or two the night before and the ice was still miles at sea. He moved behind a rock ledge that offered some protection from the wind and he dozed off there despite the freezing cold, jumping and muttering inco-herently in his sleep like a dog chasing an elusive dream rabbit. When he started awake there were flotillas of ice drifting loose in all directions, the arctic field beginning to disintegrate and the wind driving it to pieces.

The cove was chock full behind him and he turned to look across the breadth of it. On the opposite side of the harbour he saw Ada, bare-headed and wearing only her dress and apron. She was holding the heavy skirts away from her legs and step-ping down from the western arm to walk out onto the swaying quilt of ice. He shouted across to her, the wind whipping the useless words inland. He waved his arms to warn her back but she was focused on something on the ice, skipping across the loose pans to avoid sinking up to her knees or tipping face and eyes into the water.

Evered clambered down onto the ice and started across from the eastern shore to meet her, calling all the while. The vein of slob was too wide to jump and it forced him to head toward the bottom of the harbour and circle back up. He had no idea what Ada was doing and no time to consider it, watching the ice bobbing beneath his feet, kicking up salt water as he picked a way forward, glancing up now and then to be certain she hadn't fallen through. He heard the crying once he was downwind of it and registered the sound in some far-off part of his mind though he didn't connect it to Ada until he reached her.

The seal pup was lying on the only pan in the cove large enough to support a person's stationary weight. Ada was on her knees ten feet from the whitecoat, her chest heaving.

"Sister," he said and she turned to him, startled.

She pointed at the animal. It was watching them intently, wide black eyes like wet coal. The spotless coat nearly the same white as the ice it lay upon.

"That's a young one," he said. "Just born the spring."

It cried out to them in its sorrowful, nearly human voice.

"I thought it was Martha," Ada said. She wiped the snot and tears from her face with the sleeve of her dress. She laughed at the ridiculous notion though she was still crying. "I heard it bawling and I thought it was Martha."

"You thought she was out on the ice like this?" Evered said.

She raised her arms helpless from her sides and let them drop again.

"What if you'd gone through?"

"I wouldn't thinking," she said. And then, "Where's its mother?"

"Lost her somewhere I expect. When the wind broke up the ice. Or could be some creature killed and eat her out there."

Ada was without a coat or cloak and Evered could see the tremors travel through her. He helped her to her feet and took off the cloth he'd been wearing over his hat, wrapping it around her bare head and tying it under her chin.

"It really did sound like her," she said to him.

The whitecoat called behind them again as if to demonstrate the eerie similarity.

"You misses her," Evered said.

She nodded and he wiped at Ada's face with the tail end of the cloth around her head.

"We got to get in out of this," he said. "You'll catch your death so." He walked the ten feet across to the seal and struck it twice on the forehead with the blunt end of the gaff. The smack like the mallet-sound of his father's heels against the frozen dirt floor when he pulled the corpse from its bed. He unwound the hauling rope at his waist and cut a notch through the animal's tail for the hook. He handed Ada the gaff, then wrapped the end of the rope across his shoulder. He nodded toward the closest bit of shore. "Don't tarry as you goes," he told her. "Or we'll both land up drownded here this morning."

The weight of the carcass slowed Evered enough that he nearly went through on every step but he yelled at Ada to keep moving, reeling on his feet behind her, scrambling on his hands and knees.

They were both soaked through to the waist when they made shore. They straggled on to the bottom of the cove and Ada went ahead then to stir up the fire while Evered pelted the whitecoat on the landwash. He worked the knife up the abdomen to the throat, then flensed the fur from the carcass. He guessed from the meagre layer of fat the animal had been abandoned a while and would have starved or frozen before long. But there was a fine meal in the flippers and enough meat besides to salt for later in the spring. And the perfectly white coat was ready to be scraped and stretched. It was too small for a full garment or a blanket but it would do to make a vest or a hat or a pair of mitts.

When he finished dressing the animal he cut out the heart and carried it up to the tilt cupped in his hands. He set it on a plate and sliced it into sections like a fruit and they ate the flesh together, licking the blood from their lips. Ada's pale face was raw and her eyes red with the crying she'd done in the cold but there was an unmistakable glim of light beneath the skin, a look that redeemed every interminable hour Evered had spent exposed to the weather on the point.

She reached for another sliver of the heart. "Poor little thing," she said. "It's a sin to be eating it." But she could feel the fierce goodness of it flooding her senses.

She felt it right to her very toes.

The Hope. The Beadle.

After the pack ice passed through, the weather continued cold with periods of snow and sleet. But birds sang at the first sign of light and all day long, robins and other grassy birds they'd never been taught the names of. There were flocks of eiders on the cove in the evenings, a handful of lords and ladies, the drakes so flamboyantly adorned with white crescents and chestnut and slate-blue patches that Ada thought they might have been hand-painted.

Evered spent his time in the backwoods cutting spruce that he limbed and stood to dry for next year's winter fuel. At the end of each day he reefed together a small raft of ten-foot longers for the stage and dragged them out on the last of the snowpack. And as May came in he recruited Ada to help him frame up the stage on the landwash.

It was a miserable undertaking. They worked at low tide, Ada with her skirts tied up around her waist, both of them sloshing through the freezing shallows. Evered had never been much more than his father's kedger, holding logs and driving the occasional nail, and the job was bigger than he and Ada were fit for. The stage when they were done was like a child's drawing of a stage, so ill-shaped and lopsided it was barely recognizable as the thing it was meant to represent. And still they were pleased with it, that it stood at all and was sturdy enough to hold their weight.

The year's last fall of snow dusted the ground in the third week of May, then the weather turned to rain and days of unrelenting fog. They hauled loads of bladderwrack and sugar kelp up to the garden and they spread the seaweed to let it rot before turning it into the soil.

There was enough light in the evenings to pick away at handwork, mending the herring net or darning threadbare stockings. Ada hacked at Evered's hair with a set of iron shears to keep it out of his eyes. She cut and sewed the whitecoat's pelt into an approximation of a vest. By dusk they were nodding off in their chairs and the two of them crawled into the bunk together. And before falling asleep they talked awhile about when they might expect Cornelius Strapp's schooner.

Even more than the seasons, *The Hope*'s biannual visit was the fulcrum on which life in the cove turned though Ada nor Evered had so much as set foot on the vessel. It was too large to clear the skerries, anchoring off on the Barrow Ledge, and their father had always rowed out to meet it alone. In the spring he came back laden with barrels of flour and molasses and hard bread, with brown sugar and tea and butter and two hogsheads of pickling salt, with yeast and calico and twine and tar and fish hooks and nails. In the fall Evered and Ada helped their parents load the boat with salt cod and their father steered it away through the shoals. They could just make out the shape of men on deck lowering baskets on a line to hoist up the cured fish.

Eight or ten trips to ferry the season's catch and their father tied on to *The Hope* then, going aboard himself as the fish was graded and the Beadle set the figures down in his ledger. And he left the ship with all the supplies they would have to last the winter.

Ada and Evered stood on the stage waving as *The Hope* weighed anchor and sailed off for Mockbeggar. But for a rare glimpse of some unidentifiable vessel passing on the horizon, they would not lay eyes on another living soul till Strapp's schooner arrived the following spring.

There was no predicting exactly when *The Hope* would appear, its visit one element in a seasonal cycle that varied just enough to cripple the notion of certainty. The ship could sail into view any time after the ice left in March and before the caplin spawned in June. And neither youngster could guess what would happen when *The Hope* arrived this spring. The nature of those transactions and their father's obligations to Cornelius Strapp had never been discussed in the house and were completely opaque to them.

Most of their speculation centred on the figure of the Beadle who was Cornelius Strapp's man, fish culler and keeper of Strapp's ledger. Their father spoke of the man with a mix of animosity and foreboding. He married couples and read scripture at baptisms and funerals and registered every birth and death that took place in Mockbeggar. And he likewise presided over their livelihood. Their season's catch was not worth a half penny until the Beadle gave his verdict and made his mark in the pages of a leather-bound book. No supplies were loaded onto the boat without the Beadle's say-so. "There goes the bloody Beadle aboard *The Abandon Hope All Ye*," their father would say as the ship weighed anchor and left them each fall. They would never manage to work themselves clear of the Beadle's ledger, he said, not if they lived to the age of Noah.

Ada and Evered thought of him as a kind of bogey, a spectre who walked and worked among men, who governed the lives of others and lived eternally. His malevolence was the only explanation they had for their mother's refusal to allow them to visit *The Hope* with their father. Evered insisted he would row out to meet the vessel himself when it arrived and Ada didn't argue the issue for long, not willing to hazard a repeat of the rift only weeks behind them.

"Should you tell him about Mother and Father?"

"What? That they're dead, you means?"

"He might. I don't know. If you lets on we're alone here."

The thought had occurred to Evered but he hadn't wanted to kindle talk of the mortifications the Beadle might inflict upon two children without guardians or benefactors.

"Perhaps we should stay hid away when *The Hope* comes in," Evered offered. "We could pitch up in the berry hills until they leaves."

Ada was quiet awhile. Then she said, "Every barrel we got is all but empty, Brother."

They lay silently weighing whether starvation might be worse than whatever the Beadle could visit upon them. They were quiet so long that Evered thought Ada had fallen asleep, until she said, "You could tell him Mother and Father is sick."

"Why would I do the like of that?"

"You could tell him they're struck down and lying in their beds here. That Father is too poorly to row out and he sent you in he's place."

It seemed on first blush a bit of genius and they fell asleep full up with the notion. But Evered woke hours later, troubled by a doubt that he had to talk through with Ada. He waited in the dark the same as if he was walking in the woods ahead of her and sat by the path to bide until she caught up. Eventually she rustled beside him.

"Sister," he said. "What if the Beadle wants to come ashore?"

"What do you mean?"

"After I tells him they're sick and lying in bed home. What if he wants to come ashore?"

She lifted her head. "He've never once come to shore."

"And I never once rowed out to *The Hope* now have I?" he said. "What if he wants to look in on them? Or wants to send for Mary Oram to see to doctoring?"

Ada turned toward him, raising her knees to her chest and setting her icy feet between Evered's thighs to warm them. He waited quiet, letting Ada sit with the problem, hoping she might offer some solution he could sleep with.

"Sister," he said but she didn't answer him. "I think I'll have to tell him the truth of it," he said.

"I expect so," was all she said.

Evered lay awake a long time after Ada drifted off, holding the cold of her feet between his legs, that chill rising up through him as he came to grips with the grim prospect of facing the Beadle alone.

Weeks more passed without a sign of *The Hope*. They were surviving on the rind end of their salt provisions, on the bony flesh of sculpins and conners. They scavenged the first sign of green on the shoreline, chewing mouthfuls of Scotch lovage and goosetongue and oyster plant. They reused the last handfuls of tea, fortifying the miserable drink with the previous year's juniper berries. Evered managed to net a few herring off the eastern point in April and they'd gorged on the baitfish for the short week they schooled close to shore. The cod were still miles out at sea. They'd been almost a month without a morsel of bread and had long finished the bit of salted meat from the whitecoat taken in March before *The Hope* finally appeared on the horizon. The relief Evered felt at sighting the vessel almost managed to overwhelm his fear of standing supplicant in the Beadle's presence.

She was hours approaching across the open water. Ada and Evered walked down to the stagehead as the schooner swung wide of the cove and came about, hauling in and reefing its main and foresail and dropping anchor on the Barrow Ledge which was the only decent bit of holding ground near the cove. It was coming on to evening when Evered climbed down to the boat and set the oars.

"You hurry back," Ada said.

"I won't linger," he said. "You haven't got a worry."

Evered glanced over his shoulder as he approached the vessel. Three men at midships watching him come. He rowed into the lee of *The Hope* and he came around to face the schooner instead of pulling alongside, unsure of the protocol. He sat staring up at the visitors, holding the boat steady in the swell. The vessel was even larger than he'd imagined seeing it from a distance all those years, a hundred feet from bowsprit to stern. He found it hard to credit *The Hope* was shaped and built and sailed by human hands.

"You likes the look of her then?" one of the crew shouted across to him.

"Yessir," he answered. It was the first time he'd been close enough to men other than his father to see their features, to hear their voices. They looked altogether too ordinary to be the creature he was looking for. "Is one of you the Beadle?" he called.

The crewmen glanced at one another with a look that suggested Evered had said something unintentionally comic. The one who'd spoken called out a second time. "We was expecting to see Sennet."

"I'm Sennet's youngster," Evered yelled up to them.

There was a solemn pause then. The men didn't move or speak though something in their manner shifted, as if at the same moment they had all doffed their caps in their minds. The one who seemed assigned to speak for the group said, "You'd best come on aboard."

Evered turned the boat and slid under *The Hope*'s shadow where he tied on. There was a rope ladder that he clambered up to the hands of the crew. They gathered around him a moment, nodding soberly. One of the three said, "You're the very daps of Sennet you is."

His mother nor Ada had ever mentioned any resemblance between himself and his father but Evered recognized the sentiment intended. It made him feel a little less fearful. "I might be so," he said.

The man who'd spoken first said, "The fellow you wants is this way." And he walked off across the deck beckoning Evered after him.

———

Ada watched Evered all the way out to *The Hope*, a heaviness roosting in her chest. She saw him turn the boat shy of the vessel and idle there a minute before he rowed in and tied up. She watched the crewmen lift him onto the deck and that weight pressed bodily against her lungs. For months they'd been alone with the loss of their parents and Martha. Not another soul knew those people were gone from the world but that fact was about to change for good and all. And the thought of strangers carrying the news beyond the cove made it seem somehow truer.

There was a short conference before Evered walked across the deck with one of the men and disappeared through a hatchway. Where he would be initiated into the arcane adult transactions she was not privy to. Or just as likely tied up and killed and possibly eaten by the Beadle who would then come into the cove after her. She had no notion which way it would go or how long she would have to wait before she learned her fate.

Her father's visits aboard sometimes lasted most of an afternoon and into the evening. Their mother never waited on him, walking back up to the tilt as soon as he tied on at the vessel. Ada and Evered hung close to the shoreline awhile but it was a rare instance that their patience outlasted their father's business. And the longer he was aboard the more likely it was he would come back singing some maudlin song and stumbling about as he off-loaded supplies from the boat, calling up the rise for help. Evered ran down to meet him but Ada and their mother stayed clear. He smelled of something noxious and seemed a man bewitched, expansive and effusive and diminished somehow. Occasionally he'd returned so theatrically demonstrative, so unrecognizable, that Sarah Best insisted he sleep in the store. By morning their father had come back to himself though it often took him a day or more to recover completely.

Ada was about to turn for the tilt to wait there when she saw movement on the deck. Evered emerged from a knot of men and climbed down to the boat and he turned to help someone else on the rope ladder, handing him carefully to a seat in the stern. They rowed away from *The Hope* without a sign of provision aboard. She thought Evered had lost his nerve and lied about their parents being overcome in their bunk, that the Beadle had insisted on coming ashore to visit the infirm. The boat crawled toward the barred harbour mouth and then inched across the cove to the stage where she stood.

Evered's back was to the shore as he rowed in but the man at the stern was watching her steadily. He wore a shapeless black cloak and a black skullcap and his arms were folded around a book that she guessed was the ledger their father had ranted against. It could only be the Beadle, she thought, bearing down upon her and upon the cove, moving at the agonizing pace of a nightmare. He held her eye as the boat drifted into the stage and she would have turned and run for the hills if she hadn't been paralyzed by fear.

Evered shipped the oars and tied the painter to the rails. He glanced up at Ada. "This is Mr. Clinch," he said. He clambered up beside her and turned back to reach a hand to the man in the stern.

"Abraham Clinch," the stranger said to her once he was standing beside them on the rickety stagehead. "I'm sorry for your troubles," he said with a curiously lopsided mouth.

Ada looked to her brother.

Evered said, "He've come to say a service for them."

———

Compared to the rough log tilt and the bare furnishings that Evered was born to, the cabin below decks aboard *The Hope* was so finely built and finished that at first he didn't take note of the man seated at the low desk. The place was lit by porthole windows and it seemed to the youngster they'd carted the sunlight inside in buckets. It wasn't until the man who led him there stepped across the room to stand beside the desk that Evered registered the sitting figure, the massive ledger open in front of him.

"Mr. Clinch," the man said, "this is Sennet's young one."

Clinch turned in his chair and gave Evered a quick once-over. "What's become of Best?" he asked.

"Father took sick and died," Evered said. "He've been dead this months. Same as Mother."

The man who'd brought him said, "You wants to take off your cap."

"Me cap?"

"Take off your cap," the man repeated.

Evered reached to pull the worsted hat from his head and both men bristled slightly at the sight of his preternatural white hair.

Clinch cleared his throat. "Both your parents are dead you're saying?"

"Yessir," he said. "Mr. Clinch sir," he said. "Mother died before Christmastime. And Father, we lost him shortly after." He wanted to ask if this was the audience with the Beadle he'd requested or another prelude to that event. He'd never heard his father mention anyone named Clinch.

"The young miss," the nameless man said. "The one we saw on the stagehead just now."

"My sister," Evered said.

"That would be Ada. Is that right?" Clinch reached for a second, smaller ledger on the desk and opened it, running his finger down a column. "Yes," he said, "Ada." He tapped at the page with a long yellow nail. "There was a third youngster. Another girl."

Evered nodded. "She was took by the same sickness that carried off Mother and Father. I'm sorry to say, sir," he said.

"The little one," he said, "Martha. I see she wasn't yet a year old."

"Hardly so much as halfways," Evered said. There was something unsettling in seeing the intimacies of his family's history at this stranger's fingertips. He assumed he was in the ledger alongside his sisters and their parents. Like birds in a cage.

"And they all passed before the new year?"

"As best I can figure, sir."

Clinch dipped a quill and started scratching at the marks on the pages before him.

"Do you know if?" Evered said. "I was looking to speak with the Beadle."

Clinch paused his writing and glanced up at the nameless man beside him who was staring ahead and would not meet his eye. He turned back to the open ledger and spoke without lifting his gaze from the page. "That was my office in the church at Mockbeggar before Reverend Fetter passed on, may he rest in peace. We have not managed to procure a replacement in the twenty-odd years since that loss. In the absence of ordained clergy I have done my best to administer the rites and sacraments of the faith."

Evered understood almost nothing of what Clinch was saying though the gist seemed to be that he was, in fact, in the presence of the Beadle.

"Your people," Clinch said. "They are buried in the cove?"

"My sister," Evered told him. "Martha. But Mother and Father. They was both buried at sea."

Clinch regarded him a minute and Evered stared innocently back. The Beadle had all his teeth on the left side of his mouth, and nothing but gums on the right, the cheek there hollow and wrinkled. It looked to Evered like there was a different man in the chair according to whichever way he turned his head.

"How old are you?" Clinch asked.

"I couldn't rightly say," he admitted. He expected it was a question the Beadle already knew the answer to and he was at sea in the conversation, a patch of water too dark to see the bottom of.

Clinch consulted his ledger and his lips moved silently for a moment. "You are not yet twelve," he said. "Not old enough to shave," Clinch said. "It's a tender age for a head of hair so white I would venture."

The Beadle's comment was so unexpected that it threw Evered completely. He'd all but forgotten the freakish occurrence himself. Even to Ada it was an unremarkable event among the waterfall of singular events they had suffered.

"It just come over me," he said. "When Father passed."

"Your hair turned white when your father died?"

He didn't have it in him to describe dragging his father's body down to the boat and rowing into open water, of muscling that awkward package over the gunwale and staring after its descent into the black. Of the long dead sleep he fell into afterward. All he said was, "I woke up one morning like it. So Ada tells me."

Clinch watched him in silence a while longer before he pushed back his chair to stand beside his desk. "There was no funeral service for them, I assume?"

Evered shook his head. "Not so's you'd call it so."

"I will come ashore," Clinch announced, "to read the service for the dead. And then we will deal with the business at hand."

The Beadle led them up off the landwash in a pathetic little funeral procession, Ada and Evered following meekly in the wake of his black cloak. At the top of the rise the Beadle turned to take the path to the Downs and he walked on with a shocking confidence, leading them to the garden and past the potato rows to the graves set at the edge of the bog as if he had dug them and buried the dead himself. It was an act of sorcery so astonishing that Ada reached out and pinched the flesh of her brother's arm viciously. But Evered barely felt it.

The Beadle stood at the head of the smaller, more recent grave. "What is the name of the deceased?" he asked.

"Martha," Evered told him.

"Yes," Clinch said impatiently. "Was that all? Just 'Martha'?"

Evered looked to Ada. "She was the one come up with the name."

Clinch stared at her expectantly.

"We never called her anything but that," Ada said.

"Martha Best then," he said. He opened the book in his hands and dove headlong into a soliloquy that cowed the youngsters with its practised fluency, its foreign rhetoric. "Your servants, Martha Best," he said, "and Sennet Best and Sarah Best." He asked pardon for Your Servants' sins. He talked about baptism and the sacraments and a general want and deficiency in these respects, he discoursed awhile on the folly of couples being unevenly yoked, he spoke of the burden of unknown transgressions that lay on the heads of Your Servants, all of which and all of whom he surrendered to the Lord's infinite mercy. He read periodically from the black book in his hands, his voice like a spadeful of gravel against wood. Ada and Evered stood with bowed heads through the service which was as much as they knew of religious manners. Evered took in almost nothing of what was said. He felt as if he was listening under water, holding his breath against the weight of his own ignorance, wanting only to escape the suffocation of the moment.

After what felt like a small eternity Clinch said "Amen" with an air of finality that made Ada and Evered raise their heads. The three watched one another in silence awhile, as if it were sacrilegious to move too quickly back to the banalities of ordinary conversation.

"Well," Clinch offered.

"Martha died innocent," Ada said then. She didn't speak directly to the Beadle, offering the statement up as a general announcement.

"We are born into a fallen world," the Beadle said.

"Mother said Martha died innocent," Ada insisted, "and she sits at God's right hand and hears our prayers."

Clinch opened his crooked mouth and closed it again, considering. "O simple ones, learn prudence," he said, "O fools, learn sense."

Evered broke in then to stop Ada answering back a second time. "It's coming on dark," he said. "We should see about getting you out to *The Hope*."

The Beadle took a moment, his folded hands holding the book at his waist. "Given the change in circumstances," he said, "I will need to consider the best course with respect to your enterprise." He looked to Evered. "You will leave me at *The Hope* and come see me again in the morning."

Clinch started down to the landwash and Evered followed after him. But Ada stayed beside her sister's grave and waited there until she was certain the Beadle had left the cove.

They sat facing one another as Evered rowed back to *The Hope*, within an arm's length and neither speaking a word. He glanced over his shoulder after every stroke to be spared having to look steady at the Beadle's expressionless face. It had never occurred to him there would be options to consider, that the enterprise in the cove was provisional and could be voided outright. He wished Ada hadn't provoked the man at the gravesite with her talk of innocence and God's right hand. He was a little fearful of his sister suddenly, the cold brass of her.

He didn't tie on at the schooner's side when they arrived, holding the boat steady by hand as the Beadle climbed the rope ladder.

Evered said, "Mr. Clinch, sir."

The Beadle paused to stare down at him from the deck.

"We haven't got hardly a morsel of food to our names," he said. He waved listlessly toward the cove, already sorry to have revealed the extent of their want.

"We will discuss our business come morning," Clinch said.

For weeks Ada had been husbanding a last cupful of peas against some desperate hour or special occasion and she had a thin soup waiting when Evered came up from the landwash. They were both swimming in the afternoon's events and tried to talk them into sense.

"He knew right where to go to find Martha's grave," Ada said. "Same as if he'd been up there thousands of times."

"Perhaps he read a service for the one that drownded," he said. "Perhaps that's how he knew the way."

"What do it mean," she said. "Unevenly yoked?"

Evered didn't know what it meant.

"He wouldn't leave us without a lick of flour would he, Brother? I'd kill for a bit of fresh bread."

"I wish you never said something to knock him off he's bearings so."

"Fools learn sense," she said, disgusted. "I idn't a fool."

No, Evered thought, that would likely be me.

"I wish we wouldn't writ down in his book," he said. "It don't seem right he can keep us barred up there like that."

They cleaned their bowls and then cleaned the pot with their fingers for the last taste of salt and they went to bed hungry.

Evered was alone when he woke the next morning, Ada already up with a fire burning in the hearth and gone down to the stage after their breakfast. She came back with a conner too small to fillet and she fried the fish whole.

"There's already men about on *The Hope*," she said as they picked the flesh from the conner's thorny backbone. It was just enough food to make them feel how hungry they were.

He said, "I'd best get out there." He half expected her to offer to go with him again and was relieved she didn't, not knowing what she might decide to throw in the Beadle's face. "I'll have a full boat when I comes in," he told her. "Flour and peas and salt meat."

She nodded again but wouldn't meet his eyes. "Tea and molasses?"

"Please God," he said.

Ada stayed in the tilt when Evered left. Hours before the sun rose she'd startled from a dream of a Beadle-faced crow flying low over the cove with little Martha in its claws, her infant sister bawling with the same forsaken voice as the orphaned white-coat on the ice. She turned in to Evered's chest with her heart in her throat, taking in the comforting, faintly corrupt smell of his breath. His arm tucking her closer as he slept. But she could not clear her head of that image and lay awake whispering to Martha until she finally got out of bed and started the fire.

The morning had risen clear but a thick fog rolled in by the time Evered made way for the skerries. *The Hope* was within shouting distance from there but sat invisible in the fog. He rowed toward the Barrow Ledge, listening for the sound of water lapping at the hull, for the voices of the men on deck. He came around when the vessel finally appeared, its dark shape-less shape looming in the grey. Thinking it was how his father saw the world all his days.

He helloed to the crew and they called him in to the rope ladder.

"I'm not getting Mr. Clinch from he's bed I hope," he said when he climbed onto the deck.

One of the crewmen leaned in close so as not to be overheard. "Mr. Clinch don't sleep," he said. "So far as we mortals can tell."

"He's waiting on you," the man who spoke to Evered the day before said. "You knows where to find him."

He glanced back to the three men as he went across the deck to the hatchway. He could see they were all watching after him but the fog made it impossible to know what their faces might be saying.

The Beadle was at his desk when Evered stepped into the cabin, crouched over the ledger. He looked like a man gutting and cleaning a fish, the book lying open along its spine, the blade of the quill rasping across paper. Evered stood waiting in silence so long that for a time he thought Clinch hadn't registered his arrival.

"Mr. Best," the Beadle said suddenly, without lifting his head from the book.

"Yessir."

Clinch pointed to the spot beside the desk where the crewman had stood the day before, then leaned back in his chair. He gave the boy the same once-over and it was enough to remind Evered to remove his cap.

"Is it your intention," the Beadle said, "to run this enterprise on your own?"

"I expect so," he said. "Ada and me was planning to, yes."

"And you expect Mr. Strapp to underwrite the cost?"

Evered didn't know what the question meant. He kneaded the cap in his hands, feeling like he might faint.

"Mr. Strapp," the Beadle clarified, "provides the supplies you live on summer and winter. In return you sell the fish you catch to Mr. Strapp as payment."

"That was what me and Ada was planning for," he said.

Clinch turned to his ledger, tapping at the page. "At the end of last season your father's account showed a deficit of nearly thirty-seven pounds sterling."

Evered nodded. "If you says so, Mr. Clinch sir."

"Do you know what that means?"

He shook his head.

The Beadle looked down at his lap. "It means that last season, your enterprise, employing four people in total, was not able to cover the cost of the supplies Mr. Strapp gave on credit."

"We had plenty of fish," Evered said. "It was too wet last August to dry it proper is all."

"Well you know something of the business. That is a mark in your favour."

"We got the stagehead up and ready for the season."

"You built that structure on your own I presume."

"Me and Ada, yes."

"That is not a mark in your favour, Mr. Best. And there are but two of you left to prosecute the fishery."

Evered stood with his mouth open, at a loss in the moment to answer the charge.

"I can't in good conscience ask Mr. Strapp to throw good money after bad."

"There's fish galore out here, as much as you wants to catch. And Ada's a dab hand with the knife, she worked header at the splitting table some last season. And she've the nerve of a mule, she don't mind work."

The Beadle held up a hand but Evered pressed his case.

"We could get by on not half the supplies we had last year," he said.

"Mr. Best," the Beadle said. "The only sensible course is for you and your sister to come with us now to Mockbeggar. Mr. Strapp would see to finding a station for you both that over time would free you from the debt carried forward."

Evered shook his head.

"After that time you could return here if you choose, in a far better state to carry on the venture."

"Ada won't leave Martha," Evered said.

The Beadle almost smiled but stopped himself. "Your sister Martha?" he said. "The dead one?"

"Ada won't leave her alone here in the cove."

"I see," Clinch said although it wasn't at all obvious he did. He closed the ledger on the desk. "Then you must convince her to do so."

Evered shook his head again. "She got the nerve of a mule, Mr. Clinch."

"Have you ever seen a mule, Mr. Best? Do you even know what it is?"

Evered shrugged. "It's something like a horse, idn't it?"

"Have you ever seen a horse?"

"No sir," he said. "It was just something Father used to say. About the mule."

The Beadle closed his eyes and touched his fingers to his forehead.

"Maybe Mr. Strapp," Evered said. "He might find someone could come out to bunk in with us."

"You want to hire a hand to work shares with you?"

Evered wasn't completely certain what he had suggested but he nodded yessir regardless.

"There is at present," the Beadle said, "a dearth of servants on this coast. Mr. Strapp has barely enough hands to fill the positions at his various enterprises."

"One season," Evered said. "If we has one season to try our luck."

"I have to answer to Mr. Strapp."

"If we can't make a go of it come September month," Evered said, "then Ada will have to see the sense in it." He said, "We'll shift our lot into Mockbeggar as you says and we will answer to Mr. Strapp ourselves."

The Beadle rested his hand on the ledger, clicking his yellow nails against the cover. "That abomination of a stage you have built there," he said finally. There was a note of anger in his voice as if he already regretted the course he was setting. "I doubt it will stand to the end of June."

Evered tried to restrain himself but couldn't keep the smile off his face. "No sir," he said, "likely you're right on that count. It was a first go for us. We'll have to set it straight."

Clinch opened the ledger and scratched furiously at a page for several minutes. "I have one request of you," he said as he wrote. "Your mother as you know would not submit to having her children baptized outside the Papist church. Had I known her intentions in this matter I would not have consented to perform the marriage ceremony."

"It was you married them?" Evered said.

The Beadle inclined his head slightly. "Your sister Martha died without benefit of the baptismal sacrament. And I would ask you to consider it now," he said. He turned to look at Evered. "You and your sister Ada. That your name be recorded in the Book of Life."

Evered had never heard the first thing about baptism before and he wasn't at all clear what was being requested of him now. But he didn't want to risk refusing outright. "I'll have to talk to Ada about it," he said.

"Very well." The Beadle held the quill toward Evered. "You will make your mark here," he said and he pointed to the bottom of the page. He took Evered's hand to pull him a step closer to the desk. He placed the pen in the boy's fingers and enclosed them with his own, making two strokes on the paper. "Done," he said.

A Bear. The Beadle, Again.

The caplin came in to spawn along the cove's western arm a week after *The Hope* departed, each successive wave depositing a writhing mass on the grey sand like the half-drowned survivors of a shipwreck. Ada and Evered waded in the shoals with a landing net, hauling all they could lift onto dry ground. They set aside a barrel for breakfast food and two barrels to use as handline bait and as much again as they could drag up to the farm garden, turning it in with the seaweed to make something of the mean soil. And the beach was carpeted with the tens of thousands they left behind, the air clotted with the stench of that prodigal surfeit rotting on the landwash. The cod followed the caplin into shallower water, schooling in their starry numbers beyond the skerries. And the teeming downpour of the season's work fell upon them.

They were on the move hours before first light. Evered cut up his bait on the stage and rowed out through the harbour mouth into the maze of constellations reflected on the ocean's surface or through the black morning under cloud. The boat almost too much for his boyish frame, his hands coming up around his ears on each stroke. But he had a line in the water as the day broke.

He fished in fog and driving rain and in bald glassy sunshine so fierce it struck at him like a hammer. He wouldn't turn for home until he'd filled the fish pound and the little cuddy in the bow and sometimes the bilge at his feet as well, the gunwales standing barely a hands-breadth above the water. The boat riding low and sluggish with that much weight and he was next to foundering in crosswinds on occasion, his heart in his throat as he hauled for the cove.

He worked the Barrow Ledge or the Foggity Shoals or the Wester Shoal or the Razor Ledge, choosing according to some guesswork as to where the cod might be feeding that day based on the wind and which direction the tide was running. If he didn't strike within an hour's time Evered moved to some other likely spot. But once he was into the fish he worked until he had the fill of his boat, running lines fore and aft.

The ocean's drift took him off his shore marks and every hour or so he'd row back to the top of the ground to stay over the fish. Even when his father was alive it was Evered's job to watch the marks and judge when they had gone astray of them, Sennet's sight too poor to make out the Black Dog below the berry fields or the notch in the Downs. It had always seemed a striking shortcoming in his father. But the man's nearsightedness made his competence in every other sphere the more astonishing.

The cod were up in the spring and early summer, feeding on caplin near the surface. But later in the season they often pooled near the floor, thirty or forty fathom down, a long way to send and haul a line. His father had a knack to raise the fish, leaving the bait just above their heads to draw them higher each time. Evered would watch that living school of flesh ascend out of the black toward their boat and you could almost pick the fish you wanted when he was done. It was a conjuring trick he thought Sennet Best had invented.

Evered tried to raise the fish off the shoal ground himself now, once or twice saving himself a few fathoms of line though he couldn't be sure if it was his doing or just the work of the currents below. He never managed to make the school rise from the darkness as his father had and the failure made him feel he'd never be more than a youngster in the world, that he was only playing at being a man.

Ada spent the earliest hours of each indistinguishable day hauling water from the brook and baking the day's bread. When the sun was above the horizon she walked up to the farm garden where she harvested the rocks brought to the surface by last winter's frost heave before setting the seed potatoes and turnips and cabbages and beets.

From the Downs she could see the shoal ground Evered was working, and when he took in his line and turned for the harbour she walked down to help clear the morning's catch. The two children wielding knives honed to a razor's edge, up to their slender wrists in the blood and offal, their heads wreathed by galling halos of blackflies and mosquitoes. It took them hours longer to get through a boatload than it had with four at the splitting table which often meant there wasn't light enough for a second haul out and they spent the evening working the garden together instead.

When there was time enough for an afternoon run, Ada went out with Evered. They stood at the gunwale, bringing the hooked cod to the surface hand over hand like they were drawing up pitchers of water from a well. He taught her the marks for each shoal—the Black Dog close on the eastern head, the notch midway between the tilt and the Foxes' Ears— and she rowed them to the top when they were drawing off the grounds. They caught what could be taken before the sky went duckish and they sat side by side to share the burden of the oars on the trip in.

They ate before clearing the second run, standing up for fear of falling asleep if they sat, mopping their plates clean with bread and nodding over mugs of tea. It was dark by the time they walked back to the stage and they made the fish by the light of rot oil burning in a slutlamp. Midnight or later before they were done and they muddled up the rise in the dark, punch-drunk and mute. They slept together until the weather warmed enough to make the company a discomfort and they took to opposite bunks, surrendering to the leaden weight of sleep as soon as they lay down.

Evered woke before first light and hauled himself to the hearth to uncover the coals, blowing them red-hot to start the fire. He wouldn't wake Ada before the kettle boiled, wanting to give her those few minutes more to sleep. His wrists were atonic and sore, the fingers stiffened to claws. After hoisting the kettle over the fire he walked out behind the tilt to relieve himself and he pissed on his palsied hands, making fists under the burning salve to coax them to life.

Ada was up when he came back inside, a panful of caplin over the fire. She still talked aloud to Martha when she was alone, offering up a distracted commentary on the state of the weather or the day's catch or whatever physical affliction was causing her grief in the moment. But she and Evered barely spoke a word to one another, falling into the same taciturn custom their parents had kept. Once a week Ada fried a breakfast of toutons as a treat and she and Evered slathered the doughy cakes with molasses, licking their plates clean when they were done, each smiling to see the other do the same. And that was the only recognizable bit of childhood still in their lives. Martha's rag doll was abandoned on the shelf above Ada's bed, the display of shells and bric-a-brac up there ignored through most of the summer, unchanged but for a silver button Ada unearthed as she was picking rocks from the farm garden. It was an exquisite thing, fine and heavy with an elaborate engraved image that she nor Evered had encountered before. Evered guessed the thing had come from the clothes of the stranger interred beside their baby sister though it was hard to believe their parents would have buried a piece of clothing with buttons made of silver.

The object's practical function was obvious but the elegance of the graven image seemed so far from the raw austerity and moil of their lives that it almost hurt Ada to look at it. She couldn't imagine an earthly realm where the utilitarian would merit the attention the silver artifact displayed and she thought of it as something dropped from the stars, a gift from Martha. It was the last image she saw before she slept at night and the first she thought of when she woke. There were days that tiny touchstone was all that kept her from lying in a heap and bawling.

By the middle of July the cod began drifting off into deeper waters. Evered had to row further from the cove to find them and stay out longer to take a decent load aboard which meant only one trip of fish to clear and the work settled into a pace that made their lives seem less demented.

In August Ada swept the beach clean, scraping mollyfodge from the rocks on the bawn to make an untainted platform for laying out the cod that had been sitting weeks in salt bulk. Evered helped Ada scrub the excess salt from the wet fish in a tub of sea water and they carted it to the bawn on the hand barrow where Ada laid them out head to tail like youngsters in a crowded bed. She stayed close to the bawn all day with an eye on the weather, piling the fish into yaffles against a shower of rain or the sear of too much sun. Before the end of the month most of the catch was cured, each splayed crucifix of flesh hard as a plank, all of it packed in the salt shed on the stage awaiting the Beadle's stony appraisal.

It was as much a mystery to them now as ever how that sentence was arrived at and handed down. The stacks in the bulkheads looked paltry compared to previous years and neither youngster could manage the complicated conversion required to factor their current state of affairs into the final accounting. That flaming sword hung over them all season and it burned brighter every passing day as the time for *The Hope*'s return drew closer.

On one of the last bright days of August they renounced all work and walked to the brook. The water was running low that late in the summer and there was only one pool deep enough to submerge a body. They stripped off their ragged clothes, beating them wet on the rocks and spreading them in the sun, and then they scoured at themselves with homemade soap and with alder branches cut from the banks. Their hands and forearms and faces looked to have been dipped in burnt umber but their hairless torsos were a pale tuberous white like something just unearthed from a garden. After they had scoured their skin raw they settled back on the smooth stones, steeping in the moving water while they waited for their clothes to dry.

They went into the berry hills as September came in, rowing a mile along the coast beyond the brook and hauling the boat up in the lee of a granite boulder their parents called the Black Dog before walking into the backcountry. The berry hills were a stretch of woods consumed by fire a lifetime past, the burn-over colonized by low berry bushes. They bent among them hours at a stretch, their hands darting like birds among the blossoms. They didn't bring any food with them, eating from the bushes all day as they picked. They filled a brin sack halfway with blueberries and took turns carrying the deadweight of it down to the boat.

In the morning they set out for more, leaving just after sunrise. They walked up into the backcountry, chatting aimlessly, and as they came up through the spruce trees into the berry fields Ada stopped mid-sentence, reaching a hand to Evered's arm. A black bear was head down in the bushes a hundred yards off. Even from that distance the size of the animal made Ada's scalp pull tight.

"We should go," she said just before the bear rose up on its hind legs, nosing at the air. Ada took Evered's hand and squeezed hard enough to make him wince. "Brother," she whispered.

"Hold still," he said. "She's only after a few berries same as we."

"She looks like she'd eat more than berries."

"Shush," he said, and they stood watching the bear wave its massive paws like it was asleep and dreaming itself adrift in a pool of calm water. It snuffed and grunted and fell onto its fore-legs and turned suddenly, ambling into the trees away from them.

"We could come back tomorrow," Ada said then.

"Might be raining tomorrow. Or worse yet. She's likely gone on now."

They'd never encountered bears on the shore and Ada didn't know where Evered had gathered his knowledge of their habits but she didn't question him. They settled in on the edge of the field, staying close together, picking without turning away from the spot across the clearing where the bear had dis-appeared. Half an hour later they heard a rustle in the trees behind them. That unmistakable snuff at their backs, the bear circling the burn-over to get downwind.

When they turned they could see where the animal was watching them. Almost invisible in the brush but close enough they could make out the great head jigging at the air to take in their scent. Once it had satisfied its curiosity it seemed to lose interest, turning to walk back the way it came, swallowed up by the bush. They stood in silence a long time, afraid to move or speak.

"She won't likely bother with us now," Evered said finally.

"You said she was likely gone on the last going off," Ada said. And when he didn't answer her she said, "I don't want to get killed over a few berries."

"No one's getting killed here today," he said though there was no real conviction in his voice.

They started in at the picking again but couldn't concentrate on the job, jumping at every noise, real or imagined. They decided to walk back to the boat before noon and a week passed before the thought of the fall without more berries convinced them to make another visit. They found the imprint of the bear's paws among the trees where it had watched them and they measured their hands against the spread of it. But they never saw the animal again though they returned to the hills every day till the weather broke wet.

Ada often spoke to Martha about the bear when she was alone and goosebumps rose on her arms each time she described the encounter, the soft explosion of its breath behind them in the bush. The further she got from the event, the more ridiculous it seemed to have stayed in the berry hills after the bear went off into the trees. But the sight of it occupied the same place in her thoughts as the silver button with its finely graven image. She often dreamt of the bear on its hind legs and idly waving its front paws. She dreamt of the animal asleep beside her, of stroking its wide wild head in her lap.

The berry season was autumn's equivalent of the caplin scull—a rare episode of plenty in their world, a seasonal windfall that tormented them with its brevity, with its attendant, inevitable waste. They had no way to keep the cache of berries from spoiling and they gorged themselves on the sweetness morning and evening. They were unaccustomed to that richness and were overcome with the flux. But even days of stomach cramps and the bedevilment of diarrhea weren't enough to make them swear off eating the dark fruit, their lips and teeth blackened like the mouths of ghouls in a medieval painting of hell.

Ada made pots of jam from what they didn't eat, boiling the berries into a sugared confection that would keep weeks longer again in the cool of the root cellar. Come November they would be scraping the furred layer of mould from the last pots, the overripe jam spread on slices of fresh bread or spooned over flour dumplings. Even the tinge of rot was something they developed a taste for.

There had always been a celebratory feel about the ritual of boiling the berries down for jam, coming at the end of the season when the catch was put up and before the Beadle's evaluation undercut their parents' hopes for its worth, when the work had slowed enough to allow for something close to leisure, for projects that didn't touch in some way on bare survival. Their father brewed spruce beer while the jam was being boiled and it was the only time they saw their parents openly affectionate with one another. Bustling around the tiny space as if in competition for it, offering sly insults back and forth. Their father made repeated attempts to steal a taste of the jam, their mother defending it with a wooden spoon across his knuckles. The mock struggle escalated as the day progressed, Ada and Evered taking sides and adding their own racket to the contest and the whole thing devolved into shouting and wrestling and bouts of choking laughter.

The two youngsters had gone months without mentioning their mother or father, instinctively avoiding direct contact with a grief so raw. But the smell of the berries conjured their parents so viscerally they were desperate to touch those gone people. Shying from the urge all the same, each afraid what they felt might be a one-sided craving.

"Do you mind how," Ada said. She was almost whispering, her eyes on the clay pot she was filling. "How they used to fight over the jam?"

Evered nodded. "I minds it," he said.

Ada smiled down at the table. "The time I went after Father in the corner?"

"He deserved the licking," Evered said. "Every smack."

Neither could bring themselves to say more about it and they finished the work in silence, both feeling more alone for being taken over by that memory. It was the fall before Martha was born. Sarah Best would not surrender a sniff of the jam without it was taken by force and their father threw himself into the challenge with an ardent persistence. He was a small-ish man and their mother just a skiver of bone and sinew, both of them tough as corded rope. Ada and Evered stood to one side, cowed by the escalating pitch of the struggle, by the rhyme of oaths flung back and forth. Their father stole the spoon away and their mother smacked him across the ear with the flat of her hand.

"You lousy hedge whore," he shouted, grabbing at her shoulders.

"Muck spout," she said through her teeth. "Filthy beard splitter."

They wrestled nearly to exhaustion before he managed to corral her arms, cuffing her wrists together in one hand to give himself unfettered access to the cooling jam. He scooped a ladleful in his bare fingers and held their mother still a long moment then, trying to catch his breath, watching her as the thickened juice dripped from his hand.

"Don't you," Sarah Best said, weak with laughter, almost too winded to speak.

"Now my little blowsabella," he said.

"You dirty shag-bag," she said, yanking with both arms, using the last of her strength to try to pull clear.

"My bob tail," their father said, reefing her closer.

"Sennet Best," she said, "you buck fitch."

And he brought the dripping hand to her face then, smearing the jam across her cheeks and her mouth and her squinted eyes as she squirmed in his grip and laughed and cursed him all she was worth.

Ada had been fighting back a surge of tears and she charged at her father, wailing at the top of her lungs, beating at his back and his head. If she'd a knife handy she would have killed the man.

"God's nails," he shouted, leaning into their mother.

"Stop it now," Sarah Best whispered. "You're scaring the child. Stop it." She wriggled free and mopped at her face with her apron-skirt while their father cowered in a corner under the barrage of his daughter's fists.

Their mother gathered Ada into her arms from behind, shushing her. "I'm all right," she said. "I'm best kind. We was just playing about."

Ada turned into her mother's chest, holding tight as she went on sobbing. Their father knelt a few minutes longer, giggling stupidly in the corner where he'd been pinned. He glanced across the room and pointed at Evered. "And where were you," he said, "when the women ganged up on your poor old father."

Evered could barely hear the man over the noise of blood in his head. His face was so hot it felt swollen, disfigured. He had his hands folded in front of his crotch, his crupper standing on end and pulsing behind them.

"We men don't have a chance we don't stick up for one another," his father said.

Their mother turned to him and said, "Take Ada down to the landwash, see if you can't find her a wish rock or something." She wiped at the stains on her face with her sleeves, still trying to catch her breath. "We'll have bread and jam for supper when you comes back up," she said.

Their father knelt in front of Ada before she went through the door. "You're a fine girl, Daughter," he said. "You was right to act so. I deserved every smack you give me and so I did."

Ada and Evered spent the last of the afternoon scouring the landwash without speaking a word about what they had witnessed. When they were called up for supper their parents were composed and serene as if nothing out of the ordinary had happened and both Ada and Evered acted the same.

They acted the same now, filling the clay pots with jam and then setting them in the root cellar. They shared a meal of bread and jam and went to bed as soon as the sun went down. The weather had already turned toward frost at night but they were still observing the summer habit of sleeping in opposite bunks which Evered was grateful for, given the mucky agitation the memory of that afternoon had stirred up. He lay in the dark wondering if Ada was awake in her bed like himself but afraid to ask.

———

The Hope appeared on the horizon the following morning.

Ada and Evered spent the hours it took the schooner to reach the holding ground hand-barrowing the season's catch from the salt shed to the front of the stage. It looked more substantial in the open air somehow and it gave them both a sudden optimism. They packed the boat full and Evered rowed out through the skerries to meet the vessel. The same three men were on deck to greet him and take up the cured fish. It was early evening when Evered left the stage with the last boat-load and he told Ada to go on back to the tilt for her supper.

"I don't mind waiting," she said.

"I could be hours yet," he said.

Ada thought of the state of her father when he rowed back from those fall visits, the strange cast of his face, the sour smell about him. "You come home yourself," she said and Evered nodded.

"I'll be back by and by," he said.

The three crewmen were standing around the yaffled stacks of cod with their hands on their hips when Evered climbed aboard *The Hope*. The Beadle was moving in a crouch like a man in a berry patch, lifting and setting down the stiff parcels of flesh, throwing fish after fish into an untidy pile to one side. He didn't so much as glance at Evered as he went about his business.

"You two had a very good year of it," one of the crew offered.

"We done all right considering."

"Twas just the two of you?" the man said. "You and the young girl?"

"Fish galore out here the summer," Evered said. "We couldn't hardly keep ahead of it."

The Beadle turned from them and walked off toward the

hatchway, disappearing below without a word. Evered stared after him, uncertain if he was meant to follow.

"You'll want a little dawn of rum," the crewman said and he picked up a bottle tucked under the rail, handed it across to Evered.

He'd only ever had an occasional glass of his father's spruce beer in his young life and the rum burned as he swallowed, the fire of it rising through his sinuses and he had to wipe tears from his eyes.

"Go easy now," the man said, reaching for the bottle. "You wants to be able to keep your feet when you're standing in front of Himself." And he told a story about a Mr. Lucas who kept a goat aboard his coasting vessel for its milk, how a gallon of rum in a bucket was left unattended on deck and Mr Lucas's goat drank almost the whole of its contents, the animal in a state of intoxication so complete as to be unable to get upon her legs. And for days afterward the milk she gave was strong enough that a glassful sent Mr. Lucas to his bed singing scraps of My Thing Is My Own.

The crewmen laughed together in a way that suggested they'd heard the story a hundred times and never tired of it, passing the bottle among the circle and shaking their heads. "For my little fiddle," one of the crew sang out, "must not be played on." Which set them off on another round of laughter.

Abraham Clinch raised his head through the hatchway behind them. "Best," he shouted and everyone sobered immediately.

"One more nip," the crewman said, handing the rum across, "and we'll see what the Beadle has to say about it all."

Evered choked down another mouthful and went off across the deck.

"We'll have another drop when you're done," the man called after him.

Evered went down the stairs and stepped just inside the cabin's threshold. He felt himself unsteady suddenly but for the first time since his parents died almost completely without fear. The Beadle was engrossed in his ledgers, the pen nib making its peculiar sniffing noise at the paper.

"We had a very good season at it," Evered volunteered.

The Beadle stopped mid-stroke, the quill hovering in mid-air.

"We had a fair time at the fish," he tried again.

"Mr. Best," the Beadle said. He pointed to the spot beside his chair and Evered walked across the room with his hat in his hands. "You are pleased with yourself I take it."

"I expect so, sir."

Clinch nodded. He seemed younger than Evered had thought in the spring but no less severe, especially when he fronted the toothless side of his face.

"Almost half the fish you have brought to us," the Beadle said, "is dun or wet or broken and hardly saleable in the West Indies. A portion is refuse and not fit to feed dogs."

Evered stood with his mouth open.

"Yes, Mr. Best?"

"We was both standing in above our station. I only had a scatter day as splitter before the summer. And Ada was first time alone at drying the fish. It took us a while to get the hang of doing it proper." A smile crept across the Beadle's face as Evered spoke and it made him dislike the man. "We managed finest kind as we went along," he said.

"That is your studied opinion?"

Evered nodded drunkenly.

The Beadle turned back to the ledger, scratching hastily to the bottom of the open page. He said, "Your season amounts to forty-seven quintals of fish. Seven quintals are mudfish. A little more than fifteen quintals are West Indie."

"And the rest?"

"The rest is Number Two at best. And will just about cover the supplies Mr. Strapp fronted in the spring. The winter supplies will have to be set against your account."

Evered tried to hold off smiling, not certain he understood the meaning of it all.

"You are still," the Beadle said, "intent on prosecuting the fishery out here on your own?"

"I can't think why we wouldn't."

"It does not surprise me to hear you say so. I spoke to Mr. Strapp about the possibility of a hand to work shares on this enterprise and there is no one can be spared to join you. But that may change if you hold out long enough."

"I expect we'll manage."

The Beadle turned in his chair to face the boy directly. "Have you and your sister made a decision?" he asked. "On the question of baptism into the church?"

Evered shook his head. He hadn't had the stomach to raise it with Ada, knowing she would rather eat fish hooks than break faith with their mother and Martha to satisfy the Beadle. And he'd all but forgotten the issue in the sleepless churn of the season's work. "Ada won't have it," he said.

"And the girl speaks for you both on this matter?"

Evered shrugged. "She got the nerve of a mule, Mr. Clinch, sir."

The Beadle watched him silently for so long then that Evered was aware of himself wavering on his feet. He was on the verge of confessing the lie, admitting he'd never spoken to Ada, asking to be baptized there and then aboard *The Hope* before Clinch offered the quill. Evered stepped forward to take it, making his mark on the page. He surrendered the pen and stepped back to his spot.

"You will be given your supplies as you leave," Clinch said.

Evered nodded.

"I doubt it will be enough to keep you and your sister from perishing through the full of a winter," the Beadle said. "But if I am wrong, we will see you again in the spring."

"Please God, sir," Evered said.

Ada raked the floor of the tilt clean while she was waiting. She had the button in her apron pocket and she took it out now and then to study. It was too elaborate to draw in a medium as coarse as the dry sand and she experimented with simplified versions that didn't lose all sense of the thing's elegance. She tried sticks and utensils with points of various sizes, she dampened the sand to help it hold the strokes. But it would not come. She spent half an hour on a single iteration and suddenly erased the disappointment, kicking at the sand. It was a peculiar irritation that something she loved could be so far beyond her capacity to engender and she moved on to an image of the bear's paws instead, using the heel of her hand to make impressions in the wet sand.

It wasn't until she realized it was too dark to clearly see what she was doing that it struck her how much time had passed, that Evered hadn't returned from *The Hope*. It was gone a ways past duckish when she went down to the stagehead and she couldn't tell if anyone was about on deck or even if the boat was still tied on to the schooner.

She'd once asked her mother what it was kept her father so long aboard *The Hope*. Sarah Best shrugged in a way that made Ada think the question was an aggravation. "That's only men's business they're into," she said. "I don't pay no mind as long as they don't bring it in here."

There was an edge to her mother's voice that kept Ada from asking anything more. But she couldn't imagine what the flesh and bone reality beneath that vague dismissal might be. Evered, for all he was a boy, had no more insight than herself. And he was out there now learning it first-hand. She could not sort out if she should envy that fact or consider herself lucky to be free of it altogether.

It was closing in on fully dark when she saw the shape of the boat move clear of *The Hope*. There were lamps lit on the deck of the schooner and in the windows of the cabins by then. The sky was overcast and black and those lights glittered like a handful of dull stars on the horizon. Ada lit the slutlamp to guide Evered in, oily smoke spiralling off the wick. She heard the slap of the oars as he came closer and the sound of her brother singing some unfamiliar song about a fiddle.

He came around at the stage sloppily, knocking against the rails and losing his balance, and he crawled to the bow to tie on below the spot where she stood with the lamp.

"We got a winter's supply out of it," he said, gesturing at the cargo of barrels and burlap sacks in the fish pound and at the stern. Even in the poor light she could tell it was a fraction of what their father used to bring home from *The Hope*, that the winter ahead of them would be a thin stretch. Evered made several attempts to find his feet and fell on his arse each time. "Sister," he said. "I'm so bad now as old Mr. Lucas' goat." He turned to the gunwale and retched his guts up into the water.

She set the lamp on the longers and climbed down into the boat. Evered was rocking over his knees and she sat next to him and put a hand to his bare neck. She could smell the reek coming off him, the same foreign stink her father brought back from visits aboard. Men's business. And her brother like the greenest youngster beside her, on the verge of tears.

"You managed fine, Brother," she said. "You done good."

"Don't you ever leave me," he said out of nowhere.

"Why would I do the like of that?"

"Just don't," he said.

It was a cool night and much colder on the water and she moved in close to Evered for the warmth.

"Just you don't," he said again.

The season turned early toward winter, the first snow falling by mid-October, and they resumed their lifelong habit of sharing a bunk, huddling together after the dead fire's heat leaked from the room and the wind whistled through the stud walls. Once enough snow was down they went together into the backwoods to drag out the logs Evered left standing in the spring and they spent weeks cutting and splitting junks for fuel.

In the heart of the winter there were long hours of dark and enforced idleness and they passed the time with made-up games that featured elaborate rules forgotten and redrawn from one day to the next. They whiled away evenings with a call and response they knew as There's Your Answer, asking the most ludicrous or inane or troubling questions they could think of in turn—Do the dead piss and shit in heaven? Why does the brook run downhill and never up? Where do the stars sleep during the day?—and replying with belches or farts or some invented animal noise. "There's your answer," the respondent concluded each time, "and may it serve thee." They played a version of hide-and-seek within the cramped bounds of the tilt, the blinder covering their face as the other hid and keeping their eyes closed as they searched the room with their reaching hands. They sang the fragments of songs remembered from their parents' days, they rearranged the materials on Ada's shelf or drew elaborate designs in the sand near the hearth. They'd settled back into their shared sense of being of a piece and there was little enough happening in the world around them to disturb the illusion.

Evered still woke to the sound of Ada whispering aloud on occasion and he finally worked up the nerve to ask who she was speaking to. "Our Martha?" he said when she confessed.

"She's here," Ada said. "I feels her right with us still."

"Do she ever say anything back to you?"

"Not in anything like words. But I hears her inside."

"A voice like?"

"No," she said. "Just a feeling. You don't feel her with you?"

He shook his head in the dark and lay quiet awhile. It made sense to him there would be a division of aptitude and skill between them and the envy he felt for her peculiar gifts was all admiration, devoid of pettiness.

"Do you feel the same thing with Mother and Father?"

"No," she said. "It's just with Martha."

He was about to ask her why the difference when it came to him. "She died an innocent," he said.

Ada raised a hand to her brother's face. There was a fuzz of blond hair on his chin and she brushed her fingers back and forth through the downy growth. "Martha sits at God's right hand," she said, "and she hears our prayers."

It made Evered wonder where exactly it was their parents sat in the firmament. He thought that heaven might be like the ocean, that the dead were set adrift within it and that nothing in that expanse sat still for long but for their infant sister anchored at God's side. But not even Ada would venture an answer to that question. "You'll have to ask the Beadle come the spring," she said, mimicking exactly the dismissive tone their mother used when discussing the men's business that went on aboard *The Hope*.

"Perhaps I will then," Evered said, knowing all the while he lacked the spine to raise any such thing with the man. He was every day more daunted by Clinch's brusque manner, by the ledgers in which they were all of them pinned and held, by the ruthless calculations he wielded over their lives. He sometimes dreamt of the Beadle and he woke from those visions stricken, the images haunting him for days afterward. Standing naked beside the desk aboard *The Hope* as Clinch worked over his ledgers. The Beadle reaching out without turning his gaze from the page, touching him as he'd never been touched.

Evered frozen to the spot as those fingers made their cold provoking inspection.

Ada often shook him awake for the tortured noises he was
making beside her. "What is it?" she asked him.

"Nothing," he said, feeling ambushed, cornered. "Some old
foolishness." He turned to face the wall to hide the state he
was in, his ware unaccountably stiff and straining against his
small clothes.

He did what he could to push the agitation underground
but it coloured whole swaths of that winter season. He never
spoke to Ada about those harrowing dreams or the sense of
fervent infirmity they left him with. And that was the only
sliver that came between them for the longest time.

The last of the salt meat was gone before the new year and
they dwindled on the short rations, the weight dropping off
their spare frames. But the Labrador ice brought the seals in
numbers come March and Evered killed and flensed half a
dozen before the pack broke up and drifted off. They ate the
oily meat at every meal until the herring struck in a month
later and they could see the flesh slowly coming back into the
other's face.

By the time the caplin rolled on the beach they felt relatively hale and eager to get at the fish. They'd knocked together
a stage and salt shack that was idiosyncratic but sound. The
cod arrived early and stayed close to shore longer than any
year in their lives. August month was mostly dry and they put
away enough decent fish to be granted something close to a

full ration of supplies for the first time since their parents died.

And years passed in that same severe round with little variation but the ratcheting wheel of the seasons and nothing but the slow pendulum of *The Hope*'s appearances to mark time on a human scale.

A Shipwreck. Her Visitor.

The year Evered turned fourteen and Ada twelve.

They had their winter supplies in and Evered had been two full weeks at the fall fish. The days changeable and unsettled. Every September wild storms of wind and rain lashed through and they were mindful of the skies, of the light on the horizon morning and evening, trying to augur the coming weather. He went out for one last day at the cod but came off the water early, talking about sun hounds. Ada shaded her eyes to see them, two paler circles ghosting either side of the sun. There was a hesitation in the day she hadn't noticed till then, an uncertain silence. Even the gulls were quiet. They tied up the doors of the store and the empty salt shack on the stage and they hauled the boat clear of the landwash, tying it to a rock halfway up the rise. By the time they were done the sky had gone apocalyptically dark.

They were housebound the better part of two days, torrential rain sluicing down the chimney and douting the fire in the hearth, working its insidious way through so many fissures in the roof that there was nowhere they could sit that was altogether out of the steady fall. The wind brayed and howled and struck the tilt in tidal gusts they felt in their bones and they could not sleep through the night for the relentless noise of the siege they were under.

Late on the second day the window's shutter ripped free, swinging manically a few minutes before disappearing altogether and the weather invaded the room unimpeded. They tried to bar the space with a sealskin but it belled and tore free and they were forced to venture out into the wilderness of the storm to retrieve the shutter. They held on to one another and picked their way through the wind's whipping current as if they were trying to cross a flash-flood river. They found the shutter hung up in a droke of spruce trees halfway to the Downs and they managed to wrestle it back across the cove, their eyes screwed shut against the gale that threatened to take them off their feet at every step.

They hammered it into place and as they turned to make their way along the side of the tilt Ada pointed down to the cove where the waves surged up the shoreline high enough to float the boat. The little vessel hoisted aloft on a gust then and it kited in mid-air at the end of its line. The stage was loosed from its footings in the cove and the platform rose and fell like a drawbridge over a moat. It seemed a kind of madness they were witnessing and they cowered against the house, watching as long as they could stand the thrash of it before fighting their way inside.

They spent a second miserable night under the sealskin that had failed to hold to the window frame, expecting any moment the roof might be torn clear over their heads. In the early hours of the morning the wind finally moderated and the rain let up enough that the drumming was almost a soothe. They slept late and when they roused themselves they stepped out into sunshine and calm. The swaying surface of the cove dotted with storm detritus, with tree branches and driftwood, a litter of seaweed heaved thirty yards above the waterline. The stage was gone from its moorings, the longers broken up and scattered across the western arm of the cove. The boat lay on its side at the end of its line, half-filled with water. The blue of the sky and the air they breathed had a salt-scoured feel to it.

The store had stood the wind and when they untied the door they found all their supplies more or less dry and sound. But they both felt how close they had come to disaster. *The Hope* had passed through only a week before to collect their summer's catch. Delayed a week they would have lost the season and the weight of that debt would have ended their time in the cove.

They walked down to the boat and tipped it onto its belly to empty out the water. It had been smacked about and would need some work to be made seaworthy but there was plenty of time ahead of them. They'd planned to take the stage down before the snow so the loss wasn't more than an inconvenience. They spent the day retrieving the spray of longers along the western arm, hauling them back to the tilt where the logs would be sawed up for firewood.

The next morning they went back to the landwash, planning to collect the last bits of the stage and whatever lumber from the salt shack was still in the cove to use the following spring. They walked all the way out the western arm and started along the coastline beyond it. And it was Ada who stumbled on the first sign of the strange arrivals on that shore.

There was a black leather shoe thrown up on the beach, a man's shoe with a square brass buckle on its face. She turned it over to shake out the sand. She looked up the length of the shoreline and saw bottles, boxes, lumber, small mounds of unidentifiable materials. She called to Evered behind her. And then she looked back down at the unlikely article in her hand.

But for a few things rough-stitched out of sealskin, they were still wearing the only clothes they owned when their mother and father were alive. Ada's dress was barely a size to fit her then and the sleeves came halfway up her forearms now, the skirt nearly to her knees. It was as tight as a corset about her ribs and tortured her barely-there breasts and it was steadily coming apart at the seams. She still refused to put on the dress that Evered put by for her when their mother was buried though she'd relented on taking her mother's shoes when the pair she had as a child went to pieces on her feet. She'd outgrown those as well, the toes separating from the soles with the pressure, but they were in no position to add new footwear to their debt in the Beadle's ledger and she went about barefoot half the summer.

"Martha," she said aloud. "If you got any say in things atall."

They threw themselves into a feverish race back and forth the shore, dragging the materials into a pile and running off for more, as if another orphaned brother and sister was competing for the spoils. Through it all Ada was in search of the second shoe. At some point in the day their father's story of the drowned sailor came to her and it seemed entirely possible she might find it on the foot of a dead man tossed up by the storm. Which was almost but not quite enough to put her off the notion altogether.

They only stopped when it seemed dark would fall before they could get home and in the last shreds of daylight they picked through the salvage. Thirty or forty pounds of biscuit, ten pieces of salt pork, lamp oil, a small barrel of spruce beer, one demijohn of rum, five bottles of port wine. A full horn of gunpowder. A stack of lumber torn from the vessel. A woollen cassock, a door with an iron doorknob, an empty leather satchel. And in the midst of that splendour a thought brought Ada up short. "Brother," she said. "This idn't materials from *The Hope* is it?"

"I don't recognize that door," he said. He pointed to the shoe she'd found at the outset. "And I never seen anyone wearing the like of that." He shrugged. "I expect we won't know for certain before spring one way or the other."

He picked up the pork and the demijohn of rum. "We'll come out tomorrow for the rest of it. Could be more of this for miles along if we minds to look."

Ada took up the lamp oil and the woollen cassock and the one right-footed shoe and they started back in the arm toward the tilt.

They were most of a week collecting the shipwrecked materials and hauling them piecemeal into the cove. As Evered guessed, the pickings were scattered miles along the coast beyond their little harbour and they walked further each day after salvage. It was mostly pieces of the doomed ship itself they encountered, a hold cover, a stretch of the masthead still roped to a rag of sail, anonymous scraps of worked lumber. But there were pearls among the dross that made them reluctant to stop. A full round of cheese, a high-smelling comestible they'd never encountered and fell in love with from the first tentative nibbles. A cylindrical leather case thrown far above the waterline that Ada discovered when she stopped among the alders to relieve herself. It was about a foot in length and as big around as a stage longer. Ada called to her brother as she untied the toggle that held the cap tight. The interior bone-dry. She slid the object inside into her hand, a tube of dark polished wood with brass fittings at both ends.

"That's a spyglass, Sister," Evered said. "They had one aboard *The Hope*."

She looked at him quickly and he tried to reassure her. "The one I seen was altogether different than this."

He extended the three draw tubes and even that subtle mechanical adjustment seemed to Ada an act of magic. Evered took her elbow to turn her toward the cove and brought the eyepiece to her face but she ducked her head away defensively. He laughed and told her to hold still before bringing it to her eye again.

The day's last light was embering at the foot of the cove and the distant tilt and the store were on top of her suddenly. Ada jumped away from the telescope a second time. She held her hands to her face and laughed out loud.

"That'll be a dandy thing for spotting seals come March month," he said, glassing out over the ocean.

"Let me have another look," Ada said and pulled at his arm. She blinked into the lens, not quite able to credit her senses. "It don't seem like a real thing."

"More it don't," Evered said. "But neither did that storm."

Ada made a rope strap for the leather case so she could wear it across her back like a quiver when they went out beachcombing. And she wore the one salvaged shoe with moss chinked up into the toe to keep it from slipping off her foot. Happy to think she might never outgrow it. On the next to last day that they walked out the coastline she thought she'd found its mate floating in a tidal pool on the rocks. She had to stop herself screaming she was so delighted. She emptied the shoe of water and turned to hold it over her head, shouting to Evered who had gone by without seeing it. And as he made his way across the rocks to where she was standing she said a little prayer of thanks to Martha. She threw her arms around Evered's neck and they jumped up and down in each other's arms.

"Let me see now," Evered said. "I can't believe the luck of it."

He turned the shoe in his hands and his smile faltered.

Ada already had her mother's blighted shoe off her left foot and was reaching for the new discovery when she saw the look on his face.

"What is it?" she said.

"Sister." He wished she'd been on her own to figure it out, to save him being the one with the news. He said, "It's a right foot shoe."

"That's not so," she said and grabbed the thing from his hands. It was infuriating how quickly the tears came on and she bit back on them. It was a right-footed shoe and much smaller than the one she was already wearing. She lacked the words to say how malicious the turn of events seemed. She let fly with the one curse she'd learned from her mother. "Piss and corruption," she shouted.

Evered turned his face away, trying to hide the spring of laughter rising up in him.

"It's not funny, Brother."

"I knows it's not," he said.

Ada beat at his shoulder with the drowned man's shoe.

"It's not," he said, one arm raised to protect himself. "It's just," he said.

She carried on whacking at him as he crouched under the onslaught and they were both laughing then. Both overcome. Two youngsters on a raw stretch of coastline among the pitiful wrack of human enterprise. The land at their backs and the land east and west all but empty and only the dead in the firmament above for company.

Not another living soul for days.

Ada was able to wear the larger of the salvaged shoes on her left foot without much discomfort and she clodded around in the mismatched pair happily enough. They went out one more day to search the coastline though it took the best part of the morning to reach the spot they'd last left off and a river too wide to ford ahead of them. But they could see by the glass there were bits and bobs of wreckage scattered miles beyond it. They considered walking inland to find a spot that was narrow or shallow enough to cross.

"Could be miles upriver," Evered said. "And no guarantee then."

They turned back, a little despondent to think the adventure was over. But before they'd reached the cove Evered had decided to get the boat back in the water and take it coasting to satisfy themselves they weren't missing some treasure beyond the river. He was the better part of two days hammering and tarring the seams and they loaded the fish box with food and materials to keep them if they had to stay out overnight. That possibility and the powder horn they'd found persuaded him to take a closer look at his father's flintlock. The evening before they left he scraped half-heartedly at the accumulation of rust but it seemed a hopeless undertaking. The hammer spring came apart in his hands like a bit of rotten netting and he gave up the notion. They loaded the useless firearm in the boat regardless, thinking that even as a prop it might be useful to them on the unexplored shore.

They started at the oars together but the hasty repairs weren't quite equal to the beating the boat had taken and Ada shifted to bailing to keep the craft afloat. They passed the Wester Shoals mid-morning and the river mouth two hours later and by early afternoon they were sculling along a shoreline they'd never set foot upon.

There was little enough thrown up on the rocks to suggest the outing wasn't a fool's errand. Ada wore the telescope in its case across her back and she scanned ahead now and then. Splintered wood, scraps of ship's rope. She would have lobbied to turn for home if it didn't seem Evered was so set on the venture. It was passing toward evening when she realized he meant to stay out till they had travelled beyond all sign of the wreck's flotsam, which meant overnight in the open.

"We needs to find a place to put up," she said. "It'll be dark before long."

"I knows it," he said.

The coast was rocky and steep and the ocean broke heavy on the ragged stone and they'd both started to doubt they'd get safe ashore before nightfall until they came around a point into the lee of a sandy beach below a sheer bit of cliff. There were featureless mouths of darkness at the base that suggested overhangs where they could sleep out of the weather. Evered nosed the boat into the shallows and they hauled it as far clear of the sea as the beach would allow.

They'd brought a bottle of fresh water and had filled the leather satchel with bread and salt pork and thick slices cut from the round of cheese and they carried the food higher up the beach out of the wind. The coast went on in an unbroken line for miles beyond them and Evered took the glass to scan ahead.

"How do it look?" she asked.

"Same as behind," he said. "I spose we might as well head back come morning."

They scrounged enough driftwood to make a fire to boil water for tea and Evered set about sparking a ball of tinder as Ada went along the rock face to find a dry place to sleep. The caves were shallow indentations, none large enough to allow a body to sit up straight beneath the low ceiling. She came to the largest of them last. It was farthest out toward open ocean and it overlooked the setting sun, that red glow illuminating the interior. She started to crawl inside but the gravel gave slightly under her weight and she backed away. She swept a patch clear with her hand and ran her fingers over the layer of birchbark below the dirt.

Evered appeared at her side before she managed to make sense of what she was looking at. They were both on their knees which seemed right and proper after the fact. They shovelled out the gravel with their hands until the entire surface was revealed. Four sheets of bark sewn together with roots to make a panel almost the length and width of their bunks at the tilt, laid overtop of a wooden trellis.

They both knew instinctively what lay beneath it and they could not resist the urge to confirm that suspicion. The shallow depression held a shroud made of animal skin with several dozen bone pendants and bird's feet fastened along the edge. They recognized the ritual and intent and they hesitated a long time before touching the shroud.

There were two bodies set inside it, both lying on their sides, the skin of the hands and faces wizened and dried tight to the bones beneath. It was hard to judge given the posture but the largest looked to be close to their own size, adorned with a bone-and-leather necklace and dressed in pants made of the same animal skin as the shroud. The second was an infant laid naked within the other's skeletal arms. There were objects laid on either side of the bodies, small birchbark boats and miniature paddles, a wooden doll, a carved bird, a birchbark parcel in a basket made of rootlets that contained the desiccated remains of some kind of dried fish.

There was a small leather pouch set next their heads that Evered picked up and held in his hand a minute, as if trying to guess the contents by its heft. He untied the brittle string and shook the contents onto the ground. A dried bird's foot. A bone pendant carved into the shape of a feather, half a dozen bone pieces in diamond and rectangular shapes, all of them scored with intricate designs that made Ada think of the silver button and its engraving. She picked up each piece in turn, running a finger over the marks.

Evered began gathering the materials and setting them back into the bag. He reached for the piece in Ada's hand and she hesitated.

"You can't take it," he said.

She glanced across at him. "I knows that," she said. She almost said something about the dead men's shoes she was wearing and the food they had for their supper and the leather satchel they carried it in. The telescope across her back. But she knew those things were different even if she couldn't say how exactly.

She stared at the diamond-shaped piece a while longer before she surrendered it. Evered retied the bag and held it a moment as he had before he'd opened it. He returned it to the spot where it had lain and hauled the stiff leather shroud back over the bodies. They covered the grave with the sheet of bark and shovelled the gravel and rocks over the platform as best they could. They knelt a few minutes longer as if some solemnity they'd never been taught was expected in the circumstances.

Evered went off in search of more fuel after they ate their supper and they sat in the small circle of heat until they had no more wood to feed it.

"How long you think they've been set there like that?" Ada asked.

"Time out of mind I expect," Evered said.

They knew nothing about the Red Indians beyond stories they'd been told by their parents about seeing them in the distance years ago, paddling in their strange craft made of bark. Rare on the water but for all they knew the backcountry was overrun with them and they had never strayed far from the coastline, going no further than half a mile up the brook after their winter wood. Evered remembered a time when his father carted the old flintlock to guard against being set upon. The man was too blinkered at distance to hit anything smaller than a schooner and he hoped the noise of the powder might sow enough fright to drive a party off. But it was years without the first sign of a threat and he'd set the firearm in the store before Ada had learned to walk and it sat there practically forgotten.

"The little one up there," Ada said. "She can't have been much older than Martha."

It was impossible to tell in their condition if the bodies were male or female but they both guessed from the way they were laid out it was a mother and child. And they both, because of their lost sister, assumed the child was a girl. Evered thought of the graves in the cove, of Martha on her back underground and the dead stranger lying a few feet distant. It seemed an indifferent and comfortless provision in light of what they'd just uncovered.

They left the fire when it embered out and walked up to the rock cave farthest from the burial site. Evered brought the flintlock and set it beside them where they lay under the salvaged woollen cassock for a blanket. They had never spent a night outside the cove or in the open air before. Evered lay listening for the sound of footsteps on the beach scrag, hearing voices in the wind until it began to rain hours later, a cold October downpour that he considered would force even a savage to look for cover and stay put. And he finally drifted off.

Ada was thinking of the bone pendant, of its rows of intricate notching so suggestive of meaning she was convinced it would come clear if only she managed to hold the image in her mind long enough. But the details had already escaped her. She slid a hand into the front pocket of her dress to touch the object she'd sleighted from Evered's view and smuggled away from the gravesite. She rubbed her thumb across the markings scored into its surface, inspecting it blindly, memorizing each exotic detail.

It kept her awake the whole of the night.

They settled in for the winter, making a final accounting of the shipwrecked materials they'd salvaged and setting the food in the store or the root cellar. Ada presented the full list aloud to Martha, including the cheese which she had no name for, describing the high smell, the irresistible rank flavour. She couldn't help thinking the infant at God's side had a hand in their wild luck but stopped short of thanking Martha outright for fear it was *The Hope* that had been lost, a possibility she couldn't square with their good fortune. Her father used to say *The death of a horse is the life of a crow*, and Ada had never really taken in the meaning of the phrase. But she knew it in her bones now.

The floor of the tilt was ruined by the storm's rain and they raked out the sludge, replacing it with a fresh layer of sand. Evered reframed the entrance with pieces of salvaged lumber and he set the ship's door on the old door's leather hinges. The first real snow fell before the end of October and it kept coming in the weeks that followed, the drifting so heavy that even wearing a set of Indian racquets he found it a trial to haul out the trees he'd cut in the spring and left to dry in the woods.

They both felt an aimlessness about their days. They had started sharing a bed again but seemed barely to notice the other's company. Nothing in their young lives had astounded or animated them like the storm and the shipwreck's unexpected windfall and the frantic days of salvaging that followed. The urgency and resolve had drained from their world in the wake of it.

Ada felt the lack almost as a physical ailment, an oppressive aching and soreness that for days made her short and querulous. She begged off going into the woods with Evered to avoid the irritation of his company. For his part, he was happy to be clear of her peculiar crookedness and they spent as much of their days apart as the cove allowed.

She worried it might be a permanent condition she was suffering until she felt blood trailing along the inside of her thighs as she stood at the fire. She lifted the skirts of her apron and dress, knowing what she would find there and still shaken when she brought her hand away wet. "Piss and corruption," she whispered.

A visitor, her mother had called it, in a tone that managed to be diffident and still vaguely ominous. This was after Martha was buried, failing herself then and wanting to pass on what she could to Ada in the time they had left. "You'll have a little visitor every month," she said to her daughter. Her eyes sunken, the skin stretched across the bones of her face in a way that made Ada think now of the bodies they'd uncovered in the cave burial.

"Down there," she'd said and she pointed with her eyes. "It'll come calling before long."

It was never her mother's custom to offer instruction or commentary or to speak of the future beyond the season ahead and the strange talk unsettled Ada. It seemed a symptom of the woman's affliction.

"What do it mean?" Ada asked.

"It's just women's business," she said and Ada could hear Sarah Best's voice now as she stood at the hearth, a lick of her own blood on her fingers. And for the last time in her life she set to crying over her mother's loss.

For the rest of the day she talked to Martha about the development and how she might deal with the practicalities of the situation. Rags, her mother had said, or deer moss. It seemed a waste of precious material to use cloth but the moss was all frozen under snow and Ada turned to the old man's beard they had collected for tinder. She placed the dressing into her underclothes, the tree moss chafing at her thighs until it softened with the flow of blood. She threw each sodden handful into the fire and watched it burn. "Women's business that is, Sister," Ada said.

It was clear there wasn't nearly enough tinder put up to serve and she would have to sacrifice a few strips of cloth to the task. She settled on the doll she'd made for her baby sister, cutting away the strings that tied the rags into the rough shape of head and arms and legs. Asking Martha's pardon for the desecration.

She didn't speak a word about it to Evered first or last. Women's business, it was. She worried about bleeding through her clothes and they slept in separate beds for the next five nights.

Evered put it down to the queer mood that had overtaken his sister and didn't ask for an explanation, not the first night when she made up their parents' bunk across the room and not when she settled back under the covers beside him days later. It seemed a fickle act, almost spiteful, and he was tormented by it. Though not enough to risk galling her with questions.

The snow fell and continued falling through December month. It drifted past the height of the window on three sides of the tilt. It was a daily job to shovel the narrow paths waist-high, then shoulder-high, from the door to the woodpile and to the root cellar and to the space behind the store where the slops were dumped. But there was little else to occupy their time. Even with the snow's insulation against the wind it was bitterly cold inside and they spent most of their waking hours within two feet of the hearth. They had nearly outgrown the elaborate games and songs and foolishness that used to occupy their time and the short winter days seemed endless.

They drank a glass of the salvaged spruce beer with their dinner at midday and then napped an hour or longer. They had small cups of port with their supper though Ada found the sweetness of it cloying and diluted hers with water. They went to bed almost as soon as the sky went dark to save the lamp oil, lying together in alternating periods of sleep and hours of idle wakefulness. They talked through the black or looked to the other's warmth for comfort, gravitating to the familiar body beside them. And one night, half-asleep and adrift in that liminal space, Ada hooked a leg across Evered's hip and they nudged into one another.

Ada had been dreaming of the bear they'd encountered in the berry hills and the image stayed with her through the length of that flushed episode. The slow serene swing of its head among the berry bushes that she and Evered seemed to be moving in concert with. The ripple of flesh under the creature's fur like a current muscling just below the ocean's surface and she could feel something akin to it furrowing the length and breadth of herself.

May month, the year she turned nine, Ada had gone to the landwash to watch Evered and her father prepare the boat for the coming season. She stood at the bow, leaning into the curve of the upturned keel as they raked oakum from the seams, the vibration of the work travelling up through the vessel's bones into her own. She shifted on her feet instinctively to make way for that tremor, rising on her toes to rest her pelvis against the wood. She pressed against the quiver until she felt an answering quiver pass through her like an echo coming off a cliff face. A comber of goosebumps travelling the length of her arms. And for a few endless seconds she was lost to the world, her whole self compressed to the spot where she pulsed against the keel.

It was her father's voice brought her back. "She've gone to sleep there have she?" he said.

"Her eyes is open," Evered said.

They were watching as she rocked against the keel, both smiling at the studied look on her face, the blank stare. "You're all right then?" her father said when she met his eye and she turned to run off to the brook, Evered laughing behind her. She stayed there the rest of the afternoon, feeling almost stripped of her skin.

She'd experienced something cousin to that uncanny pulse on occasion, pressing into her fist as she lay in bed, though it seemed a pale shadow at best. And she forgot that first incident altogether in the grinding welter of the years since. But the nights of furtive trade with Evered revived her memory of it, the traffic between them just as acute and confounding. It felt halfways familiar and altogether new to the world. It entered their lives like a third creature with its own being and sentience, something Ada didn't wholly trust and resisted in fits and starts. She edged up to it on the sly without ever admitting to herself what she was moving toward. She never spoke of it for fear Evered would laugh at her. For fear it would disappear altogether.

It was the one thing in the interminable winter that gave her any pleasure though she never felt she had dominion over it. And the sting of being caught out on the landwash shadowed the exchange with a sour aftertaste, a residual sense of naked shame. It made her think there was no indulgence in the world that wasn't cut with regret.

The Ark of Malaga. A Blindness.

The weather went glassy in the new year, clear and sharp and windless. The pack ice moved in before the end of February and Evered used the snow drifted against the tilt to climb onto the roof with the telescope. He scanned the miles of white for seals but weeks passed with no hint of harp or hood or round.

The ice was unlike anything he'd seen before, a solid sheet of white that hugged the entire coastline and seemed to be anchored there, a blank canvas without life or movement. There were no open water leads and no patches of loose ice, there was no blue drop in the distance. No sign of the ocean at work beneath it.

In the middle of March he spotted what looked to be smoke on the ocean's horizon, a thin perplexing plume that rose all that day and the next. Eventually he made out what looked to be a vessel in the grip of the ice. He called Ada up to the rooftop to be certain he wasn't imagining the thing. The ship was a near wreck, dismasted by some misfortune at sea and all but abandoned to judge by appearances. The only sign of life was the smoke that rose each morning and sometimes the glim of a single light after dark that was too distant to be seen with a naked eye.

They talked of nothing else while it was in view, speculating on the vessel's origins and what circumstances might have brought it to them, about the smoke and the random light and who it was aboard the ship and what condition they might be in. It was lying north-northwest of the cove and was chained in the stationary grip of the ice field for weeks. And at some point in Evered's vigil there came a morning when there was no plume of smoke and the irregular light disappeared for good.

It was near the end of April when the ice was usually long gone from the coastline and the herring were about to strike in. But the field showed no sign of breakup, holding fast to the shoreline and spanning the horizon east to west. And in all that time no sign of seals. They had been surviving on the last spongy potatoes and the store of ship biscuit and pork they'd salvaged in the fall and that reserve was growing thin.

They woke in the dark one night and Evered began talking about the possibility of an expedition to the seized ship. It was miles further out than he'd ever chanced walking for seals. But the ice field had not so much as creaked in a month and a half and the vessel hadn't budged from the spot where it ground to a halt weeks before.

"Imagine what might be aboard of her," he said. "Pork and biscuit and God knows what-all."

"She could be licked clean for all we knows," Ada said.

"Might be spruce beer aboard," he said. "Or that foul-smelling stuff you loves."

Ada nodded into his shoulder at the thought of it.

"Not the first sign of spring yet the year, we'll be late getting the vegetables into the ground," he said. "Wouldn't hurt we had something to tide us over."

It was a foolish undertaking but she knew there was no bringing him to his senses. "I'm coming with you," she said.

"Sister," he said. Though he knew she would insist and didn't waste any more of his breath trying to talk her into staying back.

They spent the next three days preparing for the trek out. Evered had a kit reasonably fit for the ice but Ada was still wearing the same ragged dress and the mismatched salvaged shoes and her mother's old stockings. Evered fashioned a set of ice creepers with iron tacks driven through strips of leather that she could tie to the soles of her shoes and Ada sewed leggings cut from an old sealskin to wear under the skirt of her dress. Evered had the gaff as a walking stick and he cut the narrow end of a longer and shaved it down to make one for Ada. They tied up bundles of hard bread and salt pork and filled two of the empty port bottles with fresh water. Ada wore the vest she'd made of the whitecoat that Evered had long outgrown and they covered their heads with homemade caps and scarves. Evered considered taking the flintlock along but it was heavy and nearly his height and awkward across his back. And there was no one alive out there he was sure. Ada strapped on the telescope in its case and Evered wound the hauling rope about his waist, tucking the sculping knife and a hatchet into that belt. He beat a path ahead of his sister down to the land-wash and they walked out onto the ice in their rummage gear, looking for all the world like a pair of childish vagabonds passing through an abandoned northern kingdom.

The walking was free and easy until they cleared the harbour skerries where the ice went ragged with hillocks and rafts of shale-like outcrops that slowed them to a crawl. As the morning went on they lost the depths of shadow which made it almost impossible to read the terrain ahead and they were forced into long detours away from the vessel they were aiming for. They stopped when the sun stood overhead for noon, crouching out of the north wind behind a low ice wall and tucking into the food they'd brought. They'd set out at first light and had been on the march almost six hours, both of them famished and beat, their clothes gumboed with sweat. Evered raised up to scan out toward the vessel. It didn't look any ways closer now than when they started.

"We won't get there much ahead of dark at this pace," he said.

Ada said, "We should go back, Brother."

"Likely we should," he said. "But we come this far." He looked up over the ice wall again as if taking his bearings anew, offering his sister a chance to push for a retreat. But she did not. "We can sleep the night out there," he said. "Start back in first thing tomorrow."

She nodded. "Do you think there's anyone aboard of her?"

It was a question they'd discussed endlessly in the weeks since the ship appeared but it seemed a fresh consideration with the thought of spending the night.

"Not alive I expects," Evered said. Though he wished he'd brought the flintlock along after all.

They couldn't stop long for the cold making itself at home in the damp of their clothing and they gathered their things and trudged on across the jumble in single file. For a time they were both convinced they wouldn't reach the ship before darkness overtook them but there was nothing helpful in the thought and they kept it to themselves. Shadows stretched out on the ice field as the sun went down, adding some definition to the white terrain which made it easier to plot a useful path ahead and they made better time in the late afternoon. And they were within shouting distance of the hulk before dusk.

They stood together awhile in the lee of the ship, listening for some hint of life aboard. They saw the ship's name painted at the bow though the appellation remained a mystery to their unlettered eyes. The bowsprit was cracked and hanging by a ligament of rope, swaying in mid-air. There was no sign of boats on deck or at the stern.

She was twice the length of *The Hope* and belled wide at the hull which made them wonder what she might have carried. They walked around her in a wide circle and could see she was in worse shape than they'd guessed, not just the masts but most of the rail and the forecastle torn away and the hull on the far side caved in at the bow from the reaming pressure of the ice. It was only that frozen grip keeping the ship at the surface anymore and it was plain she would sink as soon as the field broke up.

It didn't seem likely they'd find much to scavenge aboard and Ada said as much.

"She'll do for the night anyway," Evered said.

He flung the end of the hauling rope over what was left of the rail until the hook found purchase and they hoisted themselves onto the deck. Ada stood close beside him, one hand on his elbow. They could see much of the planking along the starboard side had been ripped up.

"I guess we knows what they was using for firewood," she said, whispering as if they might be overheard.

They started aft where an iron chimney came through the decking on the starboard side and they went down a steep stair at the last hatchway into rumours of a rank smell subdued by the cold. There was a cabin door ajar in that darkness, a staff of light showing through the crack, and they stopped outside. "Hello the house," Evered called and they stood listening before pushing it wide The last of the sun shining through porthole windows that had lost their glass. A stove stood along the far wall, a body lying slack in a chair pulled close up to it, the legs covered by a rug. "Hello the house," Evered said again, quietly. They inched into the room and stood over the dead man, the face lean and unshaven, the eyes half-closed. It seemed colder inside than it had been out in the open, their breath pluming in the frost. An untidy sheaf of planking lay near the stove and they looked at one another.

"We'll have to shift him out of the way," Evered said.

They grabbed the back of the chair and scraped it to the far corner of the room and they stood a moment with their heads bowed as they had when the Beadle read the funeral service over Martha's grave. Evered was eyeing the man's coat made of a thick worsted wool. Thinking he would not be leaving the ship without it. He reached to open the jacket to see what the dead man was wearing underneath and was surprised by the bulk of the chest. Half a dozen layers of shirts and sweaters at least. Enough material there alone to have made the trip worthwhile.

He turned back to the stove to see about lighting a fire.

"What do you think it was carried him off?" Ada asked.

"No saying. But he didn't starve." Evered picked up a pot on top of the stove and waved it at his sister. She walked across to him and they peered inside at the remains of a gruel or stew with shards and splinters of bone showing through, the whole glistening with fat scum. They both reared back from the sight and Evered heaved the pot through one of the glassless porthole windows to be clear of it.

He turned to the decking in the corner for firewood and uncovered a small midden behind it. He used the blade of the hatchet to pick through the pile of discarded bone, all of them cracked and boiled and sucked clean of marrow.

"What is it you're into?" Ada asked.

"Nothing," he said.

He'd brought a pocketful of old man's beard for tinder and sparked up a fire, stoking the stove full once it took hold, and they used the last of the daylight to poke around as they waited for it to take the edge off the cold. An axe stood against the wall behind the stove, a hammer and two knives and a handful of other tools on the floor beside it. A half-puncheon with an inch or two of brackish water gathered from rain or melted snow sat under the windows and they refilled the port bottle they'd drunk dry on the trip out with it. A folded length of sail that the dead man had been using as a mattress lay opposite the stack of decking. Behind the door they found a trunk with a scatter of materials across the top, an empty tinderbox and a bladder with a handful of matches, a deck lamp with the stub of a candle.

"There's he's light," Ada said.

They lit the wick and went side by side into the gloom beyond the door, holding the deck lamp ahead of them. They could make out a second door on the port side of the vessel and another set of stairs leading further down into the hold, a long passageway into blackness toward the bow. But the little light they carried made the dark echoing space beyond it seem animate and ominous and without exchanging a word they decided to leave it all to morning. They went back into the cabin and were hauling the heavy trunk across the doorframe when Evered said, "This thing is full."

They cleared the scatter of materials off the cover and opened it. The interior stuffed to the brim with clothing that they began hauling out an item at a time, a woollen mantle, two skirts, a quilted dickey, a pair of muslin shifts. A waistcoat and three pairs of trousers, a pair of long boots. A loose nightgown made of cotton. All of different sizes and condition.

"Where did it come from?" Ada asked. The array so overwhelming she'd forgotten how terrified she'd been moments before.

Evered had already taken off his father's boots and was hauling on a pair of stockings and the boots he'd found in the trunk. "From heaven above you asks me," he said.

Ada pulled the quilted petticoat on over her leggings and tried two or three skirts for length but stripped it all in the end, opting for a pair of trousers instead. She held up the waistcoat and looked across at Evered.

"I got me eye on your man's outfit," he said, nodding toward the chair in the corner. "You go ahead."

The jacket was too large by half, the skirt falling below her knees, her hands lost in the sleeves, but she shortened the cuffs two turns and was satisfied with the fit. She put her sealskin leggings and mismatched shoes in the trunk and pulled on the red jacks her brother had just abandoned. Evered found a black tricorn among the spoils and threw it to her, as a joke, but she put it on without a second thought.

"You looks the proper Molly in that rig," Evered said to her.

She clapped at her chest and hips, delighted, and she struck something solid in one of the pockets. She hauled out a book with a cloth cover and deckle-edged papers. She knelt beside it on the floor next the deck lamp and flipped through the pages, most of which had been soaked and dried in ridges and some stuck together.

"It looks like the Beadle's ledgers," Evered said.

She thought of the book Clinch had read from at the graves. "Might be it's a Bible."

Evered shook his head. He pointed to the inked hand-writing, the blank pages at the back. "I made me mark in one the like of this on *The Hope*," he said. "With a feather pen."

She stared at him. "Whatever is your mark?"

"Like so," he said and he took her index finger and traced a phantom X on a page.

She spent minutes more flipping through the book, the enigmatic lines of writing aslant and blotted and variable. Fighting a tug of jealousy to think Evered had a mark and a place in such a thing. She might have passed the night poring over those pages but Evered made a comment about the length of the candle stub and she tucked it back into the pocket of her waistcoat and douted the wick.

———

They stood the stove door open for the shifting light of the flames. Even with the glass out of the porthole windows the fire's heat in the low-ceilinged room forced them to strip off their outer layers. They seated themselves on the floor and ate a little of the food they'd brought, taking into consideration how much they needed to save for the return. They were struck by a stony fatigue, the weight of it coming over them as they settled down and they both nodded off as they spoke. But the strangeness of their surroundings and the dead man they had for company kept them from surrendering completely. They couldn't shake their disquiet to be aboard a vessel marked by calamity and soon to sink below the ocean's surface.

Out of nowhere Evered asked, "Do she talk to you this far out? Or is it only in the cove?"

Ada lay still awhile as if she was just now listening for the infant girl's voice. "I don't think she's here," she said. "I don't think she wants anywhere near it."

"More do I," Evered whispered.

But it was the first time in their lives they'd slept with a fire burning and the heat was a delicious thing. The chill that leached into the room when the fire embered low woke them every couple of hours and Evered stirred himself to feed a handful of decking junks to the coals and blow up a flame.

At the first sign of light he left Ada by the stove and went to the dead body in its chair, wanting to deal with that job before she woke. He tried to wrestle off the boots but the feet and lower legs were swollen twice their normal size and the boots wouldn't come free until he slit the tops all the way to the ankles. The same applied to the trousers and he decided to let them be. He hefted the corpse onto the floor and flipped it side to side to shimmy the coat sleeves free of the arms. He kept his focus on the work, avoiding the dead man's stare to hold his nerve. A feeling like grit under his own lids that he couldn't blink away, as if he'd slept all night with his eyes half-open the same.

He stripped off the layers of smocks and sweaters in one thick pelt, then covered the half-naked body and the dead face with the rug that had been used as a blanket. He took up the coat and slipped it on, doing up the knitted buttons all the way to his throat. He turned back to the room still inspecting the fit and it took him a moment to take note of Ada sitting with her arms around her knees, watching him.

"How is it we plans to get all this back home?" she asked.

"I got a notion."

He took his hatchet and the axe from behind the stove and he shoved the trunk away from the door. He gestured for her to follow and they went up the stairs to a clear sky, the sun just climbing above the horizon. The day already bright and Evered squinted against the sudden needling, his eyes watering so much in the sunlight that tears rolled down his cheeks.

He wiped his face dry with the sleeve of the worsted jacket and they walked up the port side to where the last of the rail curved toward the bowsprit. He handed Ada the hatchet and wielded the axe himself and they set to chopping it free. Once it was down Evered started hacking the eight-foot length in two. The rail was made of some hardwood they'd never encountered and it was flinty as stone. Every few minutes he stopped to catch his breath, to shake some feeling back into his arms while Ada took a turn with the hatchet. Between the two of them they chipped through and they took an end each under their arms.

On their way back they passed the hatchway amidships, the cover torn free and gone, and the light was just high enough to make a gloom in that sunken space. Evered handed his piece of rail to Ada and walked down the hatch stairs, crouching in the dark below decks, waiting for his watering eyes to adjust. He could sense a second set of stairs at his feet, a smell of wet and rot rising from the bilge down there. He knelt and stuck head and shoulders into the lower deck, peering to try to pick detail from the murk. Sea water had surged in through the ruptured hull and there were bits of flotsam on the surface. Rows of bunkbeds stood out of the water's black like crops planted neatly in a peat bog.

"She had passengers aboard," he called. "They got berths down below."

Ada shook her head. She said, "I got a dark brown feeling about this, Brother."

Most of the coals in the stove had guttered to black and Evered used the sculping knife to pick through them, hooking out the dozens of decking nails that littered the bottom of the stove. They were still too hot to touch and he scooped the few he'd need on the knife's blade, dropping them in the last dregs of water in the half-puncheon to cool. He took to hacking a rough curve at the front edge of both pieces of rail and when he was satisfied they emptied all the materials out of the trunk and flipped it onto its face. They laid the improvised runners lengthwise across the bottom and Evered hammered them into the frame with the still-warm nails.

They set the axe and hammer and knives in the bottom of the trunk, along with the deck light and tinderbox and three curious instruments made of metal and glass that Evered guessed were used in wayfinding. He took one of the dead man's boots and collected the rest of the decking nails into the toe, wrapping the leather around the sole to hold them, and they stowed it with the clothes and the bottles of water and their last bit of food and fastened the trunk lid shut.

They lifted it for weight.

"She's too heavy by half for the likes of we," Ada said. "It took us near to dark to come this far with our own bit of gear."

"She've got the runners on her," Evered said. "We'll both be on the hauling line. And one night on the ice won't kill us if it comes to that." He could see she wasn't convinced. "We'll drop some ballast on the way if she slows us down too much."

They shoved the trunk through the doorway to the base of the stairs and attached the hauling rope's hook to the leather handle at one end. Ada went above deck to pull and Evered pushed from below and they managed to shimmy it up into the light of day. They were both winded by the effort, Evered still on the stairs and leaning over the hatchway to catch his breath. Ada held her tongue about their chances of dragging it miles over the ice field's anarchic snarl, wanting only to move, to put some distance between themselves and the vessel.

"I'll get the rest of our kit," he said and he went back into the cabin to gather up the hatchet and sculping knife, the gaff and Ada's walking stick. He had his foot on the bottom stair when it occurred to him they hadn't even opened the door to portside. He heard Ada call out to him.

"Be along directly," he shouted.

He still felt an irritation like sand or ash in his eyes and he wiped away the seeping liquid before he tried the door. It brought up on something as he opened it and he pushed to get inside though the smell should have been enough to warn him off. The sight coming into focus through his watering eyes and his mind reeling to stay clear of what he was seeing.

The bodies were naked and lying one on another and they seemed to number in the dozens with the jumble of limbs though the room was too small to hold more than five or six. He was backing away and still taking in the details, the raw amputations, bone exposed where strips of flesh had been flayed away. And he saw it then, the source of that ragtag collection of clothes in the trunk, the layers of shirts and sweaters the dead man by the fire had been wearing. He heard Ada's voice calling his name and turned for it, battering up the stairs and breaking wild into daylight. He came to his feet on deck and gazed around at the world with the terrified, unknowing look of a newborn.

"What is it, Brother?"

"God's nails," he whispered without looking at her. He set a shoulder to the trunk and pushed it to the rail line. He threw the gaff and walking stick to the ice below and then knelt and braced the hauling rope across his shoulders. "Go," he said to his sister, "Jesus save us, go, go." She took a grip and let herself overside, crabbing down the hull of the ship as far as the rope extended and dropping the last few feet to the ice. Evered reeled the rope back up, wanting to lower the trunk down by the hook, but he lost his hold on the container in the rush to tip it past the lip and it plunged to the ice and smashed to pieces down there. He threw the rope after it and was about to jump in his turn before Ada started waving her tricorn below. "You'll crack your neck," she shouted.

He looked behind himself and then along the length of the vessel and he ran up amidships where the deck lay a fathom closer to the surface. He shimmied himself overside, hanging by his fingers a moment before letting go his grip.

Ada saw he was limping as he came up to her but he wouldn't answer any questions about what was wrong or what had drained the colour from his face. He dug around to locate the hauling rope among the mess of clothes and smashed glass and splintered wood and he set to tying it about his waist. Stopped short when he realized what he was wearing and he stripped the dead man's jacket off as if it was on fire, kicked it away on the ice.

He picked out his old coat and wound the rope about his waist and set the hatchet and sculping knife in place. He was already hobbling away from the ship with the gaff in hand as Ada salvaged the one unbroken water bottle and the package of food from the pile of materials. All of it about to be lost to them. She picked up one of the long knives from the wreckage and turned to Evered, calling after him. He looked back to her and she waved it in his direction.

"Leave it," he said.

"We should take the axe," she said.

Evered turned and limped three more steps away from her before he dropped to his knees and vomited on the ice

and he carried on urging helplessly long after his stomach
was empty.

Hours of walking then, putting the horror ship behind them as
quickly as they could move. Ada three steps in Evered's wake,
the sun warm enough to make them strip to a single layer and
carry the excess clothing. A cloudless sky and she was grateful
for the tricorn shading her face from the worst of the brutal
glare. They finished their only bottle of water before noon and
suffered with thirst the rest of the way.

Evered was leaning on the gaff like a crutch and tripping
with a regularity that made him look drunk. But he seemed
determined to soldier on until he struck the cove. Ada couldn't
prevail on him to stop even long enough to eat the little packet
of salt pork they had left and she spread the waistcoat on a
wind-carved chaise of ice and took a seat, watching him stum-
ble across the rough surface ahead.

She'd spent the time in Evered's wake trying to guess at what
he'd encountered in those last minutes below deck and nothing
she conjured was the least plausible. And the fact she couldn't
imagine a likely scenario made her terrified to know the truth.
She hadn't so much as glanced over her shoulder as they walked,
gripped by a childish anxiety the vessel was following behind
them. She felt it looming at her back even now but wouldn't
look for fear she might turn to salt like Lot's nameless wife.

Evered was half a mile beyond her when she gathered up her
things to follow after him. He had veered dead east, as if he
planned to walk past the cove all the way to Mockbeggar. She

called to him but he was beyond hearing or ignoring her, moving at a shuffle. He'd almost come to a full stop before she reached him and she touched his shoulder. He turned his head to her, his eyes squinted shut, his cheeks and neck soaking wet. Icicles hung in the fuzz on his chin.

He said, "Perhaps you should lead on for a bit."

She wiped at his face with her bare hands. "All right," she said.

She kept an eye on him to be sure he wasn't drifting out of her track or falling too far behind. He seemed not able to see her even ten feet ahead and she called to him when he went astray. He stopped again as the sun dropped behind the western shore, leaning on the gaff and shaking his head. She put the waistcoat on and came back to him, stepping in under his shoulder to take some of the weight off his lame foot.

It was dark by the time they walked over the harbour skerries into the cove but the moon was nearly full and reflected white off the ice and off the snow on the rise and they had no trouble finding their way to the tilt. They both drank their greedy fill of water from the puncheon near the hearth and then Ada crutched Evered to the bunk. She lit the slutlamp and helped him out of his winter kit. He lay back and she tried to remove his new boots but the swelling and shooting pain in the injured foot made it impossible.

"I'll have to cut it off," she said.

Evered sat up on his elbows, his weeping eyes shut tight against the dull lamplight. "Those boots is all I got to wear," he said.

"I'll give you back Father's old ones."

"And what will you wear then? You left your shoes out on the ice." He fell back into the bed. "I'll keep the boots on," he said.

"What if you got something broke, Brother?"

"Then having the boot off won't help."

She was too tired to argue and stripped out of her own outfit. She douted the lamp and crawled under the covers beside him.

"She's still here is she?" Evered asked then. "You still hears her?"

She turned into him, her face touching his in the dark. "She'll always be here," Ada said. "She won't ever leave us."

And holding fast to that notion they were both asleep.

Hours before daylight Evered woke to a stabbing sensation in his eyes. He tried but couldn't open them, sitting up in bed and forcing the lids apart with his fingers which made the needling worse again. His eyes clenched in their sockets and he howled through the spasms. Ada was out of bed by then, at the hearth to spark up a fire, feeding it kindling for quick heat. She didn't know what was wrong and had no sense of what might help but the sound of Evered's blind torment made her want to peel off her skin and she busied herself to keep from howling along with him. She tried wiping at his eyes with a wet cloth but he pulled his face away from the sear of it. She boiled a pot of water and sat him in front of the rising steam with a blanket over his head.

"Is that helping either bit?" she asked him.

"It idn't hurting any," he said.

She kept him under the cloth for an hour before they went back to bed. They slept late and Evered was able to blink his eyelids when they woke though even in the room's permanent dusk the morning light was a torture to him. Ada insisted he wear a blindfold for the day, only removing it to bathe his eyes with steam near the hearth.

After each treatment she replaced the blindfold and helped him back to the bunk where he lay in complete darkness and varying states of misery. He assumed the affliction he was suffering was a consequence of what he'd laid eyes on aboard the ship. He thought it possible he might never see again. And he wished there was a way to blind his mind's eye as well. He slept fitfully, woken by bouts of stinging pain and he would call out to Ada to be sure she was still nearby. It was a surprise to him she hadn't asked more questions about it all but he was grateful for her reticence.

By evening the pain started to recede. Ada soaked and boiled hardtack and made a poultice of the bread mixed with lamp oil that she applied to his eyes for the night. In the morning he was able to look about the room with only mild discomfort and even managed to hobble to the door and stand in the light a few minutes at a time though Ada forced him to wear the blindfold most of the day. She collected a bucket of bergy bits off the landwash and she hammered the ice into shards, setting Evered's foot into the cold, boot and all, to ease the ache and bring the swelling down. He looked a proper fool sitting blindfolded and one leg in a bucket of ice but she was too afraid for him to make a joke of it or laugh.

Evered's sight came back to him fully within a few days but the ice field held fast for weeks longer and the ship was a daily unmentioned presence in their lives. They'd never seen the ocean iced over so late in the year and Evered began to think it wasn't the ice that was keeping the vessel afloat but the ship that was holding the ice on the shore. That it had brought some sort of curse to their time and they would starve to death in its grim shadow. When he was able to hobble about he went into the backwoods to cut longers and dragged them down to the landwash without knowing if he would live to build the stage.

The breakup when it came was sudden. Ada went out to relieve herself on the landwash early one morning and she came back in for the telescope, then called Evered outside. She handed him the glass and pointed out at the horizon where the ice drifted in long ragged strips and the sea glittered darkly where the ship had been released and disappeared below the surface.

Evered nodded at the absence though neither mentioned it directly. He returned the glass to its leather case and handed it back to Ada. He said, "I was thinking I might try to get that boot off today."

"It's like to be grown on by now," she said. "But we can have a go if you like."

As she predicted it was stubborn as a tooth. She gave Evered a strip of leather to bite down on as she reefed at the heel. The stink when his foot came free was sulphurous and feculent. Ada threw the boot out the door to air it and she left the door wide for the clearing breeze. Evered was sitting with his head thrown back, still catching his breath as she soaked the rotten stocking with water and then edged it down the calf. Below the ankle she had to use a knife to skin the material away and eventually Evered's foot lay naked to the day for the first time in a month.

He let out a long breath. "That wouldn't so bad," he said.

Ada made a face as she examined the damage. There were signs of bruising like an old water stain around the ankle and the frangible skin had peeled away with the stocking in spots. "You'll want to let that sit out a bit," she said.

Evered still walked with a limp but whatever had torn or broken in the foot seemed to have mended. And he had two unimpaired boots to his name.

The Duke of Limbs. The Beadle, Once More.

After the breakup the season skipped into the rhythm they'd
known all their lives and they could hardly keep abreast of the
pace. They managed to raise the stage on the landwash and they
scraped and recaulked and tarred the boat to be ready when the
cod struck in.

They were always gut-foundered. They'd long ago finished
the port wine and they took a shot of rum in their tea at night
to numb the worst of the hunger and the myriad ailments the
work inflicted on them. Their gums had gone grey and spongy
with the deprivations of the spring and there was a steady taste
of blood in their mouths, their teeth loose enough they could
work them like hinges with their tongues. Evered lost an eye
tooth by absently worrying it with his fingers one evening and
Ada rinsed and polished the incisor and added the ivory to her
shelf of treasures. At some point it occurred to her she hadn't
had her visitor since February month and she was surprised to
feel that absence a loss.

The caplin rolled in mid-June and the cod followed close
behind. They were up hours before dawn to make the most of

the day, both youngsters going about their duties with an exhausted deliberation. They gorged on the fish but they were still reduced with want and their privations made them child-like in their appetites. They were asleep almost before they lay down and they didn't touch each other but for warmth, for comfort. To Ada the spells that had overcome them in the first months of the winter hardly seemed real, occupying the same space as the strange stories from the Bible their mother had offered up years ago. Part of another world that might have been wholly apocryphal.

She still carried a niggling fear it was *The Hope* that had been wrecked and washed ashore on their bit of coast in the September storm and she had to tamp down the conviction they'd lost their only link to the celestial realm of dry goods and flour and salt meat and tea. She didn't know enough of the world to guess what that could mean for them besides ruination.

They had night frost all through June and Ada was weeks late setting the seed potatoes and turnips. It was hard to see the garden coming to much by the fall. And it was while that bleak thought was turning over in her head that she spotted the vessel. A speck on the horizon and hours off still but she knew it in her heart. The same as if Martha had whispered in her ear, "There now, there's *The Hope*."

Evered was home with the morning run and they had split and salted the catch and finished their dinner before *The Hope* came to anchor. Ada on the stage as Evered climbed into the boat and she waved her tricorn to the crew beyond the skerries and they every one waved back to her.

———

The crew were watching as Evered rowed out and they helloed him as he came around in the lee and reached to lift him up onto the deck. They shook his hand and clapped him on the back. They seemed as relieved to see the youngster as he was to see them.

"Half expected to find you gone," the talker said. "Hard old winter."

"We only just got clear of the ice," Evered said. "Thought we might have to walk into Mockbeggar for a bit of flour." And then he asked after Mary Oram as he did each time *The Hope* came through, she being the only soul he knew in common with the crew.

"The old witch haven't changed," a second man said. "Still wild as a goat."

"And just as contrary," the first man said and they laughed over the familiar joke.

There was a stranger aboard the ship, a boy not Evered's age to judge by his face though he was at least a head taller. He hung back from the greeting circle, eyeing Evered in a way that wasn't quite wary, that suggested he had a message to pass on when the time was right. A queer look to him, jet-black hair in tight curls and his skin a colour unlike any colour Evered knew, a barky-tea complexion.

"And what's your news?" the first man asked. "Who's the young lad?"

"Lad?"

"The one waving to us from the stagehead. Had a tricorn in he's hand."

"That's me sister. That's Ada."

"Your *sister*," the man said, incredulous. "In them trousers?"

The crewmen turned toward the cove and the strange young-ster jumped up on the rail and shaded his eyes to peer at the distant stage.

"Now he's keen to look," the man said. "The Duke of Limbs here wants to have a gander of a sudden. Watch you don't wind up overside, Jingle Brains."

"He got all the grace of a cow aboard of a dory," another said. "The gangly old stilts on him. He'll never shit a seaman's turd, that one."

The boy smiled at their teasing without looking away from the cove. Every tooth still in his head.

"We won't miss yon mongrel when he's gone," the first man said. "Look of him, the miserable wretch. I pities the crowd haves to wake up to that gob every morning. He'd put a horse off he's oats."

And there was a round of laughter so affectionate it made the Duke of Limbs blush, his dark face coming over darker still.

"Your Ada got no interest in coming aboard for a visit with you is it?" the man said, turning back to Evered. "She's like her mother God rest her," he said, answering his own question. "I spose we counted a harder crowd than she knew and a year or two in Mockbeggar was enough for her." He smiled at Evered. "You couldn't blame her wanting to keep clear of we," he said.

Evered was barely listening to the man, still staring at the Duke of Limbs gazing into the cove.

"How did that fit-out she's wearing come to hand?" some-one asked and he roused himself to tell the story of the wreck-age that washed ashore after the September storm, claiming the clothes had been part of the salvage to avoid talking about the ship frozen in the ice with its pot of fatty flesh and bone on the stove.

"That was some blow we had," the first man said. "Three ships in Mockbeggar parted their chains and wound up wrecked ashore. We was worried you crowd out here might be blasted to hell and gone."

"We come through it all right," Evered said.

"God in His mercy," the first man said. And then, "Himself is waiting on you. We'll get your provisions up."

Evered took a last glance at the Duke of Limbs before limping off across the deck.

"I see you got yourself good and gimped up," the second man called after him.

"It was a hard old winter," Evered said.

They renewed their acquaintances in the accustomed manner, the Beadle pointing Evered to his spot beside the desk and giving him the usual once-over.

"You've survived another winter, Mr. Best."

"Still got all me teeth but one," Evered said before he thought of the state of the mouth he was speaking to.

Clinch watched the youngster steadily. Nearly a man to look at now but beaten down and spent, the filthy white hair looking less and less incongruous with each passing season. A grizzly bit of blond beard on the chin.

"We're out at the fish this weeks now," Evered said to break the silence. "I expects we'll have a decent summer at it if we don't founder altogether."

"On that subject," the Beadle said. "You met the boy on your way along?"

Evered glanced over his shoulder at the doorway as if the youngster might be standing behind him. "The Duke of Limbs you means?"

"Who?"

"The dusky-faced one."

"He has a lick of the tar brush I grant you. But he's a Christian soul."

"What of him?" Evered asked.

"You requested Mr. Strapp find a hand to go shares with you and your sister out here," Clinch said.

"That was ages since."

"And Mr. Strapp has endeavoured every year to find a suitable servant."

"That's an unlicked cub if ever I seen one."

"He is accustomed to work," the Beadle said. "And a great favourite among the crew. I'm sure you and your sister," he said and he paused to give extra weight to this point, "would be happy for the company."

"Mr. Long Shanks is too bockity to be any use in a boat. He nearly fell overboard just now."

Clinch looked Evered up and down a second time. "He is a quick study to judge by his time aboard *The Hope*."

Evered shook his head. He felt a pall blooming in his chest and he wanted done and off the ship. "I don't see paying a share to a green hand who never fished a day in he's life."

"Mr. Best," the Beadle said. "You can never hope for more than meagre trade without you will take on help."

"Me and Ada have muddled through this long. We'll get by all right."

"I will tell you that Mr. Strapp went out of his way to accommodate you in this matter."

Evered plowed ahead, goaded by some squalid thing worming in his gut. "If you could thank Mr. Strapp for the trouble he went to on our account," he said.

"It's up to you of course," the Beadle said and he paused, looking for a delicate way forward. "But I know how much you value your sister's opinion. Do you think you should speak to her before we decide things?"

Evered said, "I knows Ada's mind well enough."

Clinch rubbed his hands along his thighs. "If you say so," he said and he turned to the ledger, stroking items from the list, altering amounts to be off-loaded.

"Mr. Clinch sir," Evered said. He felt emboldened to have faced the man down and to still be standing. And beneath that little triumph a recklessness inspired by the fetid creature turning his insides over. "If you could front us a drop of rum with the rest, sir."

The Beadle stared at Evered. "Your mother did not approve of the stronger spirits as I recall."

"Mother is dead this years," Evered said.

Clinch offered a clipped nod and added a line at the bottom of the list. He held the quill toward Evered. "Your mark, Mr. Best," he said.

Ada was waiting on the stage as he rowed in and she helped unload the materials and carry them up the rise to the tilt. They had a celebratory meal of fresh baked bread and molasses and sugary tea and before they went to bed they each had two fingers of rum cut with a splash of water which was enough to make them briefly feel blessed in their circumstances. And in the full of that glow Ada said, "Who was the young one aboard *The Hope?*"

"Which?"

"How many young ones was aboard? The new hand. The one with the curly black hair."

Evered looked into his glass. The worm rolling inside him. "How'd you know there was a young one with curly hair?"

She brandished the spyglass in its leather case. "I had a gander while you was out."

"You liked the look of the Duke of Limbs I imagine."

She smiled at the fire.

"You wouldn't mind adding him to the collection," Evered said. "Sitting him up on your shelf with that book and me tooth and such."

Ada shrugged. She wasn't sure what he was implying but she could tell he wasn't intending a compliment. "I just never seen the like of him," she said.

"He's a green hand," Evered said. "And a bit of an eejit to judge by what they was saying."

She felt surprisingly defensive of the stranger, of the interest she'd made the mistake of showing in him. "He didn't look like no eejit," she said.

"You can't tell by looks now can you."

"I don't spose you can," she said. "A person wouldn't know it to look at you."

Evered drank off the last of his rum and they sat with the unfamiliar heat of animosity awhile. Finally he said, "How come you never put that piece of Indian bone up on your shelf?"

Ada shrugged again. "What bone?"

He smiled at her. "You snuck one of them pieces of bone from the grave. Where is it you keeps it hid?"

She was about to deny it all before she saw the obvious lie would give Evered a measure of satisfaction. "I got a place," she said.

Her brother stared across at her. She could see he was waiting for more but she left it there.

It was still light and Evered went outside to cleave a bit of wood. Every junk he set on the block he imagined was the jingle-brained head of the Duke of Limbs.

Ada went to bed while he was outside and pretended she was asleep when he followed after. It was still cold enough they hadn't shifted to separate bunks for the season but he settled across the room from his sister. Hours later he woke from a miserable dream of the Beadle, of his own naked flesh being worked over as the Duke of Limbs stood watching the cold molestation from a corner, smiling at Evered with his white, white teeth.

It was the first time in months there'd been any sign of vigour down below and he turned to the wall to take advantage of the surprise. It had been an incessant activity the previous summer, laying in the cuddy after he ate his bit of lunch, working his trousers down around his arse. Or standing with his back to the cove to piss overside and the simple fact of having his tackle to hand making him swell up. Having a go at himself, thinking of the Beadle's cold fingers upon him. Of Ada standing in his place beside the desk, the Beadle holding her wrists in one spidery

hand and spreading some viscous concoction across her face
with the other.

He still remembered the shock of that first hot spill pump-
ing across his hand and stomach. Almost a year since. Feeling
on the verge of some imminent arrival with no clue who or
what was coming, the sudden convulsion bringing his knees to
his chest. Ada stirring in the opposite bed, asking was something wrong. And he honestly did not know. Snapping at her to
go to sleep, muddling his confusion with belligerence.

Every private moment that followed was an opportunity to
indulge that obsessive release and he squirrelled away twice,
sometimes three times a day to abuse himself.

It was the loneliest affliction.

He felt he'd fallen into a lurid dwall he couldn't pull clear of,
halfways out of the world altogether. He swore off the habit a
hundred times but there was some corruption in him, some
soiled thing, and he surrendered to it without fail. He took to
nicking his forearms with a knife to lock the urge away in the
narrow windowless cell of that burn. But it did little more than
delay the activity and he gave up on it when Ada began asking
about the scars.

When the fish were done he insisted on hiking into the
backwoods after their winter wood alone. "You got enough to
mind around here," he told Ada. He went about the work with
a ruthless focus that didn't admit time or space for any other
consideration on its face. But at some point each day he found
himself kneeling in the snow with his pants around his ankles,
the cold and wet adding a strangely pleasurable layer of discomfort to the undertaking.

The close quarters in the tilt compelled some restraint after the heavy weather set in though his dreams were no less insistent or troubling. Early in the winter he'd surfaced from a vision of the Beadle's outstretched hand and he nestled closer to Ada to push it aside, still half-asleep. They tucked into one another, Ada lifting her leg across his hips and rocking against him. And he was suddenly, vibrantly awake. He leaned into the heat of her, barely moving, letting Ada work against him, moving his hand to the small of her back to add weight to that drowsy agitation. They didn't speak or acknowledge one another at any point and Evered thought it was possible she was dreaming, that she was insensible to the waking world the entire time they were engaged. And that was his fervent hope in the aftermath.

He spent the days that followed outside at the chopping block or widening the snow paths or nosing some useless project in the store, enduring the bitter cold to avoid his sister's company, to spare himself having to talk to her. Whatever might have been in Ada's mind he didn't doubt it was altogether different from the thoughts that consumed him. And he would sooner cut out his tongue with a fish knife than speak them aloud.

He slept with his back to her after that first rogue encounter, intending to shield the girl from more of the same. Expecting Ada would want nothing more to do with the base exchange. But it was not always Evered who tapped quietly at that door between them. He thought less of himself every time it opened. And without admitting as much to himself he thought something less of Ada as well.

He'd lost his nature altogether after the pilgrimage to the icebound ship. They were both at a low ebb, half-starved and dull on their feet, and he slept chaste beside Ada. He didn't even feel the urge to touch himself and it was a relief to be clear of that turmoil awhile, until the gloom of the endless winter made him think it was a permanent state he'd fallen into. Waking to the slow rolling boil of a toothache or from dreams of the amputated limbs in that wretched abattoir, he rooted at himself while Ada slept, hoping to escape the pain a few minutes, hoping to blot out the sight of those naked corpses. But he was altogether dead down there. He tried to summon some semblance of life with the basest thoughts he could conceive, to no effect, and he drifted off despondent, his flaccid shuttle in his hand.

He examined it quizzically as he took a piss, wondering at the drastic change in its humour. "You're as bad now," he said, "as old Mr. Lucas' goat." And he laughed ruefully at the thing and at himself. It was hard to believe the wormy bit of flesh had wielded so much sway over him. And he mourned the loss as if a creature he loved had died.

He fell back into that habit now with a religious fervour, the old images playing through his head as he jigged at himself and the Duke of Limbs arrived unbidden among them. Evered came over himself as he pictured Ada astraddle the dusky youngster in the opposite bed, both of them naked as the day they were born. He lay still a long while afterward, his mettle going cold against his skin, stirred and repulsed by that image of his sister and the strange boy in raw congress.

By the Beadle's count he was handy about fifteen years old. And more a mystery to himself with every passing season. He felt he was being slowly turned on a spit over an open fire and he suffered hours of that misery before he finally lost himself to sleep.

A Bear Cub; Its Dam. The Abandon Hope.

The summer was a season of sullen estrangement.

The barbed conversation about the Duke of Limbs and the Indian pendant picked at them both and they slept in opposite bunks and spoke only as much as was needed for the work at hand. Standing hours at the splitting table's methodical drudge in silence and eating in silence and generally keeping their minds to themselves. And all their thoughts of the other. Both youngsters suffering and neither willing to raise the white flag. When there was a second run to the grounds in the afternoon Evered rowed out alone. When there wasn't Ada asked for no help at the farm garden and he made himself busy with other things.

Ada had been hiding the bone pendant up there, secreted under one of the stones marking the border of Martha's grave. It was carved to the shape of a feather, tapered near the top, with a driven hole where a person might run a string to wear it as a necklace. Every time she unearthed and held it a little chill ran through her. The beauty of the thing. And a nick of shame to have stolen it for its beauty. Ada could still bring to mind the figurines and toy boats in that grave, the elaborate necklace of shell and bone and animal teeth around the mother's neck. If she'd been there alone she might have taken it all.

It felt like love, this hunger of hers. Though part of her suspected it was closer to greed at its heart and that suspicion chimed like a bell when Evered asked about the pendant. Even in her incessant conversations with Martha she'd never mentioned the object or how it came into her possession. To spare herself looking too closely at the shadow cast by her inclinations.

Past the shock of seeing what Evered had known all along it seemed natural enough she was an open book to him, that he would have a view of what she'd thought her most secret self. What stung was his blindsiding her. The realization he'd been holding that bit of information in reserve for some occasion when she needed to be knocked down a peg.

The guilt and resentment worked at her in tandem through the first weeks of the season, as if she was hobbling through her days with a rock in each shoe. Until she buried both guilt and resentment under a stone at Martha's grave and brought the pendant down to the tilt. She set it up on her shelf of treasures. She raked the sand around the hearth clean and scored the pendant's shape and markings there, daring Evered to say something. But he ignored the provocation. Which felt to Ada like a victory of sorts.

After the caplin scull the cod were unusually scarce on the shore. Evered spent hours rowing the empty boat between the Barrow Ledge and the Foggity Shoals and the Razor Ledge and even when he struck in there was hardly enough some days to fill the fish pound. The back end of the summer was cold and inclement and what they'd managed to catch cured poorly, laid out on the bawn in the scuddy intermission between showers. The flesh went slimy and maggoty and they carried dipping tubs to the bawn to rewash the fish and they laid it out in the same miserable run of weather. The garden fared no better. What didn't go to rot in the steady rains was undersized and soft and wouldn't keep through to March month in the root cellar.

They didn't speak of it though the implications were obvious. And that impending disaster sobered them both, taking the edge off the animosity that had soured their time together. As if they regretted the petty damage in light of the scourge they'd shortly be facing. It wasn't a reconciliation exactly but they managed to be civil in each other's company.

Evered found himself filling the vacant time on those long fruitless rows between the shoal grounds reliving his visit aboard *The Hope* in the spring, the offer of the Duke of Limbs as a share hand and what possessed him to refuse. It seemed a lunatic decision in hindsight. He could still feel that fecal ooze in his gut, the panic to be clear of the ship. He knew the dusky boy was somehow to blame for his keeping Ada at a remove through the summer. But playing it over in his head left him none the wiser and made him feel no better about it all and he circled the outskirts of that maze against his will, chafing at every step.

He'd outgrown the childish habit of speculation and conjecture that had occupied himself and Ada in their wakeful hours and in this one particular he felt barely related to his sister anymore. Ada was one not satisfied until she hammered every raised nailhead flush to the boards. Months after he taught her the shore marks on the water she'd turned to him one night to ask how it was he knew them.

"Father taught me," he'd said.

She nodded in the darkness. "Who was it taught Father then?"

"What?"

"Sure Father's eyes was too poor to make them out he's self."

"He couldn't mark them from the water, no."

"Someone must have taught him," she said.

"What, out in the boat with him you mean?"

"How else is it he'd've managed?"

"Might be so," Evered said and he shrugged away from it. The question had never occurred to him before and didn't particularly interest him then.

He'd almost drifted off when Ada said, "Might be he's eyes got worse."

"What?"

"Could be Father marked them when he was younger and lost them before we come along."

"God's reeven nails," Evered said. "Are we going to sleep here this night?"

Beyond figuring the province or works of some article or charge, he preferred to keep his head down and marl along. Puzzling over the Duke of Limbs and his own murky motivations was such a torture it was almost a relief to turn his thoughts to the winter's looming privations instead.

There wasn't a real break in the miserable run of rain and drizzle until the beginning of September, a mocking sliver of summer too late to be any use. Ada crossed the brook and walked the beach to the berry hills every day while the decent stretch lasted. The berries were sparse and small and sour but even so she persisted, stooping to the work and carrying on a long one-sided conversation with Martha until the afternoon showed late and she started for home. On her last trip out she stumbled on a bear cub as she came up through the spruce trees into the berry fields, the animal as startled and shy as herself, rearing to its full height twenty paces away. Even on its hind legs it was not much taller than Ada and after a brief stare-down it turned tail and scooted across the open ground.

"Now Martha," Ada whispered. She caught sight of the mother on the far side of the clearing. Raising her head at the sound of her young coming in a rush, bulling into the open until the cub was behind her. The dam stood straight, making a growling racket that prickled the skin on Ada's neck. The exhalation when she dropped to all fours like the wet chuff of a whale as it breaks the surface. Turning to the cub and shep-herding it into the underbrush, glancing over her shoulder repeatedly before disappearing into the trees.

Ada remembered how the bear had circled on them the previous year and she backed into the spruce behind her, then turned and ran all she was worth. She didn't stop until she reached the brook and fell to her knees there, winded, a taste of blood in her throat. "Piss and corruption," she said, her hands shaking, an incongruous smile on her face. She turned and shouted her mother's curse out over the ocean. For the first time in months she felt alive in every nook and cranny, all the lamps of her self trimmed and lit and burning bright.

It wasn't quite mid-morning, almost warm out of the wind. She couldn't imagine going back to the berry hills this day, maybe ever. She gathered a handful of alder branches and then stripped out of her boots, out of her shift and trousers and

stockings, and she stepped into the brook, completely naked for
the first time since she'd bathed there the year before. The water
was running high and cold from the steady rains, it stippled her
skin head to toe and she yelled against the icy shock of it.

"Piss and corruption!"

She took a breath and went under all at once and she stayed
down as long as she could hold it.

Evered was on the stage splitting the few fish he'd caught in
the early hours of the morning when he heard a voice yelling
over by the brook. Their mother's curse and sounding eerily
like the dead woman. Ada was still in the tilt when he left before
first light and she was planning to walk up to the berry hills, he
thought. He cocked his head to listen but there was nothing
more and he turned back to the fish on the splitting table until
he heard her shout again, an edge to it this time, pain or fear.

He tore off the stage, running up the rise far enough to look
down toward the brook. Her clothes in a pile on the bank and
no sign of Ada until she erupted from the bathing pool, gasping
for air. She stood knee-deep in the running current, reaching
up to wring water from her hair. She crawled a little ways up the
bank to grab the trousers and stockings and her shift and she
pushed them under the surface, trampling them underfoot
before beating each one against the rocks.

Evered stood considering he might walk down and join her.
It might be the last halfways warm day of the year. He imagined
it wouldn't go astray to give himself and his clothes a scrubbing.
But the sight of Ada made him hesitate. He did not recognize
the youngster he'd bathed with in that same spot a year since.
The thick patch of dark hair between her legs, her new breasts.
A woman's body he was looking at and he was embarrassed to

be watching as if it was a stranger standing in the brook below him. Ada laid her clothes out on the rocks to dry and when she took up a handful of alder leaves to scrub at herself Evered turned away.

Ada had seen him standing on the rise, watching her. She half expected he would make his way down to the brook and was of two minds about the prospect so she ignored him there as she wrung out her clothes and scrubbed at herself with the alder leaves. Wondering which way things would settle, until it occurred to her Evered was likely waiting on her to raise a hand, to offer an invitation. She glanced up the rise then but he was gone.

She lay back on her elbows in the chill of the brook, letting the rushing water skin over her, surprised to see her breasts riding above the current like little dumplings in a pot. Ada pictured the bear cub at the berry hills, the animal coming up on its hind legs a stone's throw in front of her. The dam on the opposite side of the clearing. She was likely the same bear they'd encountered the previous year, Ada guessed, though there was nothing she knew of bears and their habits to say so.

And the notion of sleeping beside Evered came over her unexpected then, a transparent hankering, as if her body was having a thought all on its wordless lonesome. She dipped her head back till it cradled in the water, staring up at the sky with the noise across her ears. Of two minds again though she could feel all her weight sliding wordlessly to one side of the scale.

When she lifted her head there was a slender line of blood flowing down the brook away from her and out to sea. Her visitor had arrived. The first time in months.

Evered was at the tilt when she made her way up from the brook, her clothes still wet on her frame, her hair dripping water.

"Thought you was going up after some berries," Evered said to her.

"I guess I changed me mind about it."

He watched her a few moments and then nodded. "Everything all right?" he asked.

"Everything's best kind," she said, with a dissenting edge she couldn't quite keep clear of the words. Miserable in her soaking kit but not able to hang her trousers over the hearth for fear she had bled through the pad of moss between her legs. Angry with Evered for no clear reason. She'd already started resenting the urge that had come over her as she lay naked in the brook. It felt like something foisted upon her against her will and she didn't know who to blame for it but him. Though she was not so ignorant of her own self to ride that thought all the way to the Promised Land.

Her visitor's arrival had saved her surrendering to something she would likely regret was the truth of it. And she halfways resented being spared her own recklessness.

"Piss and corruption," she said under her breath.

"You sure everything's all right?"

She nodded. She considered telling Evered about the bear cub and its dam at the berry hills as a kind of peace offering but kept it to herself in the end. Too bound up in it all to offer even so private an apology.

It was pissing down rain the day *The Hope* anchored off on the Barrow Ledge.

Ada and Evered filled the boat with their meagre store of cured fish and Evered ferried it out through the skerries. Bailing the accumulated inches of rainwater from the bilge before the next haul could be loaded in. Both of them soaked to the skin. Every time Ada dipped her head forward water funnelled through the gutter of her soggy tricorn in a wave.

"This is all a mess of cullage," Evered said before he shoved off with the last of the season's work.

"Let's see how the Beadle marks it down," Ada said. They were shouting to be heard over the rain drumming on the water and the stage and their sopping clothes.

"I got eyes, maid," Evered said. "Every bit of it is refuse. It idn't worth the salt we set it in." He looked up to her on the stage from where he sat at the oars. "I'm going to ask the Beadle if he might see his way to taking us into Mockbeggar. Set us up working for Mr. Strapp."

Ada looked away across the cove a moment and then back down at Evered, water sluicing off the front corner of the hat.

"We got no choice," Evered said. "As I sees it."

"If you says so," she said.

"I'll ask then will I?"

"You says we got no choice."

He nodded. "That's what I says," he said, "yes." He pushed away from the stage and set the oars. And he watched her where she stood watching him all the way out the cove.

Ada stepped into the lean-to shelter over the splitting table. She took the glass out of its leather case and scanned the deck of *The Hope*. Without knowing it she'd been looking toward this moment all summer, that she might lay eyes on the Duke of Limbs again, his curly black hair, his gangly boyishness. But there was no sign of him aboard. There was no one visible at all on the deck now, the crew waiting somewhere out of the rain until

Evered tied up alongside. It was possible the youngster was in Mockbeggar, she thought, if that's where they were going to end up. Though she couldn't imagine what would become of them there. She thought on Martha a moment, of her grave up by the failing farm garden. And then she forced herself to think about something other.

She watched the fish brought up to the deck in baskets and Evered climbing aboard, then disappearing into the hatchway toward the stern. The three crewmen bringing barrels and sacks out of the hold and stacking them along the rail. Evered reappearing sooner than she expected and spidering back down to the boat, the materials passed overside to his out-stretched hands.

The Hope weighed anchor to catch the tide before Evered slipped through the skerries and Ada stepped out from under the shelter to wave the tricorn as the sails were set and took wind. Only one man turned her way to wave back.

She helped Evered unload the supplies at the stage but they didn't say a word over the sound of the rain. Not half enough for the winter. Evered walked past her and hefted the flour barrel onto a shoulder. He headed up the rise and she followed after him with a brin sack of peas under her arm. They made two more trips for the rest and then sat next the fire in the tilt, picking spots where the rain wasn't dripping through the ceiling.

"I guess we wouldn't welcome in Mockbeggar," Ada offered.

"They've had as bad a time of it as we," Evered said. One side of his face was swollen up with the toothache that had been tormenting him off and on since the spring. They'd run out of rum halfway through the summer with what he'd been drinking as a medicinal and there was none came in with the new supplies. "They'll be lucky folks don't starve there the winter the Beadle says. We'd only be more burden to them."

They sat quiet a long time. Ada felt she'd been unfaithful to Martha even letting Evered raise the question with the Beadle and part of her was relieved despite what staying meant.

"He give us what he could spare," Evered said. "It was more than what the season was worth."

"We'll make do," Ada said. "We always does." And almost as an afterthought she added, "Our Martha will look out to us."

Evered stared at the girl, fighting the urge to take her by the shoulders and shake her. He said, "Martha's dead, Sister."

She glanced across at him and he turned to the struggling bit of fire, rubbing absently at his swollen cheek.

"I knows she's dead," she whispered.

There was an illness running among the crew of *The Hope* and Evered took sick in the days after the ship left them. He was bedridden a week with fever and headaches and a fierce cough, insensible half the time and waking only to talk gibberish to people who were not in the room. Ada made a poultice of cod-liver oil and wet bread for his chest and she sat up with him to bathe his face with a cold cloth until she fell ill herself. And they passed by each other in the fever's long dark hallway, Evered coming slowly to himself as Ada descended deeper into bouts of the shakes and delirium and periods of near oblivion.

Evered was too fragile and woolly-headed to help his sister beyond keeping her warm and trying to recreate the useless poultice she'd concocted for him. She couldn't be coaxed into eating even hardtack soaked in sweet tea. When she opened her eyes she didn't know her brother and she spoke only to Martha though there was no logic or sense to her rambling. With each passing day he was more convinced she was going to die in her bed and he sat holding her clammy hand hours at a time as if that might be enough to tether her to him.

He left her only long enough to carry in wood for the fire and to bring water up from the brook and to empty the chamber pot in the landwash and rinse it in the cove's bitter cold. At the top of the rise he would stand scanning the empty horizon, the breadth of the barren grey sea. Nothing out there and nothing out there.

Until a morning at the beginning of October, a slur of blowing snow like a haze over the water and the vague apparition of a vessel in the distance. A fever dream, a ghost ship that winked in and out of sight among the drift. He was barely well enough to be taken in by the illusion, to feel even a rote imitation of hope. He shuffled inside to find Ada's spyglass and spent a while watching the schooner making way across his field of vision. It wasn't until he could see the bowsprit with his naked eye that he gave in to the fact of it.

He made a torch of a handful of blasty boughs and stood waving that noisy flag on the rise as the ship leaked past the cove, just visible through the snow's blowing curtain, and he knew the little light he held up was useless. He dropped his eyes to the cove, to the stage still standing on the landwash, waiting to be taken down. He gathered an armful of dry brush and carried it to the salt shed, piled the tinder in a bulkhead and set it alight. The structure was weather-cured wood and went up in a rush, along with the lean-to shelter and the cutting table and Evered had to scramble down to the boat and slip it free of the stage to row it away from the flames. He drifted out toward the skerries with the oily black smoke's distress signal billowing above him. But the schooner was beyond the cove by then. And because there was nothing more to be done he said, "Please Martha." Hating himself to be reduced to the helpless plea. And he repeated those two words aloud until he saw the sails of the vessel dropped and furled and a wherry let down overside and two figures rowing through the blowing snow toward the cove.

Captain Truss and Mrs. Brace. A Bitch-Bear; Her Cub.

Captain Solomon Truss was an Englishman from Oxfordshire and for many years an officer in the King's army where he rose to the rank by which he still introduced himself. He was sent as a young cadet to the East Indies where he obtained an ensigncy in Colonel Alderson's regiment by the death of Captain Lyon. In Germany he served the late Marquis de Canby as aide-de-camp and expected to be in the sure line of promotion but took a pension to avoid the mortification of serving under two junior officers who purchased companies that Truss would otherwise have been offered. He spent a year hunting in the Scottish Highlands where it became apparent his pension would not suffice to keep himself and two servants and three brace of dogs in meat and out of the rain. He'd followed a younger brother to Newfoundland almost on a whim and returned several summers running for the abundant fish and game and ten years ago he borrowed the money to set up a handful of enterprises on the Labrador coast, seining for cod in summer, hunting and trapping through the winter, and trading with the Eskimos for fur and tusks. He was just now bound for

England by way of Fogo Island to settle his father's affairs as executor of the will, having lately received his brother's news of the man's passing some months earlier. There was no inheritance of substance but there was a family manor and some property, the sale of which would be enough to settle the debts Truss had fallen into in the prosecution of his trade and to allow him to live a gentleman's life somewhere outside of London's extravagance. Portsmouth was his notion at the moment though he allowed that might change.

Evered nodded yessir, yessir as Truss carried on with his exhaustive autobiographical recital though the man might have been speaking a language other than English altogether. It reminded him of the Beadle's description of his church office and of the funeral service he'd performed for its alien vocabulary, its rush of incomprehensible notions waterfalling one on top of the other. He'd never heard of ranks or pensions or hunting dogs or any such place as Oxfordshire or the East Indies or Portsmouth. Even Fogo Island and Labrador existed on the very fringes of his knowledge of the world.

"Captain Truss," Mrs. Brace interrupted, "I'm sure the young one has heard enough for an evening."

Truss looked across the room to where the woman was seated at Ada's bedside. "Your concern for our host's tender ears is commendable, Mrs. Brace. I suspect he is not alone in having heard enough?"

"No sir," Evered said. "No such thing." He was willing to let the man speak till Kingdom Come if that was the price to be paid for their improbable rescue.

"He might like to rest is my meaning," Mrs. Brace said. "He's not long past the girl's condition himself."

"Of course," Truss said. "I have forgotten myself."

"Would that we were so lucky," Mrs. Brace said under her breath and Evered saw Truss give her a look and deciding not to address the comment.

"I'm best kind where I'm to," Evered said. "Don't bother about me."

Truss stood from his chair to lay more wood on the fire, stooping low to keep from smacking his head against the rafters, and Evered marvelled again at the man's compass. He had hands the size of platters and a wingspan that allowed him to nearly touch opposite walls of the tilt at once. His mutton-chopped face was as long and narrow as a fox's tail.

He'd rowed into the cove from the passing schooner and stepped from the boat onto the shore like he was stepping over the lintel of a doorway. He carried a rifle that stood almost to his height when he rested the stock on the ground. He introduced himself and shook Evered's hand and loomed over him as the youngster tried to explain the nature of the emergency. Truss turned to the man at the oars of the wherry. "You'd best go back for Mrs. Brace," he said. "I'll want the black bag from my cabin. And I suppose you'd better send in my shotgun." And he lifted the bow of the boat with one hand and pushed it out into the cove.

Evered led the man up the rise away from the collapsed and still burning stage and directly to Ada in her bed.

Truss knelt on the sand beside her. "Have you candles or a lamp?"

"We got an old slutlamp."

Truss got to his feet and ran out the door in a hunch and Evered heard him bellowing across the cove to the man in the boat to bring candles and matches as well. He came back in, walking in the same hunch to Ada's bedside. "The lamp," he said to Evered. "The smoke may choke us but it will be better than nothing."

In the shadowy light they could see that Ada's face was flushed a bright partridgeberry red. She was staring at the ceiling with a fierce fixed look and seemed not to know they were with her and she fainted dead away for a few moments.

"Sister," Evered called to her.

He shook her shoulder and shouted again and she opened her eyes, flicking a blank stare left and right. And a few minutes later she went under a second time.

Evered reached to shake her again but Truss stopped his hand. "How long has your sister been in this state?"

"I don't rightly know. I was laid up myself when she took sick. Days," he said. "A week?"

"Fainting in this manner?"

He shook his head. "First time ever I seen it."

Ada opened her eyes again and watched them blankly awhile and fell away again.

Truss rubbed his massive palms against his mutton chops a moment. "I'm sorry for your troubles," he said.

"She idn't going to die is she, sir?"

"I'm afraid it's quite likely," Truss said. "Evered, I will need a sharp knife and a bowl of some sort."

"A knife?"

"A sharp one," he said. "And stoke up the fire, it's too damp in here to do the girl any good."

By the time Mrs. Brace was delivered to the cove with the black bag and candles and shotgun Truss had opened a vein in

Ada's arm and taken off twelve ounces of blood. He handed the bowl of nearly black liquid to the boy beside him. Evered could feel the warmth of it seeping through the bowl's cold clay.

"What do we do now?" he asked.

"Now we wait," Truss said, "and pray that God in His mercy." And he left the thought there.

The strangers had been in the cove with Ada and Evered two days and two nights since.

When Mrs. Brace arrived Truss lit a handful of candles on the crowded shelf above the sickbed and he rummaged in the black bag. He gave Ada seven grains of James's Powder and then he left Evered in the tilt with Mrs. Brace at his sister's bedside with orders to look for him if the situation deteriorated.

"Where's he after going?" Evered asked the woman.

"Hunting for his supper," she said. "You look poorly yourself, Evered Best."

"I been better."

"You should sleep."

"Don't think I could," he said but she tucked him into the bed opposite Ada and against his own desire he drifted off, startled now and then by the sound of Truss's rifle firing and echoing around the cove. Each time he rose up on his elbows in a panic, asking after Ada, and Mrs. Brace settled him back.

"She's still with us," the woman said. "You sleep."

Truss returned hours later with three shell-birds and two grey plover and a saddleback gull. He turned the game over to Mrs. Brace and looked in on the patients. He administered another dose of James's Powder to Ada and set about making a pot of Labrador tea with leaves foraged near the brook. He let it steep several hours and in the evening he sugared it and gave a mug to Evered to drink and then set about bleeding Ada a second time.

"Will she be all right after all?" Evered asked.

"If she makes it through the night, she might recover."

"She got the nerve of a mule Ada have."

"Evidently," Truss said and he smiled at the youngster.

Ada made it through the night and through the night that followed as well. On the second day she was able to keep down a few spoonfuls of broth and a little of Truss's Labrador tea. But she was awake only minutes at a time before falling back into a state more like unconsciousness than sleep.

The schooner had come around to anchor off on the Barrow Ledge. Truss spent his days in the backwoods or being sculled along the coast by a manservant in the wherry, shooting at anything that moved. He bagged a goose and a bottle-nosed diver, three ducks and four strangers, seven ptarmigan, two brace of hares and a silver fox and he sent most of the game back with the wherry for the servants and crew still on board The Hydra, save for his favoured meat of the haul which he brought to the tilt and delivered into the hands of Mrs. Brace.

Evered had never been in the company of a strange woman other than Mary Oram and he was almost struck dumb to be left two days alone with Mrs. Brace who he was belatedly taking in now that Ada seemed past the worst. She was somewhere between his mother and Mary Oram in age but more than that he couldn't guess. A bit wide in the boughs his father would have said. Sturdy. A bosom the likes of which Evered hadn't considered possible. When he wasn't asleep in bed he sat near the hearth, as far from the woman as the room allowed.

"Is it just the two of you on this property?" she asked from the bedside.

He nodded.

"Has it always been just you two?"

He shook his head and she smiled down at her hands.

"We been on our own the last little bit," Evered managed. "Mother and Father is both dead for long ago."

Mrs. Brace nodded. She seemed embarrassed suddenly and for a moment Evered was afraid he'd said something indecent or impolite.

"Where were they from?" she said then. "Your parents?"

"From?" he said.

"Their people," Mrs. Brace said. "Is there no one you could have gone to?" she said. "After they passed on?"

He shook his head, embarrassed himself now. "They never said one way or the other," he admitted.

They had a stew of rabbit and potatoes for their supper. Evered's mouth was so swollen up with a toothache he could barely chew his food but he felt well enough afterward to sit in front of the fire as the evening came on—which Truss took as an invitation to recite the details of his life story, until Mrs. Brace intervened with her jab about the Captain forgetting himself.

He didn't know what to make of their exchanges. Truss referred to her as his housekeeper which Evered took to mean a servant in the Captain's employ, the same as the men aboard *The Hope* were the Beadle's underlings. As little as he knew of the world Evered could sense she took liberties no servant would dare or be permitted. He slept beside Ada in the sickbed and Truss hung a blanket down the middle of the room, lying on the other side of that thin wall with Mrs. Brace. And both nights Evered woke to the half-strangled sounds of two people struggling against each other.

"Mrs. Brace," Truss said as he placed a junk of wood on the fire, "has expressed some concern about your provisioning for the winter."

"It was a late spring," Evered said. "And we had a wet August month besides. We're in a bit of a blind look-out the winter I imagine."

"I took a look at your store today," Truss said, "and at your cellar. Forgive my intrusion. You will need some luck with that flintlock of yours to carry you through."

Evered glanced at the firearm standing in the corner near the hearth. "That old thing was Father's," he said. "The works is rusted solid and the spring is gone. It idn't much good to us."

Truss picked up the gun and weighed it in his hands. "You don't hunt for meat over the winter?"

"I sets a few snares for rabbit."

"You don't use this at all?"

He shrugged. "I can't say as I knows the first thing about it."

"Well," Truss said. He turned to smile at Mrs. Brace. "We have a virgin on our hands." He squinted down the sights. "If I can set this thing to rights and you're feeling up to it perhaps I could teach you to shoot?"

Evered couldn't keep the grin from his face at the prospect and that act caused him so much pain that he doubled over in his seat, massaging his jaw furiously.

"First thing tomorrow we will deal with that tooth," Truss said. "And then we will go shoot something."

They all stopped still then at the sound of Ada calling weakly. "Brother," she said.

He went to sit beside her on the bed and touched her face. "Now, Sister," he said. "You're back in the land of the living are you?"

"Who are these people, Brother?"

"Angels from heaven you asks me," he said.

In the morning Evered rowed Truss out to *The Hydra* and they returned with bags of shot and powder, a set of iron smithy tongs and a bottle of brandy. Truss poured Evered a full glass of the liquor and set about reaming out the barrel of the flintlock and oiling the works as the youngster drank. He poured Evered a second glass when the first was gone.

"I won't be no use today if I haves another drop of this," Evered said.

"I expect by the time we are done here this morning," Truss said, "you will be stone cold sober."

Truss replaced the lock spring and used the smithy tongs to fire the hammer red-hot to reharden it. When Evered's second glass was empty he cooled the tongs in the water barrel and sat Evered in a chair beneath the open window for the light. "Mrs. Brace," he said, "if you would hold his head steady."

Evered was vaguely, drunkenly aware of her hand across his forehead, of his crown cradled in the valley between those remarkable breasts, until Truss straddled his lap and forced the tongs into his mouth and the searing clamp of it blotted out the world. The three of them locked in a hellish little struggle, Truss's long face reddening with the effort, grunting inches above Evered's wide eyes. Truss adjusted his purchase on the tooth as Evered tried to beg him to stop around the mouthful of iron. Mrs. Brace wrapped her forearm across the top of his head as Truss reamed back and forth, the molar clinging relentless to its place until the moment it surrendered completely, Truss falling off Evered's lap with the tooth in the grip of the tongs.

Blood was pouring from Evered's mouth but the relief was so immediate he paid no mind. He felt wildly, joyously sober. Mrs. Brace held the bowl that Ada had been bled into under his chin. She poured him another drop of brandy. "Swish that around," she said, "and spit." Evered grimaced against the burn but even that felt purifying, almost pleasurable. Mrs. Brace folded a piece of rag and reached into his mouth to stuff it into the gaping crater. "Bite down," she said and she smiled at him, her hands on either side of his face. "Are you all right?"

"It wouldn't so bad," he said through his clenched teeth.

Truss had the molar in the palm of his hand. "What shall we do with this beast?"

"Ada," Evered mumbled. "For her shelf."

"Yes," Truss said. "I wondered who was responsible for that. Quite the collection."

They stayed another five days in the cove.

Truss took Evered into the backwoods hunting every morning but for the second day which he announced was Sunday. He sat the youngster and Mrs. Brace at the hearth and read prayers from a calfskin-bound book and then Evered rowed him out to *The Hydra* and listened to the man read prayers to those on board.

The enforced indolence made Evered itch to get back to the glory of shooting. He had a natural aptitude for the weapon, for leading a moving target, and he was already addicted to the sport. They shot grouse and geese, a handful of squirrels, two otters, a great horned owl. "There is plenty of fat on the owl," Truss told him, "but it is tough eating." They shot curlews and a raven and a handful of jays and nameless grassy birds. And the day after the Sabbath observance he took down a falcon that was circling the cove just as they were setting out.

The bird fell on the eastern arm and they walked out to retrieve it. Truss spent a few minutes examining the speckled plumage, the talons and hooked beak and the black black eyes. "Beautiful," he murmured. "A beautiful creature." He put a platter-sized hand on Evered's shoulder. "A shame you weren't shown the use of that flintlock sooner," he said.

Evered looked down at the firearm in his hands, feeling his father was being slighted somehow. "Father couldn't see proper," he said. "Not past thirty paces. The gun wouldn't much use to him." He shrugged over the inadequacy of his defence. "I guess it fell from his mind," he said. And as if to compensate for his father's shortcoming he went on to talk about the mysterious blindness that came over him during their trek across the ice the previous spring, the days of torment with a poultice strapped to his eyes. The fear he might never recover his sight.

"Snow blindness," Truss said matter-of-factly. "I suffered a bout myself our first winter in Labrador. It's prolonged exposure to the ice glare that causes it."

"It never bothered Ada none."

"You were leading the way?"

"Till me eyes give out," he said.

"She was watching your back as she followed behind. You were staring at the ice."

Evered nodded, relieved to think there was an unremarkable explanation for the affliction that had come over him. That no less a man than Truss himself had once succumbed to it.

The weather was cold but fair and they walked into the backcountry along the shore of the brook, miles further than Evered and his father had ever dared. He kept his discomfort to himself for fear of calling his upbringing into question again, holding tight to the Captain's wake. Truss striding brassy into the wastes of strangled bush, looking for open ground where caribou might congregate after the snow fell. They hadn't seen any game large enough to warrant using the Hanoverian rifle and Truss was eager to show what it could do beyond the target practice Evered had taken to feel its weight and kick. He told endless tales of the deer and wolves and white bear he'd killed in Labrador as they walked.

They skirted the shorelines of three boggy ponds and at the last came upon a beaver house that they watched for an hour without making a sighting. "Keep this place in mind," Truss said. He described the animal's buck teeth and flat tail and ornery disposition. "An old one can weigh forty-five pounds or more," he said.

On the way back down the brook he taught Evered to build and set deadfall traps for foxes that he baited with old Cheshire cheese and honey.

"What do you call that," Evered asked. He was pointing to the bait.

"This?" Truss said. "Cheese?"

"We had a load of it wash ashore from a wreck last fall. Ada just about loved it more than the world. Never knew what it was called."

Truss looked at the youngster steady though Evered couldn't read his expression. "Who told thee that thou wast naked?" he said.

Evered nodded yessir, as he did whenever Truss said something beyond his understanding.

"You aren't lonely out here, Evered?" the Captain asked. "You and Ada?"

The question struck him nearly as peculiar as the one about being naked. "We idn't alone," he said.

"Of course not, no." Truss watched him a moment as if weighing how far down that road he wanted to travel with the boy. And he gestured it away with a wave. "Boiled fox is decent meat," he said. "Not as good as beaver but better than owl by a long shot."

They were licked out with the rough walking when they returned each evening, carting the day's carnage over their shoulders. Truss fired a powder shot as a signal to *The Hydra* and the wherry was sent in to take the bulk of the catch. Before they ate themselves, Truss made an examination of Ada's condition and pronounced himself encouraged by her progress. And then the man sat to a plate of meat so gargantuan as to beggar belief. Evered thought the housekeeper was making fun of her employer the first time she set food in front of the Captain. But Truss calmly ate the full of it and a second helping just as preposterous besides.

Mrs. Brace smiled at the look on Evered's face. "The man is all appetite," she said, a hint of mockery in her voice. But Truss did not dispute the claim.

Ada seemed to brighten by the hour and she was soon enough able to sit up for short spells and keep down solid food and she carried on a languid centreless conversation with Mrs. Brace between her bouts of sleep. She'd hired herself out as a house-keeper, Mrs. Brace told her, after her husband died of consump-tion fifteen years ago. They'd had no children. "I was young to be a widow," she said. "But not quite young enough to interest another husband." She'd been in the service of Captain Truss a decade, coming over from England when he began his enterprise in Labrador.

"Will you stay with him?" Ada asked. "When you gets back to England?"

"If he will have me, yes."

Ada nodded thoughtfully.

"What is it?" Mrs. Brace asked.

"I wondered if you and the Captain," she said. She'd been hearing the same stricken intimacies across the room that Evered had. "I thought you two was married."

"Because we share a bed?"

"Is there more to it?"

"Sometimes it seems there is and more times there does not," Mrs. Brace said. "But the Captain," she said, "refuses to tie a knot with his tongue that he can't untie with his teeth." She laughed to herself then though Ada didn't see the joke exactly. "Don't ever be beholden to a man if you can help it," Mrs. Brace said and she pointed a finger to underline the lesson. "That is my advice to you, my maid." And she smiled in a way that made it impossible for Ada to say if she was being serious.

On their next to last night Ada dressed in her trousers and waist-coat and sat with them to eat her supper. Truss had procured a half-pound wedge of cheese from the schooner and he laid it on her plate whole. "I understand you have a taste for this," he said.

Ada covered her mouth with her hands, looking from one face to another and shaking her head as if the fruit of Paradise had been placed before her.

"It's cheese is the name of it," Evered said.

"I don't recommend eating the thing entire this evening," Truss told her, smiling. "In your delicate condition."

She got up from her seat and went to the shelf above the bed. She came back and set the Indian pendant and the silver button in the Captain's hand. He examined each in turn, nodding over them.

"Fleur-de-lys," he murmured and the youngsters stared at him. He held up the button. "It's French," he said. "A fleur-de-lys it's called."

"I found it up to the farm garden," Ada said. "Next the graves."

"The French were great raiders on this coast during Queen Anne's War."

"It was off the clothes of a drownded fellow," Evered said, "washed ashore when Father was first come out from Mockbeggar."

"Well," Truss said, "Queen Anne's War was long before your father's time. It could have been a sailor wrecked off a French vessel." He made a skeptical face. "Though no common sailor would be sporting silver buttons. An officer possibly."

Mrs. Brace said, "As with many things of the like I suppose we will never know for certain."

"The voice of common sense as always," Truss said, not unkindly. "Now this," he said, holding up the pendant. "This is a relict of the Red Indians, of that I have no doubt."

"We come upon a grave," Ada said, avoiding Evered's eyes. "A ways along the coast. There was lots more pieces the like of this one laid with them."

"I'd been meaning to ask if you had any dealings with the Indians. I saw numbers of them when I first travelled along this shore but only from a spyglass distance. They were not keen to make our acquaintance."

"Never laid eyes on a one of them ourselves," Evered said. "Not on the hoof anyway. Father claimed to seen them paddling by in their queer little boats once or twice."

"They paddled those little boats out to the Funks for bird eggs, did you know?" He looked up at Evered and could see he did not know. "A flat bit of rock sixty miles off of Fogo Island," he said. "The middle of the Atlantic Ocean. How could they have known it even existed out there?" He shook his head, incredulous. "Remarkable creatures," he said. And he went off on a lengthy treatise on the Indians, their habit of painting themselves and everything they own with red ochre, their expertise in the manufacture and use of bows and arrows of sycamore and Weymouth pine, their jerking of venison and seal meat and fish for times of scarcity. He was running his fingers over the markings on the pendant as he spoke. "And for all their cleverness they are the most forlorn of any human species I ever heard of. Excluded from all intercourse with the rest of mankind. And they are not even possessed of the useful services of a dog."

"Captain Truss," Mrs. Brace interrupted.

He came back to them then, looking up from the pendant. "Yes," he said. "Well."

Evered said, "I half expected we might run into some when we wandered up the brook."

"Not at all likely," Truss said quietly. "Up the brook or any-where else. I predict the entire race will be extinct before many more years have passed."

"Extinct?" Ada said.

"Eradicated," Truss said. "Wiped off the face of the earth. Blotted from the Book of Life." He passed both the button and pendant back to Ada. "I could not possibly take these," he said. "But it would be a great privilege if Evered was willing to escort me to the burial site."

Evered stared down at his plate. "Was only chance we landed on it to begin with. I doubts I'd spot it a second time."

"I'm willing to take a stab. If you would indulge me."

"I could go with you," Ada said.

Evered glanced across at her. "It's a fair haul, Captain," he said, though he kept his eyes on his sister. "We was out over-night with the boat."

"We will take the wherry of course. And two men to the oars. We'll have you back before dark." Truss turned to Ada. "You may have the nerve of a mule," he said, "but I will not allow you to try it on my account. You will stay here and rest. If we are lucky enough to strike upon the burial I will bring you a few treasures to add to your collection. How would that suit you?"

"That would be the finest kind of a thing," she said.

Before it had gone fully to dark Evered rowed Truss out to the schooner to prepare for the morning's expedition. Mrs. Brace took the pots to the brook and Ada insisted on walking down with her though Mrs. Brace refused to let her help with the work. "Sit there and be still," she said. And a moment later she said, "Your Evered seemed none too pleased to be talking about Indians this evening."

Ada couldn't say if it was a question or a simple statement of fact but she wanted no part of it either way. "Did you see any yourself back then?" she asked. "Red Indians?"

"I did not," Mrs. Brace said. "But I saw enough of their like in Labrador to do me a lifetime."

"Captain Truss seems right taken with them."

"He'd sooner sup with savages than Christians is the truth of it. Trying to teach them to behave like sensible creatures when sense is not in their nature. Even the ones that go to church and say their prayers will still eat their meat raw." And as if that uncivilized behaviour highlighted another she said, "I was wondering, Ada, have you not got something other than your brother's trousers to wear in mixed company?"

Ada smiled at the notion a person might put on different clothes according to who they were sitting with. "They're not Evered's trousers," she said.

"I found a dress tucked away when I was putting the place to rights," Mrs. Brace said. "Is that not yours?"

Ada shook her head.

"Oh," Mrs. Brace said and she turned back to the pot in her hand. "You never said what became of them. Your mother and father." She scoured away at the perfectly clean surface awhile and when it was clear the girl wasn't going to answer she said, "She would have wanted you to wear it I'm certain."

"I'm happy enough with what I got," Ada said.

Evered spent the night aboard the schooner with Captain Truss and they started out in the wherry before light. The wind was with them and Evered was stunned by the time they made with two hands at the oars. They passed over the Wester Shoals before dawn was fully upon them and reached the mouth of the river before mid-morning. Truss scanned up-country with a pocket Dollond as they sculled past.

"What's the name of this river?" he asked.

"Can't say as I knows," Evered said. "We never laid eyes on it before last fall."

"If we have time on the return we might wander in a ways. See what we can see?"

It sounded almost like a request and Evered nodded yessir.

Within an hour they were rowing wide of the small beach where he and Ada had landed. Truss stood in the bow and glassed the cliffs, the low caves at the base. "That looks a likely spot," he said.

"We had a gander in there," Evered said. "The gravesite was further on."

Truss pocketed his telescope and they travelled on in silence, the two men at the oars in lockstep and apparently tireless. An hour later Evered said, "I feels like we must have passed it. I doubt we come this far."

Truss gave the order to come about and they landed at a stretch of low beach to make a fire for tea and to eat their lunch. The two servants sat a little ways apart, talking about England and what they would do when they set foot home in the Old Country. The Captain was uncharacteristically quiet and Evered could feel the man's eyes on him as he ate.

"I can take a turn at the oars," Evered suggested as they finished up and walked back to the wherry.

"No," Truss said. "I want your eyes on the coastline. Perhaps approaching from the opposite direction will make the burial site plain to you."

"Perhaps it might."

Truss looked at him directly. "You don't approve of this expedition."

But Evered only shrugged.

"Speak freely," Truss offered.

"You said that crowd was just about." He searched for the word.

"Extinct. Wiped out."

"What was it happened to them?"

"We happened to them."

Evered let that notion hang in the air.

"Don't we owe it to them to learn what we can of their ways before they disappear altogether?" Truss said. "To keep something of them alive?"

They'd reached the boat, the oarsmen up to their knees and holding the gunwales to steady her.

Evered said, "If it was me, I expect I'd want to be left alone out of it."

Truss stared at the youngster as if the sentiment surprised him. Evered stood aside to allow the Captain to step in and he took a seat at the transom.

"Perhaps that's all they ever wanted," Truss said. "To be left alone. But we will likely never know for certain now."

Evered knelt at the bow and watched the coast as it passed. They approached the cliff cave and its gravesite and he expected any moment to hear Truss order a landing to investigate. But when he finally spoke up Truss said, "We'll make a little detour up the river on our way along. Perhaps we'll find something to shoot and the day won't have been a total loss."

And he nodded yessir without looking back to the stern.

Ada woke that morning to a relapse of infirmity. Dressing and sitting up for the meal, walking down to the brook with Mrs. Brace, even that little had asked too much of her. She'd slept poorly, awake half the night with violent coughing spells and was too weak to leave the bed. Mid-morning Mrs. Brace offered a concoction of Labrador tea laced with a medicinal helping of brandy and Ada travelled the rest of the day through swampy dreams that she had trouble distinguishing from the waking world when she stirred.

At times she thought she had climbed from her bunk and called to Mrs. Brace for help and then came to herself still lying in the bed, all of her senses swollen and logy. She woke to the sound of the woman crying at some point and lifted her head to see Mrs. Brace sitting on the lap of a man, her arms about his neck, her face pushed into his shoulder to muffle the mewling sound of her weeping. All she could see of the man was the bald crown of his head. She drifted off again when she laid back, trying to puzzle who he might be and what grief was being consoled.

It was near dark when she sat up, fully awake for the first time in hours, shaky and parched. Mrs. Brace was sitting alone by the hearth and brought her water when she called. Ada had forgotten the man in the chair and Mrs. Brace made no mention of his presence. It was hours later that the image came back to her, too precise and unambiguous to be from a dream she decided, though Mrs. Brace offered no hint and showed no trace of that sad encounter. It made Ada think the heartbreak was too private a concern to raise and she never asked after it.

The river was forty to fifty feet wide at the mouth and fathoms deep in the middle. They rowed almost a mile inland where the first whitewater rattle made it impossible to go further by boat. "We'll have a wander," Truss said, "and see what we shall see." He and Evered were landed on the eastern shore and they walked up beyond the rapids where the river turned sharply west and deepened again. The trees grew almost to the water which forced them to walk single file. There were signs of otter on the banks and rainbow trout in the deepest pools. But no game crossed their path and Truss was about ready to turn back when he held his hand in the air, signalling for Evered to keep still.

The Captain was blocking his view ahead and it was a minute later before he saw them, two black bears in the river and riding the current downstream. Truss unslung his Hanoverian and dropped to one knee on the bank. "Bitch-bear and cub," he whispered. "The young one is a yearling at least to judge by its size."

He passed the rifle to the youngster. "Your game, Mr. Best. The mother first," he said softly. "You'll want to aim for the head, just behind the eye."

They were six feet above the water and the bears were directly below them when Evered fired and the animal went slack in the water. The cub was startled by the shot and bewildered by the dam's unresponsiveness as it pawed at her hind quarters. It glared up at the two men on the bank and seemed to come to some understanding of its mother's condition and those responsible for it in the same moment.

"You'll want to reload," Truss said evenly.

Evered took a ball from a compartment in the rifle's stock and wadded it home with the ramrod as the cub came out of the river thirty yards below them, roaring as if it had been wounded itself. The sight put Evered into a panic and he snapped the rod in the barrel.

"God's nails," he said.

Truss stepped in front of the youngster and raised the shotgun. "What have you loaded her with?"

"A bit of small shot. Enough to kill a bird is all."

"It will have to do."

Truss fired at the bear's face and sat the creature back on its haunches, the left eye riven and extinguished in its socket. It turned in circles, howling and pawing at its forehead and snout which were covered in blood. "And if thy right eye offend thee," Truss said as he poured powder into the barrel. He rammed a handful of shot without wadding as the bear shook itself and surged toward them. "Pluck it out," Truss said, "and cast it from thee." The second shot blinded the creature and it pawed at its ruined face again, turning wildly before it struck the ground with its front legs and blundered into the woods, bawling helplessly and smacking its head off every rock and every tree in its way.

Truss took the Hanoverian from Evered's hands and managed to free the ramrod from the barrel. He reloaded it as best he could with the broken instrument.

"I made a shaggery of that," Evered said.

"A lot of men would have turned tail and run," Truss said. "And you have meat enough to get you a ways through the winter. That is some consolation."

And Evered nodded yessir.

The bitch-bear had floated a hundred yards downstream before bringing up on the near shore and they walked down to it, past the noise of the cub bellowing as it knocked blindly through the woods. They had as much as they could manage with the mother and Truss decided against wasting a ball to dispatch the yearling, unsure if he would be able to reload a second time. The carcass had rolled in the water's current and was lying on its back. They each grabbed a limb and tried to haul it further from the river but they couldn't budge the massive weight of the animal.

Truss sent Evered to collect the men waiting with the boat and together they shifted the bear a little ways out of the water. The cub was still crying in the woods behind them, floundering through the trees as Truss measured its mother's body from nose to tail and the span of its limbs. "She's as big as the white bears I've shot in Labrador," he said. And they fell to gutting and quartering the animal on the riverbank.

Truss worked a blade up through the paunch and he tipped the offal in handfuls into the moving current. He picked out the kidney and liver and set them on a rock. "In Scotland," he said to Evered, "they have a tradition for a hunter who makes his first kill." And without warning he brought both his hands up to the youngster's face. Evered reared back but couldn't escape the reach of the Captain's arms, his head disappearing in the grip of those huge mitts as they smeared his cheeks and mouth, his white hair and forehead and closed eyes with the guts and blood of the bear. The two servants laughing and applauding the baptism as Evered spat the iron muck from his mouth. He shook his head like a wet dog, he wiped at his anointed eyes with a sleeve. The stink of the gore in his nostrils.

"You must wear that," Truss said, "until we get the meat back to the cove." And he smiled. "Be grateful it's too late in the season for flies."

It was all tainted a little by his breaking the ramrod in a green panic, by the transparency of his misdirection to steer the Captain clear of the Indian grave. But Evered was almost happy, standing knee-deep in the river with a rank skim of viscera drying on his face, hacking at the bear's shoulder joint with a hatchet. Happier, he thought, than any time since his father and mother were alive.

They spent the rest of the afternoon butchering the animal and transporting the meat to the boat. The quarters weighed over a hundred pounds apiece and they tied each to a line to float them one at a time through the rapids to the wherry. They tied up the creature's humbles in a square of canvas and it took both oarsmen to cart the weight of the heart and liver and kidney and lights downriver. Truss made a last trip to the remains of the carcass with a hatchet as they loaded the spoils into the boat and he came back with the bear's eye teeth for Ada's collection.

And they abandoned the blind cub to the indiscriminate work of nature.

The Blind Cub. Her Cross Fox.

It snowed all morning and all afternoon of the day *The Hydra* left them, a solemn windless fall that gave a funereal air to the departure. It fell on the landwash and on the tilt and the farm garden and on the stack of blackened wood where Evered had collected the remains of the stage. It fell on him and on Ada where they stood watching the ship's boat making for the skerries with Captain Truss and Mrs. Brace aboard. Both knowing they would never lay eyes on their chance benefactors again.

Truss had taken the bulk of the bear meat for the voyage to England but he left a quarter with the youngsters. When they'd arrived with the butchered carcass and Truss presented Ada with the prize teeth she'd asked if the bear was a dam and if there was a young one with her.

"A yearling or so, yes," Truss said. "How did you know?"

Evered was washing the crusted blood from his face and hair in a bucket of water at the hearth. "She's a bit of a witch that one," he said.

Ada pushed the Indian pendant on Truss before they left. As trade for the bear teeth she said. Though she meant it as compensation for his missing the burial site which she never doubted Evered steered clear of deliberately. Truss insisted in turn on paying for the pendant with two gallons of powder, a box of twenty balls and three bags of shot. Even the youngsters could see it was an extravagance, a grant Truss presented in hopes of keeping them from starving through the winter. Mrs. Brace left them a long woollen gansey that the youngsters traded back and forth at intervals.

It carried on snowing for most of the week that followed as if to lay a muffle over the quiet that descended on the cove in the vessel's absence. Ada and Evered so thrown by the rhythm of regular company that they couldn't quite recover the kilter of being left to themselves. Ada was still suffering the lingering effects of the illness that had all but killed her and Evered went alone into the hills to haul out the season's firewood. Ada set as much of the bear meat as could be fit into the brine that kept their pork and she salted the rest and hung it from the storehouse rafters. When Evered was done sawing and junking the firewood he spent most of his days in the backcountry with his father's flintlock.

He was happiest that winter on his own in the woods. There was the simple pleasure of hunting. And there were the onanistic indulgences that the privacy of the woods afforded him, these latter activities focused now on the figure of Mrs. Brace, on the memory of her breasts cradling his head, of the lewd nickers he heard in the dark each night she'd slept at the tilt.

It was a relief to have an object for his attention that didn't inspire a residual shame. But he couldn't avoid the sense he was being an unfaithful servant to the Captain and edited all signs of Truss from his imaginings. Placing the housekeeper naked before the Beadle's desk to hear her whispering helpless with that cadaverous hand upon her. Or lying back to take the Duke of Limbs between her legs, the cold slap of skin on skin as he'd heard it from the other side of the blanket. It was the one intimacy that everything between the siblings seemed a prelude to. But some hesitation had always stopped them short, a shared vertigo that stayed them at the edge. Though it was sometimes Evered and sometimes Ada alone who turned away from that sheer, sudden drop.

Even after it turned too cold and inclement to satisfy his prurient habit in the wild Evered was out the door at first light. He followed the brook upstream past the necklace of ponds, tailing rabbit slips along the way. He stopped an hour or two near the beaver house on Third Pond, hoping to catch a glimpse of the mythical creature, to get a clear shot at the thing.

Wherever he found a flat stone heavy enough for the job Evered set a deadfall trap, baiting the trigger with rancid strips of bear fat. But he had no luck. There were often fox tracks criss-crossing the snow around the sets and sometimes the ledge rock had fallen but the animal always managed to escape. Sometimes the bait was stolen, the rock still standing on the set post. And on occasion a fox left him a little gift in trade, a jay's wing or the head of a ptarmigan laid beside the trigger stick. It seemed a deliberate taunt. Evered was judicious with the gun, husbanding the powder and shot to make it last the winter. But he sometimes sat vigil in a blind near a deadfall, thinking he would have to shoot a fox to take one. Keeping still until the cold and his own impatience forced him to move on.

It was a torment and a respite to be away from his sister, to escape the confines of time spent with someone he would have died for and could hardly manage to speak to anymore. All the days of his life had been inclined to her orbit and he canted toward her still though she seemed as distant as the moon. Even when they were together in the tilt she sat somewhere out of reach. Where Ada was concerned he felt he was the blinder in their childhood game, reeving around sightless with his useless hands before his face.

After the mid-winter freeze-up the snow was firm enough he didn't need his Indian racquets and he was able to cut directly across the iced-over ponds. He expanded the range of his travel each time out, following the brook into a treeless stretch of bog where even from the low ground he spotted three beaver dams and the mounds of several houses. He stayed with the brook which broadened as he went and eventually it led him to a sprawling inland lake, the far shore miles across the surface. He skirted the beach westward until he struck a river that still ran free where it was deepest.

The sun was crossing mid-afternoon and he turned for home to avoid being caught out too long in darkness. But he considered he'd likely struck the head of Black Bear River as Truss had christened it that fall afternoon. And before he made it back to the tilt he was already planning to box the compass of that circle.

Evered laid out the scheme to Ada as he tucked into a stew of bear meat and root vegetables, ravenous and exhausted and surprisingly talkative. Describing the countryside beyond the beaver pond, the size of the lake in there, Sister, twice the breadth of the cove or more, and the riverhead he'd struck walking the northern end.

It was a relief to Ada to hear him talking, overtaken by a new enthusiasm and unselfconscious in her company for the first time since *The Hydra* left the shore. Since long before that, she thought. She felt a rush of affection for him as he shovelled food into his gob and waxed on about the minutiae of what he'd done and seen since the last time they spoke. As if he hadn't fully experienced his own life until his sister was apprised of its every detail.

"Perhaps I could go along with you," she said.

He glanced up from his bowl with the expression of someone who'd caught himself slipping off a cliff edge and was still falling in his mind's eye. "You're only just on your feet," he said.

"I won't hold you up," she said. "A rank cripple like yourself." She tried to smile across at him though her face felt wooden.

He shook his head again. "We'd be out in the woods one night the least," he said. "And we'd be coming back to a cold house. I'd sooner there was a fire and a mug of tea waiting when I gets in."

Ada nodded and watched him eat his food. He carried on discussing his plans but there was a muted air to his talk suddenly. And she could hardly hear him over the noise in her head. It seemed a frightening prospect, she thought, to spend any length of time in her company.

"When do you expect you'll be going?"

"Day after tomorrow if the weather holds decent." And as an afterthought he said, "You'll be all right here while I'm gone will you?"

"You needn't worry about me," she said.

His absences through the winter she'd taken in stride. She'd never spent as long a time alone and indolent but wasn't well enough to go with him after *The Hydra* departed. And she was nursing her own small sense of loss that satisfied her to brood in private awhile. She puttered around the tilt aimlessly, repacking the log seams with moss harvested before the illness struck them, scrubbing and oiling the cast-iron pots. She filed a notch at the root of the bear teeth that she circled with fishing twine, ran leather strings through the knotted loop to make necklaces after the fashion she recalled from the Indian burial.

She spent time leafing through the curled and bleary pages of the cloth-covered book from the icebound ship. She raked the floor and mimicked some of the handwriting's inscrutable patterns in the sand, that curious landscape of headlands and valleys and waves and trees and stones.

She went through the other contents of her shelf, culling the shells and rocks and feathers that had lost their lustre, objects that had once possessed a hint of magic or beauty or mystery and now seemed merely ordinary. It was confounding to see magic and beauty and mystery leach out of a thing, to think it could be used up like a store of winter supplies.

She watched Evered finish the last of his meal, wondering if the same might be true of a person, of how two people felt about each other.

Evered went to bed almost as soon as he was done eating but Ada sat up for a time, wanting to be sure he was asleep before she crawled in beside him.

Once the fire burned off she banked a circle of coals under ash and turned an iron pot over top to keep the embers alive through the night. It was already cold in the tilt, currents of frost sieving through the log seams, through the closed window shutter and the ship door's frame. She stripped down to her shift in the black, the chill raising goosebumps the length of her arms. Evered was snoring softly as she lifted the covers and eased in beside him. She curled toward his back, close enough she could feel the radiating heat without touching him.

She missed her brother, missed the easy physical affection that had been the only constant source of comfort in her life. But all through the fall she'd felt Evered waiting, expecting Ada would be the one to make amends, to bridge what remained of the gap between them. His waiting was like a hand at her back and she bristled against the nudge. Against the part of herself that nudged in the same fashion, in the same direction. His refusal to take her into the backcountry seemed part of a long penance imposed as punishment for that.

He was strangely unaware of his own nature. He liked to think himself constant and selfless but Ada knew him a moody creature, someone who could disappear from her life for days and weeks at a stretch. He was put out every time her visitor arrived and she took to the opposite bed for fear of the blood bespoiling him. He never said a word directly, retaliating for the unexplained absence with a sulk, a clipped note to all their interactions. It was almost sweet those first months to see he could be hurt so easily. She tried to make it up to him when she came back to the shared bed, drawing him into her heat, giving herself over to the small pleasure that seemed innocent and equal to each in the moment. But using it so brazenly added another sour note to the aftertaste of regret.

If not for the arrival of her visitor as she lay naked in the brook at the end of the season, angling toward Evered, they might have found the old way back to each other. But that urge had ebbed away by the time her bleeding was done. And even after the weather forced them into the same bed that winter she refused the easy device.

In some obscure way Mrs. Brace lay at the heart of her refusal. That fever image of the housekeeper in the lap of an unfamiliar man picking at her, details she'd been too listless to take in at the time asserting themselves. Mrs. Brace straddling the chair, her bare legs braced against the floor. The stranger's hands high up under the skirt of her dress. The subtle steady rocking motion. Evered and the Captain had taken the wherry in search of the Indian grave and Mrs. Brace's visitor had rowed Evered's boat in from *The Hydra*, she saw now, to take advantage of their absence. Heartbreak there might have been between them. But Mrs. Brace was not weeping.

The sound was altogether different from anything Ada heard behind the blanket. And recognizing that difference amplified something she suspected about the Captain and his housekeeper. There was a suffocating nakedness to their transactions that attracted and repelled her by turns. Something in it reminded her of the hitch in Evered's breathing during the solitary ministrations she pretended to sleep through. Of her brother ferreting through her small clothes to find the place she was warmest and wet, her hips rising to his hand as he figured the works of her. Fiercely intimate and somehow impersonal still, as if it was a stranger opening her up. As if she was a stranger to herself in the moment.

Ada was up and out of bed with a fire burning before Evered stirred the next morning.

After his breakfast he set about preparing for the river trip. He tied up a sealskin blanket as a bedroll and picked through the salt fish for a half-dozen pieces that hadn't gone green with rot, packing them with strips of dried bear meat and hardtack and a few potatoes. He added a handful of dried moss to his tinderbox. Ada sat with him at the hearth as he carved set and trigger sticks for deadfalls, trying to refine the points and notches to match the guile of the creature he was hunting.

He'd told Ada about the gifts left behind by the scavengers who made off with his bait and she smiled at him now. "They seems too clever by half for the likes of you, Brother," she said.

"You thinks you might fare better is it?"

She shrugged. "What did the Captain use for bait?"

"Cheese," Evered said. "But you got every bit of what he give us eat up."

"It idn't that they don't like the bear fat," Ada said. "They likes it well enough to steal off with it. What stopped them making off with the cheese?"

"He gobbed it on there with honey. So's they had to work at it I spose."

"You wants to do the same you asks me."

"We got no honey, Sister."

"We got molasses."

Evered nodded at her. Feeling thick not to have thought of it himself. "Could be it might work," he said.

Ada watched him whittle at the trap sticks a few minutes longer and then hauled on her winter outfit and went to the door.

"Where you off to?"

"Thought I might say hello to Martha. Maybe cleave up some wood."

"I'll look after the wood," Evered said, in a way that might have been a veiled thank-you.

"You carry on with what you're doing," Ada said. "I'll look after mine."

And that was the last bit of real conversation they had before he left the following morning. They ate their supper in silence but for talk about what the weather might bring in the next few days and what Evered's hopes for his traps were.

"You'll be all right here?" he'd asked her again.

She was poisoned with him and was having trouble holding still in her chair. "I can look out to me own self, Brother."

He nodded and let it drop. He said, "I wish we had a splash of rum in the house."

"You and me the same," she said.

Ada went to bed ahead of him that night and turned her back when he crawled in beside her. A sick little roil in her belly as he tucked into her. The hatch lifting on the pit of her stomach where the echo of Mrs. Brace and the Captain writhed and twisted in the black.

She placed her hand on Evered's hip behind her and then down between them, finding her way to bare skin. He put an arm around her waist and moved to reach under her shift but she grabbed it with her free hand. She did not want to be touched. Or to turn toward him or to speak. She moved against the rigid bit of gristle in her hand, working toward that hitch in his breath, that spastic release.

Afterward they both lay completely still. Ada waited until she thought Evered was asleep before she extracted her hand, the slurry across her fingers and the back of her wrist already crusting dry. And she didn't move again through the night.

It was clear but blowing fresh and cold when Evered started out, almost too cold for walking before he struck the brook and turned into the cover of the trees. An hour's tramp to First Pond and another half-hour beyond it to the first deadfall on a flat outcrop of stone above the brook where the snow didn't drift in.

There were fresh tracks around the set and the ledge rock was down but there was nothing in the trap and he went about resetting it with the newly notched sticks. He took off his mitts to lather molasses from a little jar onto the bait and onto the trigger stick before angling the rock over the set post. The cold was so fierce that his numbed fingers fumbled about the delicate business and the thirty-pound ledge came down twice, almost catching a forearm both times.

Evered shoved his hands up to the wrist into snow to bring the blood back into them. Thinking what a crushed arm would mean out here. He took a breath to steady himself and leaned the weight of the ledge rock onto the post, levering the trigger stick into its notch. Backed away like someone trying to exit a room without disturbing a sleeping dog.

He hauled his mitts over his hands with his teeth and carried on upstream. There was a buck hare in a slip above Second Pond, the body stretched full out and frozen solid. He reset the snare and tied the rabbit by the feet, the carcass knocking like a junk of wood against his back as he walked on.

There were two more deadfalls below Third Pond and both had been looted of their bait without tripping the trigger stick. The feathered leg of a ptarmigan placed under the ledge rock at the last. He reset them both with the molasses and bear fat and carried on to Third Pond where he built a fire in a droke of trees with a view of the beaver house. He opened his jacket to the heat and gnawed at a cake of hardtack as he watched the pond. Thinking all the while about Ada.

He'd long ago given up the notion his sister could be told what to do or when or how simply because he was the older sibling, because he was the man of the house. She was the more clever of the two and Evered could admit that to himself if not to her. But he couldn't escape the sense he'd relinquished all say in their affairs. Ada could offer or withhold at her whim was how it seemed and he took what came his way as it came. It made him feel like a green youngster being bidden about by a mother's silent say-so. And he overstepped in other ways to counter the imbalance or he swung at shadows and fell on his face for his efforts.

He was still galled by his refusing her offer to come with him. It was a thoughtless reflex, the same as pulling his arm clear of the ledge rock as it fell. Getting out from under as the sudden and unexpected clapped down. He regretted the words the moment they were uttered but didn't know how to recant without looking foolish. The rest of his time at the tilt he was looking for a way to offer an invitation that wouldn't seem servile or false. Trying to work up the nerve as he sat at the hearth with the trap sticks to say he'd thought it through and Ada might come along if she still wanted the jaunt. And then they fell into the business about the honey and molasses and he felt too much the idiot already to let Ada think he didn't know his own mind.

She'd gone to bed ahead of him and turned her back when he crawled in beside her. Poisoned, he could tell. Then the shock of her hand snaking into his small clothes. And even that managed to feel like an act of hostility, holding him at bay as she went about the business. A hum of choler rising from the stillness she settled into after he came and Evered too stunned and alarmed and uncertain to move himself.

He spat into the fire, itching to move suddenly, to busy his head with something. Idleness was the root of all trouble, he could vouch for the truth of that right enough.

He walked the brook's frozen road into the boggy country above Third Pond.

At the lake he cut for the head of Black Bear River and he had three full hours of daylight when he started north toward the coastline. The river ran through a valley of forested hillsides and there was almost no wind. The trees were spruce and pine and fir and they were the tallest living things Evered had ever laid eyes on, fathoms higher than the scrub trees near the coast that were stunted by the constant wind and the thin soil and the bleak weather. He walked most of the way on the river which was iced over except where it ran fastest, the rattles forcing him to scramble through the bush.

There were signs of otter and marten and rabbit and fox along the bank and he scouted for likely spots to set deadfalls and snares as he went. Just as he was beginning to lose the light he flushed a brace of ptarmigan and felled them both on the wing with a single spray of shot. He tied them by the feet to the strap of the bag he carried, famished suddenly.

He could hear the rumble of a falls ahead and was of two minds about stopping above it or making the climb down to look for a campsite below. The water ran free for a hundred yards to the falls and the shoreline rose steep from the bank. There was nowhere that looked flat enough to lie down for the night and he decided he would have to make the climb though the light was poor and failing fast in the valley's shadow. The open water forced him up into the trees and he was on top of the falls before he got a glimpse of the height of it, a rocky drop of almost fifty feet. He looked downriver to see how the country below shaped up for a night's shelter. And at the farthest bend where the ice caught over the moving water again he saw a fire burning on the shore.

For a moment he was shot through with terror, thinking he might have stumbled on an Indian camp or some other wild unknown. But in the next moment he knew it was Ada down there, waiting for him.

Ada didn't move when Evered crawled from bed that morning. He didn't light the lamp or kindle a fire, picking around in the dark to pull his materials together. He'd stopped at the open door and turned back to the room where Ada pretended to sleep.

"Sister," he said.

She ignored him until he called a second time. She sat up to look at her brother in the new light through the door, the sun just rising.

"I'll be back tomorrow. Next day the latest," he said.

"All right."

He nodded and waited a moment longer as if he hoped she might say something more before he went on his way. She could hear the sound of his footsteps over frozen snow as he passed by the side of the tilt and headed down toward the brook. The room was bitterly cold and she got up to light a fire, to make herself breakfast. But she couldn't eat when she sat to the food, her insides bound up by a chalky disgust. With Evered or with herself she couldn't say.

She'd set about packing tinder and a flint then, a blanket, fish hooks and a bit of line. Pulled together what she could find of her kit from the walk over the ice to the ship. She didn't examine her motivation in any detail. For fear she would talk herself into being reasonable.

She headed around the western arm of the cove and along the coast toward Black Bear River. Wind gusting out of the north and blowing almost face-on, strong enough at times she had to angle her head away to breathe. She knew it would take most of the morning to reach the river and the biting cold and the contrary wind convinced her to turn back half a dozen times. And in the end she kept walking.

By the time she turned upriver from the coast the wind had dropped off and after the first bend she was well into the trees where the air was almost still. But she was too cold to stop and carried on past the first rattle before considering a place to make a fire. She crouched into the woods behind a massive granite boulder where the ground was mostly free of snow. She set her pack down and wandered further in after firewood.

She stumbled on the bear cub's skeleton about thirty yards from the river, frozen into the snow. Most of the flesh gone from the bone that was visible though there were ragged tufts of fur stuck to the spine, to the crown of the skull. The bared teeth of the muzzle angled up from the ground as if the cub was trying to keep its nose above the snow. Ada pried it loose, using the hatchet to break the ice that held it and then chopping through the dried ligaments running up from the spine. And she carried the skull back to the boulder with her armful of dead branches.

There wasn't enough light in the gloom of the trees to see the object clearly. She could feel a stubble of tiny holes across the forehead and she held it close to the fire. The bone around the brow thickly pocked and the bone at the back of the sockets as well. A scatter of lead shot embedded in the white.

She packed the relic away in her bag with the rest of her materials and she walked on through the afternoon, stopping in the lee of a rock face below a waterfall at the first hint of darkness. She spent an hour gathering wood and while she was striking sparks into the tinder to start a fire she heard the clap of a rifle shot above the falls. She walked up to the open water below the cataract and she caught three trout in the deep pool there, covering them in snow back at the campsite and settling in to wait. She took out the bear skull and scraped away the last of the fur and dried fascia with a knife and she used the tip to pick the shot from the bone. She held it up in one hand to stare into the empty eyes and a shiver passed through her.

It was a steep tricky climb down the waterfall. Evered tied up his rifle and pack, the telescope and shot bags and racquets and the rabbit carcass, and he lowered them to a ledge below with the hauling rope, then followed after. And he repeated the manoeuver three times more before he reached the foot of the falls.

Ada was sitting with her back to a low rock face looking out over the fire toward the frozen river when he came up to her. It was nearly dark and he called out as he approached so as not to give her a fright though he knew she was expecting him. She turned her head toward the sound of his voice and waited until he came into the fire's halo.

"I almost give up on finding you tonight," she said. "Till I heard the gun go off."

He held up the ptarmigan. "Bit of fresh craft for supper," he said.

He took off the rifle and shot bags and laid the frozen rabbit carcass out of the fire's heat and sat beside her. They plucked the birds and cleaned them and Evered cut alder sticks to roast them over the fire, grease spitting as it fell into the coals. They roasted the potatoes in the same way and ate the meal with their bare hands, picking the last bits of meat from the rames with their fingers.

When they were just about done Ada said, "You idn't mad with me, Brother?"

Evered considered the question a long time before he answered, unsure exactly what it encompassed. "I left it too long," he said, "finding a place to set. Dark come on quicker than I expected." He gestured at the night's worth of wood she'd collected and stacked under the rock face. "I'd've had a cold time of it on me own out here."

It was a misstatement of what he felt, the sense of relief and reprieve that welled up when he realized who was on the river ahead of him. But it was all he could manage. It occurred to him then to ask if Ada was angry in turn but he was afraid of what her answer might be.

"Run into any trouble on the way up?" he asked instead.

"Fair going most of it," she said. "I come upon this above the first rattle."

She took the skull from her bag and handed it across to Evered and he turned it in the firelight, glancing across at his sister. He rubbed his fingers across the pocked bone.

"You plans on carting this all the way back to the cove?"

"Thought I might."

He shook his head. "You're a queer creature, Ada Best."

"Me and you both," she said.

They sat up a while longer. The deep dark strangeness of the country, the black amphitheatre of hills topped by a glittering strip of stars, made them feel new to the world. They slept side by side, the ground beneath them alive with the rumble of the falls. They woke to the cold whenever the fire burned low and one or the other would add wood to the coals and breathe it to life and they fell immediately back to sleep.

In the morning they boiled water for tea and roasted the trout fillets for their breakfast. Evered said, "You carrying on upriver?"

"That's what I had in me mind."

"That's the worst of the walk right ahead," he said. "You gets above the falls there and the rest of the way is pretty much clear."

Ada looked toward the noise of the cataract. "I could come back down with you," she said. "If you wants."

He took a moment to think through the offer. Sensing it was a test of some sort. "Best you goes on," he said finally. "You could look in on the deadfalls on your way down the brook. See if that molasses is doing any work."

The sun was up but the valley still sat in a dusky twilight. Evered described where she should look for the deadfall traps and about where she might find his snares. He handed off the telescope in its leather case to her and he stayed at the fire to watch her climb the falls. Picking her slow way up with all her gear on her back. That bear skull in her pack. She paused on the face two or three times, considering a way ahead. And Evered had to force himself to sit still at the fire.

Once she'd topped the falls she turned back to the campsite and waved her tricorn hat and he raised an arm to see her off. He stood to pack his materials and when he glanced back upriver she was gone.

It snowed off and on through the morning but not enough to slow the travel. He stopped twice in likely spots and set deadfalls in both locations. Just past noon he built a fire over the remains of Ada's fire in the lee of the boulder above the first rattle on the river. And he carried on then to the coast and along the shore to the cove. Trying to guess how far along Ada might be on her twinned journey.

It was still daylight when he made it home and he set a fire going in the hearth to take the chill out of the room, then skinned and cleaned the rabbit. He baked the haunches in a covered pot with potatoes and onion and carrot and turnip. He was planning to wait for Ada before eating but the evening was gone to dark with no sign and he ate his meal alone. Listening for some sound of her on the snow outside. She had the harder haul of travel, he knew, and might have kipped down somewhere as the night closed in. It might have snowed heavier inland and forced her to hole up around the lake. She had never seen a deadfall trap and could have crushed a hand or foot trying to reset a downed rock ledge.

He should have asked her to travel back with him when she offered. Or gone up the river with her himself. But he knew that was not what she wanted.

He should at least have shown her the use of the flintlock and sent it on with her.

He was hours in bed without so much as shutting his eyes when she stamped through the door, shedding snow from her boots and trousers. He could feel the frost steaming off her clothes when he came up beside her at the hearth to light the slutlamp.

"I waited awhile before I eat me supper," he said.

She'd glassed what she guessed were deer out on the lake, she told him, and tracked after them a couple of hours which set her behind.

"And what did you plan to do if you come abreast of them?"

"I just wanted to get close," she said.

Neither of them had laid eyes on the creatures except in Truss's stories of hunting in Labrador and Ada described the implausible spread of antlers on their heads that looked as if they were carting a load of deadfall branches to a fire.

"I thought about putting up somewhere after dark," she said. "But the sky was clear by then and I had no trouble following the brook with the moon out. So I come on."

Evered uncovered the coals and stirred up a fire as she stripped away the layers of her kit. He was absently singing *My Thing Is My Own* under his breath, unaware he was singing until Ada took up the chorus with him. He set the kettle over the new heat to boil and warmed the rest of the rabbit stew.

He could see the body of a fox laid among the shadows of her materials and he brought it out into the lamplight. A cross fox, its coat a mix of red and silver but for the muzzle and breast and the legs which were black, like some hand had dipped the animal so far in ink and lifted it out before the eyes went under. The face crushed askew by the weight of the ledge rock hammering down.

"That was at the last set," Ada said. "Almost walked past it in the dark."

He stroked the animal's plush winter coat. "Spose you was right about the molasses," he said.

"I had a go at resetting the thing but couldn't figure it."

"I'll show you the works of it," he told her. "Next time out."

It was too late to pelt the animal and he went up to the store in the moonlight to hang the fox from the rafters. When he came back Ada was sound on the bed in all her clothes and she didn't stir when he worked her boots free of her feet and covered her with the blankets. He banked the coals and douted the lamp and then he lay beside her and fell asleep himself.

———

They travelled together the rest of the winter before the ice on the brook gave way and the snow began to rot. They expanded the sets on the trapline to eleven and they went out twice a week to check them. They built a halfway lean-to below the falls on Black Bear River where they spent their nights on those rounds. They snared rabbit and shot ptarmigan and marten and three otters and, on their last trip of the season, a forty-five-pound beaver they stumbled on in the woods a hundred yards from the water. They trapped four more fox, three red and a silver, and they spent much of their time at the tilt scraping and curing the pelts.

They seemed more or less content with their lives. They spent all their time in each other's company and slept innocent in the same bed. Nothing at all was resolved between them but they both felt they'd reached a truce in some undeclared conflict. That they had returned to neutral corners and settled into an equilibrium that might last them.

They turned their attention to the fish and the farm garden when the mackerel started running and fell into the relentless round of work they'd known their whole lives. When *The Hope* arrived in the middle of May Evered brought out the cured pelts of the fox and otter and marten and the lone beaver and the Beadle paid for them with powder and shot, with extra flour and twine and calico and two demijohns of rum and a promise to set them up with iron traps come the fall.

And as they lay one evening in the mulish sleep of over-work, before the sun had even set, they were startled awake by a stark *rap rap rap* that went on a long while before they managed to sort out what was happening and how they were meant to respond.

Someone was knocking at their door.

Bungs Forever! Josephus Rex. Noah's Ark.

Evered presented himself in his undershirt and drawers and the man standing outside smiled at the youngster's state of undress.

"We've woken you," he said. He apologized and introduced himself, John Warren, he said, of HMS *Medusa*. He glanced past Evered and saw the girl standing slack-jawed in her shift and he turned away, his face blushing crimson so quickly it seemed to glow.

"We are unexpected company," he said and he apologized again for the interruption without ever taking his eyes off the hills behind the tilt. The man had a queer rolling accent that made it difficult to follow his meaning. He suggested he give them a few minutes to make themselves presentable and they could return to their introductions then.

"All right," Evered said and he watched Warren walk up the path to the store where he stood with his hands at his back. Evered closed the door and went to the window across the room, unlatching the shutter to open it a crack. There was a thirty-foot bully boat tied up at the newly raised stagehead, the crew of oarsmen loitering on the landwash.

"What do he want, Brother?" Ada whispered.

"He wants us to get our clothes on."

"*After* that," Ada said. "What is it he wants of us?"

"We won't ever know we don't get dressed," he said. He threw her trousers to her and pulled on his own pants and shirt, his boots. He took the flintlock from its corner and poured in a charge of powder. He debated a moment whether to load it with shot or ball and came to the conclusion they would be equally useless if things went badly. But shot offered a wider swath of damage and confusion and he rammed in as large a load as he thought the barrel could manage.

"What do you want with the rifle?" Ada asked.

"There's a crew of them down below, Sister."

She felt something the size of a fist clench at the crown of her head, a numbing heat there that made her scalp contract. "How many?"

"A dozen or more," he said. "We could make a run for the brook, head into the country."

Ada went still under the weight of that number. There would be no outrunning twelve or more. She conjured the man at the door, the calm lilting tone of his voice, the crimson shade of his face as he apologized for the intrusion. "We'll be all right," she said with a conviction born of knowing there was no contemplating the alternative. She finished pulling on her clothes and went to the hearth to start a fire. There was a knock at the door again and Evered looked to Ada.

"All right," she said.

And he set the gun back in its corner before he opened the door.

The *Medusa* had been laid up in St. John's harbour since the previous June. She was a twenty-gun vessel, an old East India-man fit more for use as a prison hulk now than for Navy service, Warren said. Her mainmast had split in an Atlantic storm and they'd limped into port looking to replace it. They'd sent crews four miles into the woods around the town but found no mate-rials fit to the purpose and the trees for twenty miles north and south had been cut back to bare scrub. Warren was engaged on shore for the summer months brewing spruce beer for the Navy ships in the harbour but in September he was sent north with the bully boat to find a suitable column of pine. They'd sailed as far as Fogo Island in the fall without sighting anything passable and they put up there over the winter, starting north-wards again after the pack ice ground through. For two months since they'd been sculling into every bay and tickle and likely-looking river mouth without luck, coming as far as Mockbeggar and on the verge of abandoning the quest altogether before they were told about a river valley beyond Orphan Cove that might offer what they were searching for.

"Is this it then?" Warren asked. "Is this Orphan Cove?"

The youngsters looked at each other.

"Was never no name to it," Evered said. "But there's a river a ways to the west. Black Bear River. Biggest kind of trees in there."

Warren bowed his head slightly as a thank-you for the infor-mation. "You two now," he said. He blushed again in anticipation of a delicate inquiry. "You don't have children?"

"Children?" Evered said.

"You're not?" Warren said uncertainly and his face glowed darker again. "Are you two wedded?"

Ada covered her face with her hands, mortified by the suggestion.

"She's me sister," Evered told him.

"Well bless me for a fool," Warren said. "Yes, I see it now. Your hair," he said to Evered, "made me think you the older by a stretch. And I'm under the influence of my time in St. John's. Nothing," he said, "surprised me more than the early marriage of girls in that town. I encountered twelve-year-olds who were already mothers to children of their own. Are your parents not with you?"

"They both passed," Evered said. "Years since."

"Ah," Warren said and he nodded over the name of the cove as it had been given him in Mockbeggar.

They could see something in his bearing shift slightly, a barely discernible acknowledgement. It reminded Evered of the first time he rowed out to *The Hope*, that moment when the crewmen all seemed to doff their caps in their minds.

"I'm an orphan myself," Warren said and he smiled at them. "My mother died giving birth to my youngest brother. And my father died after I went to sea, when I was eleven. I have no family at all to speak of anymore," he said. "Two brothers were taken as infants. And a brother in the Navy succumbed to his wounds in the West Indies. And the last went off to America before the war and I've not heard a word of him since."

They had no idea what war he was referring to. "How long ago was that?" Ada asked.

"What, the war?" He smiled at her in a way that made her want to kiss his cheeks. He had a gold ring in one ear and a blue kerchief about his neck. "Before you were born, I'm certain. I don't know if Brother Lewis is alive or dead. But that's as good as dead to me, I suppose."

They were all quiet a moment then.

"Did you say," Evered said, "you brewed spruce beer?"

"That is one of the tasks set for me, yes."

Evered had brewed a batch in the fall the first two years he and Ada were alone but he'd fouled the concoction somehow. Both times it made him feel bloated and nauseous and he'd poured the bulk of it away. He abandoned the undertaking then though there was still a bag of hops in the store. "I'd give my right hand to know how to go about the job," he said.

Warren laughed. "Well now. There's no cause to go to extremes. First thing tomorrow we will head for Black Bear River. And if we find what we need, we'll be back this way within the week. A long haul to St. John's ahead of us and the crowd below wouldn't say no to a few days' rest before we start."

The crewmen slept that night above the landwash, huddled in a shelter manged together with a tarpaulin to keep them out of the wind. Ada offered John Warren the bunk across the room but he declined for the delicacy of sharing a room with the girl. Evered crawled into the bunk they'd been roused from an hour before and turned to the wall, sound asleep before Ada had her boots and trousers off.

It wasn't until after the caplin rolled and sometimes on to July that warmer weather forced them into separate bunks. But something in Warren's blush to have thought she and Evered were wed made Ada shy about lying beside her brother. She settled opposite him and she was awake much of the night. Trying to guess how old their mother was when she took up with their father. Orphans, Warren had called Ada and her brother. It was a peculiar feeling to learn there was a word for it. That they were not the only people in the world to suffer the condition.

She imagined Evered lost to her forever in some far-flung corner of the earth, not knowing if he was quick or dead, and that seemed worse somehow than the thought of her parents adrift in the waters off the cove, of Martha lying in her grave of peat on the Downs. She thought for a long time about the fist-sized clutch of terror that had come over her after Evered announced the strangers on the landwash. That sense of dread absolute and amorphous though there was nothing vague about what lay at its root.

She'd only been asleep an hour or two when the chorus of men's voices woke them. It was still dark and Warren knocked before they'd managed to get a fire burning. Evered lit the lamp as Ada greeted him at the door.

"You'll have breakfast," she said.

"Already had our victuals below, Miss Ada."

"You'll have tea then," she insisted. She took him by the forearms and sat him in a chair over his protests and she turned back to the fire, stacking kindling for a quick heat.

They heard voices from the landwash calling "Hallo, Bungs! Bungs ho!"

"They're anxious to set out," Warren said.

"What is it they're shouting? Bungs?"

"That's me," he said. "I'm Bungs. Every vessel's cooper is called the same."

"We'll walk down," Ada said, "to see you off."

Warren tried to talk them out of the courtesy but they insisted. Ada put on her waistcoat which she had almost grown into and the drooping tricorn and they set off. It was a cool morning with a fair wind off the water and she thought she could smell the men below. The rising sun threw a little light into the cove as they walked out on the stagehead with Warren, the sailors already aboard the bully boat and waiting.

"Ho, Bungs!" one of the sailors shouted at the sight of him and there was a general round of catcalling.

"Easy, ye nest of vipers," Warren called. "Hush up." He extended a hand to Ada and Evered. "Our hosts were kind enough to come see us off."

The sailors sat in neat rows at the oars, a sour garden funk rising from the boat. Brother and sister struck dumb in the presence of that thewy squalid audience and they could only nod their hellos.

"That's a fine pair of madge culls you set on, Bungs," one of the men said and laughter exploded up at them like a flock of birds flushed from cover.

"Is that why you want a stop here on return, Bungs?" another shouted. "A voyage up the windward passage?" And the laughter ticked a notch higher.

Ada took half a step behind Evered in the face of the strapping racket and he put a hand to her hip to tuck her further in. The exact meaning of the words were beyond them though there was no mistaking the tenor, the implication. Warren stepped in front of them both, nodding and smiling, a rabid blush turning his earlobes purple.

"A sauce box at every oar is what I've got here," he said. He had the beleaguered air of a parent embarrassed in public by his offspring. He climbed down to the stern and they cast off. "We will see you before long, God willing," Warren said to them.

The sailors rowed out beyond the skerries at what seemed a lightning speed and they set the lugsails to take the wind westward when they were in open water. Ada keeping halfways behind her brother until the boat was out of sight.

The caplin were beginning to shoal offshore and were only days away from rolling on the western arm and there was work enough to occupy them as they waited for the sailors' return. But they spent hours the next two mornings hooking crabs. The crustaceans had overrun the waters along the shore that spring and they picked half a hundred from the shallows, filling a puncheon tub halfway with salt water to keep them until the bully boat came back to the cove.

Ada was walking down from the farm garden the afternoon of the third day when she saw them sculling up the coast. Evered was on the water handlining beyond the shoal grounds and she watched the sailors pull up beside him briefly before carrying on toward the skerries. There was a massive tree tied to the lugsail masts that extended ten feet beyond the bow and ten feet beyond the stern.

Evered hauled in his line and set for the cove after them though he trailed further and further behind. And Ada was suddenly shy of greeting them on her own. She went to the tilt instead, starting a fire and setting the kettle, going about the makings of enough fresh bread to feed the crew. She heard the sailors as they came ashore on the landwash and a few minutes later there was a knock at the door.

"Miss Ada," Warren said with a little bow of his head.

She ushered him in and set him in a chair with a cup of tea as she carried on kneading the dough.

"They thought you were a lad," Warren said to her, "when you came down to see us off. In your jacket and trousers. A pretty lad mind," he said and he smiled at her. "They all wanted to know how old the pretty lad was."

Ada felt herself blushing and she slapped viciously at the loaves to break any air bubbles still in the dough before she left it to rise. A little uproar reached them from the landwash as Evered came ashore and was greeted with some raillery that they couldn't make out.

"They're all fine sailors," Warren said. "Good-hearted. But the roughest kind of men. When I first went to sea I was placed in charge of the ship's fowl and I was rendered most uncomfortable from the swearing and loose talk of the men in the tender. Father raised us to use the strictest conversation, prayers night and morning. It was a relief when I was appointed cooper and shifted to mess with the steward." He leaned forward on his thighs. "I said my prayers and read my Bible in private in those early days. But truth makes me confess I became more and more remiss through the years. And before long I was a sailor like the rest. Though my mind is uneasy to have fallen so and I make many weak attempts to amend even now."

His face took on its high colour again. It was like a lamp, Ada thought, lit and douted at regular intervals.

"Miss Ada, I would ask you," he said. "As a favour to me. I would ask you not to go among the crew without myself or your brother for company."

Evered came through the door as if on cue, smiling stupidly, buoyed up by whatever foolishness had been visited upon him below. Warren stood to shake the youngster's hand and they fell into an affable back-and-forth that seemed to Ada peculiar to the company of men. She'd never seen Evered engaged in the easy banter but he seemed born to it.

She sat quiet while they carried on in their way, mulling Warren's request. Thinking she was right to have been afraid of the men on the landwash though it was a mystery to her how she knew. How specific and certain the knowing was. She considered maybe it was something a woman was born to.

Evered was telling Warren about the puncheon full of crab that was to be cooked for their supper and the cooper raised his hands.

"The men will tuck in and happily," he said. "But you will forgive me if I sup on bread alone."

He could see the look of raw disappointment on the youngsters' faces. "I apologize for being a difficult guest," he said. "But when first I sailed to the West Indies I took the country fever while we lay at St. Kitts. I was taken to hospital where I was like to have died for most of a week. And for days afterward I was only well enough to crawl about the hospital. I'd see men from my ship brought in sick one day and buried the next in graves only deep enough to hold the body, an inch or two of earth to cover them is all. And the graveyard was overrun by land crabs, about the size of your hand they are, I'd watch them burrow into the ground where those men lay. And they ate up every bit of flesh below."

Ada and Evered stared at him, incredulous.

"It was the same in every graveyard down there. And you know the black fellows eat those crabs. I used to ask how they could stand to make a meal of such loathsome creatures. And to a man they would say, 'Why, they eat me!'" Warren laughed. "I haven't been able to stomach a morsel of crab since."

"You seen half the world in your time it sounds like," Ada said.

"Half and then some," he said. And he stayed the rest of the afternoon in the tilt, describing his experiences at sea and the countries and creatures and people he'd encountered, one story following on another like knots in a rope he was hauling hand over hand from a bottomless well. The Tartar girls in Hong Kong who washed the sailors' clothes in exchange for whatever rice they left at mess. The torpid heat in the hills of Peru where everyone moved as if they wished someone to carry them. Voyages so rife with disease and bad luck that every morning they threw overboard a dead sailor or a dead sheep.

They had never met anyone other than Mary Oram as relentlessly talkative but his tales were so strange and diverting they only whet the youngsters' appetite and they pressed him for more. Evered poured them each a glass of rum as Warren drew maps in the sand at their feet, tracing the voyages of the various ships he'd sailed on, the naval vessels and traders and South Sea whalers. Ada placed the risen loaves into covered iron pots and set them over the coals as he described the action on the *Surprise* during the American war, serving powder to the guns with shot and splinters flying past. "Half our crew were Irishmen," he said. "They fought like the very devils and they were great favourites with our captain on that account. We were engaged with the *Jason* out of Boston and I heard them calling from one of their guns, 'Halloo, Bungs, where are you?' And when I looked I saw the two horns of my anvil across the mouth of it. I'd hidden it when the action started, you see, hoping to keep it from them. The next moment it was fired through the *Jason*'s side. And when the Irishmen saw what a dreadful hole it made they all sang out, 'Bungs forever!'"

Evered refilled his own and Warren's glass but Ada demurred for fear of saying or doing something foolish before company.

Warren described the Indians in Nootka Sound who blacked their faces and powdered their hair with the down of birds. The Frenchmen in Canada who spoke the parley-voo and ate their fill of serpents that abound in the woods,

"Serpents?" Ada said.

Each new detail picked at the scab of the youngsters' ignorance and Warren answered their endless questions with a nurse's patience for the infirm. He sang a song he'd learned while drinking three-bit mauby with the slaves in Grenada, *ting a ring ting, tarro*, and he tried to explain how some people came to be owned by others the same as if they were a horse or a piece of land.

"We were the first Christians to visit the Sandwich Islands after Captain Cook was murdered by the natives," Warren said and he answered them the location of the islands and who Captain Cook was and what he was doing there. He described hills that smoked like torches and beaches of white sand and a sea as tranquil and blue as heaven's eye. The dances the women performed, the battles the men fought in pantomime to entertain their visitors. They were mad for the Englishman's iron, he said, and he spent his days cutting coopering rings into ten-inch lengths and filing the ends to points, trading those for all manner of materials.

When the bread was ready Ada turned the loaves out to cool.

Warren said, "The weather was sudden on those islands. We were caught ashore at Onehow by a gale that forced the ship to cut her chains and stand out to sea. There were sixteen of us sailors left behind and almost three weeks before our vessel was able to make its way back to claim us. And the natives set us up two and two to a dwelling and fed and watered us and gave us liberty to ramble as we wished. We never lived so well in any Christian village. But there was one grumbletonian among us, an old bo'sun who thought we were any minute about to be killed. If he saw two or three of the native men in conversation he would shake with fear, convinced they were plotting against us. 'Now,' he'd say, 'this is the night we'll all be murdered in our beds.' He was a perfect annoyance to us all." Warren laughed. "It was a kind of paradise we were in," he said. "And the old sinner was too blind to see it."

Voices started calling "Hallo, Bungs!" from below and the three of them went down together to the landwash where a fire was burning on the beach and half a hundred crabs were boiling in a riveted copper pot nearly the size of a puncheon tub as the day went to dusk and night came on.

Evered was feeling his rum when they reached the fire and another cup of liquor was placed in his hand, the blood-red full moon of a crab passed along by its claw. Ada had carried down fresh bread and he tore a hunk from a loaf as it made the round. He saw Warren sat close to Ada and that was the last sober thought he gave to his sister for the evening.

Most of the crew were already rammaged and ready to make a night of it knowing they were staying put for a time. They were face and eyes into the crab, cracking the shells with stones and sucking the flesh into their mouths, cheeks and chins awash and firelight glinting in the souse. They were almost indistinguishable one from another in the falling dark, Evered thought, though they were nothing alike in age or size or appearance. They were of the one demeanour and bearing, their voices and shouted conversation interchangeable.

"Have he got you two rinded to the core?" someone called.

"He's a bit of a bagpipe our Bungs is."

"Did you tell them your exploits fighting the Americans, Bungs? In the reign of Queen Dick?"

The man sitting closest to Evered said, "Talking bilge about Scotland, was he? He've enough tongue for two sets of teeth when he gets onto ole Itchland."

A voice from across the fire said, "Did he tell ye about his position as duck fucker on the *Proteus* when he was but a lad?" And the circle erupted with laughter.

Evered had just turned seventeen. He felt all at sea among the raunch and candour and artless generosity of these strangers, their vulgar cant so unfamiliar it was almost a private language. And the welcome they offered so genuine he managed to feel nearly at home regardless. They had christened him Sixpence for his pate of silver hair and they called out to him by that name now and then, they threatened to shave the currency from his head as Delilah had shaved Samson's locks and to spend it all in the grog shops of St. John's.

"Now Sixpence," a voice shouted, "your sister has gone adrift."

He looked around the fire but there was no sign of Ada or the talker who had been sitting beside her. What was his name?

"Was our Bungs flashing the gentleman for the pretty lad?" someone called. "Was he putting on airs?"

Evered tried to get to his feet and almost fell face-first into the fire. Four hands reached for him and hauled him back to his arse. The man next him put his arm around Evered's neck and he had trouble shouldering that drunken halter.

"No worries now, lad," the man said. "Once our Bungs has a drink or two he's rabbit hunting with a dead ferret."

The fire roared ha ha ha ha.

Someone told a story about a sailor who had enjoyed a bit of relish with a fetching fire ship in London and caught a case of the clap so bad he had to be shaved smack smooth, his man Thomas and tarrywags and all.

"You are Josephus Rex," a voice said.

They were each in their turn called Josephus Rex in the wake of an outlandish story or dubious claim and Evered began to think of them all by that singular moniker. He found it increasingly difficult to distinguish one sailor from the next and himself from the company that surrounded him. He felt himself disappearing among Josephus Rex as the light of day had disappeared into the night and it was an entirely pleasurable sensation.

Someone crawled a little ways away from the circle of men to puke in the darkness.

"He's calling up his accounts now," a voice announced. "He's shooting the cat."

He might have fallen asleep for a time.

There was a ructions close by, a sudden clinch of sailors

mauled by drink, the lot of them cursing and shoving and hauling at each other like crabs trying to build a ladder of crabs to
escape a copper pot. Josephus Rex walked over Evered's legs
and stepped through the outskirts of the fire. Someone's trousers were set alight and there was a general panic to put out the
flames, Evered on his hands and knees to slap at the burning
fabric. Evered and two other men picked up the sailor with the
still-smoking trousers and threw him into the shallows of
the cove. The two men picked Evered up and threw him in
after for good measure. He crawled soaking wet back to the fire
where someone kissed him on both cheeks and handed him a
mug full of something he couldn't taste.

It was the best night of Evered's life. He thought it might
never end, please God.

He fell asleep for a time.

It was iron grey light when he woke and he could not tell if
that blade was in the air or only pulsing in his head. He sat up
from the bare stone. Bodies of the sailors and smashed crab
shells around the dead fire like flotsam thrown up by a high tide.
His mouth stuffed with tinder. Everything hurt. His body was
an iron cage and he clanged against the bars whichever way he
moved, his head rang if he so much as lifted his face. He looked
carefully up the rise to the tilt, squinting against the cold gleam.

His first cogent sober thought: Ada.

She'd left the fire and walked to the tilt with Warren before it
was properly dark. She was sorry to leave her seat front row to
the simmering riot on display. The sailors were roary-eyed and
foolhardy and obscene. They cursed and sang and threatened

violence upon one another with casual affection. They wandered out of the fire's circle to piss into the cove, still carrying on conversations with the sailors at their back. They told stories about storms with waves running higher than the ship's topmast and the native women they took for wives in the Sandwich Islands.

"We should go," Warren had said then and she nodded yes but didn't move.

"Every man aboard had a wife the whole time we were at anchor," a sailor said.

"You are Josephus Rex," a voice called.

"God's truth," the sailor insisted. "A man had only to offer a couple of iron nails and he was as good as married. The women would arrive at the beach every evening and call for their husbands by name. And they would come aboard after dark and stay till morning."

A second sailor said, "The fattest woman ever I saw our gunner chose for a wife. Her thighs were big around as my waist. We had to winch her aboard every evening. And not a hammock in the ship could hold her."

"And the gunner was gaunt as Job's turkey," the first sailor said. "He had to tie a picket across his arse to stop himself falling body and bones into her water-mill."

Ada could feel Warren's raw distress as he sat po-faced beside her, having admitted he was a sailor like the rest and would be in the throes of it but for her presence. He leaned toward her ear. "Miss Ada," he said over the laughter. He was sober and ashamed to look upon himself cup-shot and profane through the young girl's eyes. "We should leave them to their diversions," he said and Ada couldn't bring herself to inflict more punishment on the man.

At the tilt he apologized for the display and she shook her head to say no apology was necessary though it was plain he did not want her to protest. She couldn't see the earnest cooper offering an iron nail to take a wife as the other sailors had or making a farce of it in the aftermath. But she was anxious now finding herself alone with the man. He seemed on the verge of an avowal, some personal declaration that Ada wasn't sure she was prepared to hear. It had been hours since she'd had her single glass of rum but the mercurial sensation of drunkenness was still with her. A vague impression of being set adrift.

Warren lit the lamp and announced he would sit at the hearth for the night while she slept. Ada took the blanket the Captain had fashioned into a divider and drafted Warren into hanging it between the beds to answer his concern about modesty and that seemed enough to satisfy him. He jammed a chair against the door and they went to their bunks on opposite sides of the blanket without saying more than their good-nights. They could hear the sailors' jubilant feuding as it barrelled up the rise for hours afterward.

Ada was paging through what she'd retained of the voyages Warren had described that afternoon, the maps he'd traced in the sand. Still trying to make room in her head for the size and variety and strangeness of the world he revealed. She'd long suspected there was more to creation than the cove and its mingy handful of satellites but she was shocked by the manifest truth of it—the earth's vast labyrinth and the teeming lives within it, numberless as the stars. The sailors' racket like the sharp edge of a ferment that roared endlessly beyond the quiet of the cove.

———

The sound of Warren at the hearth woke her. It was still dark outside and she dressed in the near black. She filled the kettle from the water barrel and set it over the fire. She took a seat beside him.

"You're an early riser," she said.

"Long since," he said and he smiled at her, the same sense of gravid anticipation about the man that she had avoided the night before. She thought to move from the chair to escape it now when he said, "I have a daughter, Ada."

"Oh," she said.

"She would be about your age. If she's still in the world."

Ada tried to keep her rising confusion from her features. Not relief exactly, not disappointment, but a mongrel creature born of both. "But you idn't married," she said.

"Not in the eyes of the church," he said. "But there's more to a marriage than the banns."

She waited.

He said, "I'd been to every continent on earth but one before I was thirty years of age. And I had always wanted to see Australia. I took a berth on the *Lady Julia* transporting female convicts to New South Wales. I did not by any means like her cargo but I was resolved to submit to a great deal to see the country."

"What was it they did wrong?" Ada said. "The women?"

"Petty crimes mostly. Theft. Or being disorderly."

"I don't know what that means."

"Streetwalkers," he said. And a moment later, "Prostitutes."

Warren paused again as if he anticipated more questions or was hesitant to carry on with the story.

"When we were fairly out to sea," he said, "every man on

board took a wife from among the convicts. And I was as bad in this point as the others. She was from Lincoln and like all the girls from the country she came on board in irons. They were riveted rather than locked and the country jailer paid me half a crown to strike them off on my anvil. And I'd set my fancy upon her from that moment. She was modest," he said, "and reserved. And as kind and true a creature as ever lived. That was my impression of her you understand."

"What was her name?"

"Nancy," he said. "Nance Phair."

"Was she?" Ada said. "What was it? Disorderly?"

"She was banished, she told me, for a mantle she'd borrowed from an acquaintance. And the friend prosecuted her for stealing it."

"That idn't true," Ada said.

Warren laughed at the vehemence in the girl's voice. "Well it was such as she told me," he said. "And some in this world are more credulous than yourself, Miss Ada. I would have married her on the spot had there been a clergyman aboard. And I was resolved to bring her back to England my lawful wife when her seven years' sentence was done. She bore us a daughter on the voyage out."

"You didn't leave them there?"

"We were six weeks in Port Jackson after our arrival in New South Wales. I offered the captain to lose my wages if he would permit me to stay but he was short of hands. And it was not without the aid of the military I was brought aboard all the same. I left Nance my Bible which had been the companion of all my voyages, with both our names written in it. I told her I would come for her when her time expired."

The door of the tilt swung wide then and Evered fell into the room. He looked up from his hands and knees, staring first at his sister and then the stranger beside her and back again. "You're all right then," he said.

"The brother of the bung has arrived," Warren said. He seemed relieved to be interrupted. "Shall we get to work, Evered?"

But the youngster crawled past them and into his bed. Ada turned to Warren who showed no interest in carrying on with the story.

"So," she said. "You never went back."

He shook his head. "I looked two years for a berth without luck. I made it as far as the Cape and paid off there, intending to stay until I could flag a position on to New South Wales. The *Venus* came into port under Captain Coffin. She had taken convicts to Port Jackson and there was an escapee aboard who had stowed away and kept himself hidden till they were well out to sea. He told me he had seen me in Port Jackson with the *Lady Julia* and my heart fair burst in my chest. I asked if he had any news of Nance and he claimed she had left the colony for India. I didn't know what to think of it. Every day for a week I went back to him to ask again, thinking he had confused my Nance for some other woman. I described her in detail and her parents and place of birth and anything else that might distinguish her. But he never wavered. She'd left Port Jackson within a year of arriving. With her daughter. And her infant son. And her husband."

"That idn't true," Ada said again.

"I didn't believe it could be," he said. "I went to Lincoln when next I was in England and found her mother and father but they knew nothing more than myself. I tried for a while to find a berth to Bombay to track her there. Until it occurred to me I was the only one looking."

"What do you mean?"

"I mean she had never made the slightest effort to find me, not in all those years we were apart. There were no letters or messages. Even if she wasn't married and living in India, for all her talk of faithfulness she had discarded me."

"Maybe," Ada said, "it could be she died."

"I wished it," Warren said. "So I did. But the heat has left me long since. If she had died in Port Jackson her parents would have heard. And I would rather think her alive now and looking after my daughter." He turned to Ada. He looked as if he were about to bawl. "It galls my heart to think of a girl abandoned to the world without mother or father to tend to her."

She saw it then, the knot Warren had been trying to tie since their first encounter, and she could hardly speak around the lump in her throat. She shook her head. "I got Evered," she said. "He been good to me."

Warren wiped the tears from his face with the palms of his hands. "Amen to that then," he said.

Ada roused Evered from his rum stupor before noon and Warren took him into the woods to clip new growth from a spruce. They boiled the branches to make a tea that was added to the mash of hops and yeast and molasses cooking over the fire on the landwash. Warren salvaged and rehooped a puncheon from the remains of two crippled tubs in the store and after the brew cooled enough they set it to work in that vessel and in the beer barrel recovered from the shipwreck.

"That should be fit to drink in two days," Warren said. "But those hops are old enough you might want to leave it a week or more."

The sailors stayed three nights longer with them. Their needling debates and catcalls and laughter like a rattling brook running through the cove, a steady racket at the centre of their days, a cold rushing current they waded into and kicked up and soaked in.

Outside of the few hours he worked on the batch of spruce beer, Evered spent every moment with Josephus Rex. They rowed the bully boat out along the coast that first afternoon, placing him in the bow where he leaned over the ocean with his rifle like a vessel's figurehead. He bagged a brace of loons, a goose, five turr and seven strangers, the sailors giving a roar of approval every time he took a bird they'd set to wing. "Ho, Sixpence!" they shouted. They cleaned and roasted the game for their supper and there was enough left over to make a meal of it the following evening.

Evered got drunk with the men each night and he wore his vibrant daylong hangovers like a starry crown. He slept among them in the improvised shelter they'd built at the treeline and when he started from a dream of walking through the bowels of a drowned ship with mutilated corpses in his wake one man or other would lay a hand on his head and whisper drunkenly to him until he'd fallen back to sleep.

The caplin struck in on the morning of the third day, rolling on the grey sand beach in a wall-eyed churning mass. The sailors had never experienced the like and all hands were in the shallows with dip nets and buckets and hand seines, hauling the suicidal harvest above the landwash. Evered and the crew hand-barrowed several hundred pounds to the farm garden where they turned the soil and spread the caplin to compost. When they were done they lit a fire on the plateau and sat with pipes and cigarettes to tamp down the blackflies swarming to life off the Downs and they dozed and gossiped lazily, waiting to be called down to their dinner.

"Who is it you got buried up here, Sixpence?" one of the men asked.

They'd lit the fire at the head of the garden rows and within spitting distance of the graves.

"The little one there," Evered said, "is our sister Martha. She was carried off by the same sickness took Mother and Father. But they two was buried at sea."

"And what about the other then?" a voice asked. "Next your sister?"

"Before my time," Evered said. He considered telling them about the drowned French sailor but the conversation with Captain Truss had made him uncertain of the tale.

"I was told a story while we were in Fogo last winter," the first man said. "There was a grave in a peat bog was part of it."

"I heard that one too," a second sailor said.

The first man said, "There were two brothers came out along this coast, oh this was long and long ago it was. Two brothers came over from England as servants in the fishery and worked off their indenture and they came out to raise an enterprise of their own in a little cove like this one. And they hired an Irish girl to work the shore crew and cook and the like."

"She wasn't Irish," the second sailor said.

"Well she was born in Newfoundland right enough but she was Irish stock. Twelve or thirteen years old she was and all her people left behind, out in the world on her own. And the brothers of course they both coveted the girl. And the brothers loved each other you see and couldn't decide who should marry the lass. So they resolved to make themselves known to her and let the girl choose."

"That's a mistake right there," someone said. "Never let the girl decide."

And there was a quiet round of agreement on this point.

"Well each of them made his declarations and pledged his offerings of love and fidelity and children if she would choose him. And for her part she was taken with them both but by one more than the other. And she gave her hand to the younger of the two. Now the older brother was in a bad skin over it. He never said as much but all along he'd thought it his right as the older to have the girl. He'd agreed to the arrangement only to spare a falling-out with his brother and it bedevilled him to be passed over."

"What did he do?" Evered asked.

"He slew his brother is what he did," the second man said, "with a blow to the head."

"You are Josephus Rex," two voices called.

"And so he did," the first man said. "When they next went out on the grounds he struck his brother a blow across the head and tipped him into the ocean. And told the girl a tale of her intended falling overside trying to bring in a fish and sinking like a stone. And he comforted her in her grief as a good man would. When the body washed up on shore days later the two eyes were eaten out by sea lice. And the older brother carried it up off the beach and buried it at the edge of a peat bog much like this one here."

There was a murmur around the fire and then a voice asked, "What did the girl do?"

"Well what choice did the young one have?" the first man said. "Likely no more than a blanket hung between their beds," he said and then shrugged. "A parson or some such came into the cove in the fall of the year and he said a funeral service over the dead man's grave and wedded the older brother and the girl on the same afternoon. And they two joined giblets that night in the shadow of the brother's final resting place."

There was a round of sober scandalized laughter. A voice across the fire asked, "What became of them after?"

"They never said. Perhaps they're still on the coast somewhere. Surrounded by youngsters who don't even know the poor uncle's name."

Something in the details reminded Evered of a story his mother told about a murderous brother from the childhood of creation though he couldn't recall her version well enough to say how close they tracked. "Is it true?" he asked. "The story?"

The sailors both made a face as if they were tasting some strange new flavour they weren't sure they liked.

"It was told to me as if it were so," the first man said.

Evered felt like a fly trapped in honey. Each turn he made to haul clear of the tale sank him deeper into the sticky mess. What he knew of his father was at odds with most every detail. But the telling of it alone seemed nearly enough to make it real. He said, "Don't you be talking any of your old mash to Ada."

"It's only a story, lad."

"Just you don't," he said. Someday it would get put down in a book somewhere, he thought, and that would be the fact of it.

"All right, Rusty Guts, no need to get up in the boughs over it."

"Young Sixpence must think his Ada is some delicate creature," a third sailor said.

"Easy now. He's only looking out to the young maid."

"What does he think our Bungs is up to with the girl all this time I wonder? Other than joining giblets?"

The circle of men came to attention without seeming to move a muscle, their eyes flicking across Evered and away.

"Bungs has tapped that dirty puzzle and no mistake."

"On Saint Geoffrey's Day he has."

"He's been taking a stroll up cock alley is what."

"You'll be getting a dowse on the chops you don't watch your mouth."

"What, from Sixpence here? Fart-catcher to his little sister? That will be when the devil is blind and he—"

Evered was on the man before he'd finished and all the sailors came to their feet in the youngster's wake, forming a seething ring around Evered astraddle the man. He had a handful of hair in his fist and swung wildly with his free arm, Josephus Rex cheering him on. "Blacken his lamps," someone yelled. He took an elbow across the bridge of his nose and the shock of it made his head buzz like a hive of bees. The sailor beneath him twisted sideways and they found themselves on the ground in a useless clench, grunting at one another. Every fibre straining to cause the other pain and irreparable damage and they managed only to rock back and forth in a vehement interminable hug until the other sailors stepped in to break up the stalemate. "All right, lads," they kept saying, pulling at their limbs. "All right, lads."

"Well done yourself, Sixpence," someone said to Evered as he was helped to his feet. Several hands clapped him on the back.

"Sure I was only having a bit of fun," the sailor said. His lip was split and swelling and he spat a thick clot of blood. He laughed and reached for the youngster's hand. "But you were right to come aboard of me for it. Fair play to you," he said.

Evered shook the proffered hand and sat back at the fire. His eyes still watering from the smack to his face. He'd wanted someone or something killed dead for a hot instant but every ounce of that malice had drained away. There was a round of celebratory chatter among the men, he and the sailor sitting beside each other and joking. Evered felt diminished and lifted up. As if he'd passed a particularly sly and gruelling test and been admitted to a fraternity he'd aspired to all his days without knowing what he hankered after.

They heard Warren hailing from down below for them to come eat their dinner.

Ada spent most of those three days baking bread with the sailors' store of flour in a vain attempt to stanch their relentless appetites and she kept company with Warren who slept in the bunk behind the blanket curtain and was hardly out of her sight when she was awake.

He talked through his days growing up in Scotland and the shock of arriving in London as a boy, the taverns and beggars and street thieves, the playhouses where men wore costumes on a stage and pretended to be other than themselves for three hours of an evening. She walked him through his voyages again, asking after additional details and clarification on the circumstances of one episode or another. She asked him to redraw the map of each of his journeys in the sand. She had him place the cove on an outline of Newfoundland and to sketch in the continents around the island, moving chairs and table and the water barrel to make room for the expanding atlas.

Warren asked after her parents and where their people hailed from, if they were Newfoundlanders or had come over from somewhere in the British Isles to the cove. The question had never occurred to Ada and she had no answers for him. And that lack made her feel almost as naked and pitiable as her baby sister before the infant was bestowed with a name.

He asked how they had managed in the cove on their own and for the first time Ada had to consider their lives as they might look from the outside, as a story she might tell a stranger. She spoke of Mary Oram and of the infant Martha who was gone but still with them, of the Beadle aboard *The Hope* and the whitecoat they almost died taking off the ice. There was the storm that wrecked the ship on the coast, the icebound vessel with its dead man at the stove and the trunk of clothes where she salvaged her trousers and waistcoat and tricorn. She mentioned the bear and her cub, she told Warren about the unlikely Captain Truss and Mrs. Brace who had saved her life, about trapping with Evered up the brook and along Black Bear River over the winter. Even to Ada's mind there was detail enough she was satisfied she hadn't left out anything significant.

They ate with the sailors at the fire above the landwash on the second evening, the men offering to take Evered aboard as a stowaway and to leave Warren behind with the pretty lad in his place.

"Bungs have been of a strange kidney since he set foot here," a sailor said. "We'd be happy to be clear of him."

"I'd be happy enough to see the back of you lot myself," Warren said. "But I'm afraid His Majesty might object." He turned to Ada to ask her pardon and he walked into the darkness to relieve himself.

"You see now, Sixpence," a voice called, loud enough for Warren to hear, "why we want to be rid of old Screw Jaws. His Majesty this and His Majesty that. Grand talk for a dogsbody who served as duck fucker on the *Proteus*."

"I remind you we are in mixed company," Warren shouted from the water's edge.

"Where?" a voice called. "Everyone present is wearing trousers."

"An imposter among us," another said and he climbed to his feet. "Let's go, lads—your credentials." He dropped his pants to his knees and a handful of others stood to do the same.

"Come on, Sixpence," a sailor called. "Are ye fish or fowl?"

And Evered got to his feet with the rest as they wagged their lobcocks in the dark light of the fire.

"The pretty lad now," someone shouted over the naked laughter. "Make a signal, young sir! Hoist your flag!"

Warren was at her shoulder then and lifting her from her seat, turning her up the rise toward the tilt. A chorus of boos following after them. Ada half-sorry to be escorted away, the display too farcical to carry any real menace. It was the threat she'd felt radiating off the sailors when they first arrived turned on its head, tatted up in a fool's rags to be ridiculed. And as long as Warren was with her she felt safe enough to laugh.

Ada tried to imagine her protector with his pants at his ankles and casually waving his bits, a sailor like the rest, and the thought brought on a fit of giggles that she refused to explain. It seemed impossible to her that Warren would have joined in the exhibition at a different time in his life or under different circumstances. Though she was beginning to suspect a person might not be one simple thing, uniform and constant. They ate alone at the tilt the next evening, Warren not willing to expose Ada to the men in their cups again though it seemed a loss to her.

On the last morning they had together Ada asked again about the convict ship and Warren's time with Nance Phair.

"You haven't heard enough of my troubles?"

"I can't believe she was transported for borrowing a friend's mantle is all."

"Why would anyone?" he said.

She waited.

He said, "When I went to see her mother and father in Lincoln I discovered she'd stolen six yards of black chintz cotton, a Coventry tammy gown, a quilted petticoat, a black silk hat, a pair of leather shoes." He waved his hand. "A pair of stays, half a dozen silk handkerchiefs. I've forgotten the entire list. She was a thief, my Nance. Every finger a fish hook." He looked across at Ada with a sad wry smile. "I've never told anyone the truth of that before," he said and he seemed relieved to offer it up without prevarication finally.

"Do you ever worry," Ada said. "About how your daughter? I mean." She trailed off, sorry to have raised the issue.

"Nance used to read my Bible on the voyage out," he said. "More than ever I did. Which is why I left it with her when I sailed away." He shrugged helplessly. "It might be something in her was changed by what she read there. I pray it was so."

Ada was quiet then, long enough that Warren asked her if everything was all right, if he'd said something to upset her.

"I was just wondering why it is some people come to read and not others," she said.

"I was taught from the time I was a little one. And my brothers the same."

"It was taught you?" Ada said.

"Of course," he said and he laughed.

"I thought it was something you was born knowing," she said. "Or not knowing."

He shook his head but knew better than to laugh a second time. "Anyone can learn to read," he said.

Ada got up from her chair and went to fetch the cloth-bound journal on the shelf over her bed. She said, "I wants you to read this. If you would. As a favour to me."

"Where did you come across this then?"

"In the pocket of me waistcoat," she said. "Out on the ship was icebound."

Warren turned it over in his hands several times before he opened it and flipped through. The pages were water-buckled and some stuck together and much of the writing was illegible with having been soaked sometime before. "Most of it is ruined of course," he said. He turned to the opening page. "'Joseph Knott,'" he read. "'His Book. Consisting of A Journey from Saint John, New Brunswick to Limerick, Ireland aboard *The Ark of Malaga*.'" Warren smiled and shook his head. "I knew the vessel," he said.

"That idn't true," Ada shouted.

"Sure and it is," Warren insisted. "I could list half the British ships at sea, crossing paths with them in one port or another. When I knew her she was captained by a man name of Noah. *Noah's Ark* we called her. But he's long since dead now." He turned back to the journal, whisper-read phrases as he turned the pages. "'Departed Saint John, September 15th . . . passing through the Strait of Belle Isle, cold stormy weather . . . inclement, most passengers ill and myself among them.'" He turned past a number of indecipherable pages and then read silently a minute. "Mr. Knott records they struck a storm out on the Banks," he said. "It blew the better part of three days and the *Ark* lost her rigging and her masts and most of the rail besides."

"She was in a sorry state when we went out to her," Ada said.

Warren turned a page, made a noise in his chest. "The crew thought the ship lost and abandoned her," he said. "They took every boat and left the passengers to their fate." He whisper-read again. "'Still adrift and no sign of land or rescue . . . fall of snow for seven days and everything above decks encased in ice . . . this morning we buried five of our number at sea . . . as forlorn a Christmastide as ever a man could pass . . . two more have perished overnight.'"

Warren looked up from the journal and took a breath. "When was it you walked out to this ship?" he asked.

"April or May month a year ago," she said.

"And there was someone keeping a fire in the stove out there?"

"Up to a week or so before we walked out."

Warren stared at the ceiling, his lips moving as he counted up the months. "Miss Ada," he said. "I don't think we should carry on with this."

"Evered saw something," she said. "When we was leaving the ship. He've never said a word about it. But I knows it torments him still."

"You knowing what he knows won't spare him that."

She said, "He wouldn't be alone with it at least."

Warren considered her a few moments before reading silently ahead. "They drifted into ice in January," he reported. "I imagine they'd been driven up around Greenland. I was icebound on a whaling vessel off that coast for seventeen days years ago. I expected we would die there like that, stuck fast." He tried to separate several pages held together but couldn't manage the delicate job and turned past them. "They were weeks in that condition when the ice cracked the timbers amidships and sea water filled the lower decks."

"We saw that," Ada said. "Evered did. When he went snooping below."

"There were only ten of them left alive by this time," he said. "They burned wood pried from the decks to keep warm." He turned the page. "They ate the last of the ship's provisions before the end of February."

"They still had food aboard," Ada said. "There was a pot of food on the stove when we was there."

Warren reached a hand and placed it over hers. He said, "You didn't eat any of what was in that pot did you, Ada?" His face was glowing red again, like a lamp warning off catastrophe.

"No," she said. "We. It wouldn't fit from the look of it. We eat the bit of food we carried out with us."

Warren sat back in his chair. He looked exhausted. He flipped ahead a few pages and then closed the book on his lap. "Your man Mr. Knott," he said and he tapped the journal with an index finger, "was among the last few alive. He saw the worst of it." And then he said, "I think we would do well to stop there. If you will permit me."

She nodded without looking at him. "Could it be true?" she whispered. "They could do that to other people?"

"I've heard the like," Warren said. "In circumstances of similar distress."

"Distress don't seem warrant enough for such a thing."

"We live in a fallen world," he said. "And easy enough to judge anchored at a fire with a plate of food and a pocket full of tender."

Warren got up to place a junk of wood on the coals and he passed the journal to Ada. "You ought to burn this," he said.

"Why?" she said. "Would that change what happened?"

"I suppose not, no. It wouldn't. Not one whit."

He shook his head.

"Still," he said.

There was a fire on the landwash the last night the sailors were with them though they were relatively subdued and judicious in their drinking with a full day's rowing ahead and untold days beyond that to St. John's. They roasted caplin over the open flame until they were blackened and ate them head and tail together. They had nearly run through their liquor supply and they broke into the smaller barrel of spruce beer Bungs had brewed, adding a shot of rum to each glass, a drink they said Americans called callibogus. Ada convinced Warren to walk down for a few minutes before it was gone to dark and they stayed an hour with the crowd, listening as the men traded songs and stories and insults.

Ada watched Evered across the fire. Picturing him with his pants at his knees among the troop of half-naked men, the drunken grin on his face. And a queasy shudder passed through her, thinking of what it was he might have seen aboard *Noah's Ark* that caught in his flesh like a hook. It hardly seemed possible both those experiences could inhabit the same frame at the one time. They should be different people, she thought, those two boys.

Warren took her up to the tilt before the cove was dark enough to reflect the moon, Ada saying her good-nights to the men as they coaxed her to stay longer.

"Pity us," one sailor said. "We'll have nothing to look at but Bungs' ugly mug for days on end. Spare us a few more minutes."

Evered watched them as they left the fire, his sister walking close enough to the older man that their shoulders touched. He didn't know if the sailor he'd fought on the Downs was only having a bit of fun or if there was some truth to his insinuation. He thought of their stories of the Sandwich Islands where the sailors took a wife among the local women while they were at anchor.

"Ho, Sixpence," one of the sailors said, "have you a song for us?"

He shook his head and Josephus Rex groaned in disbelief.

"One song, John-a-Nokes," someone said.

"Every nigmenog got a song in them."

And because it was the only one he knew beginning to end he told the sailors the story of old Mr. Lucas's goat and offered up a rendition of *My Thing Is My Own*.

Ada and Warren were at the hearth by then, listening to the voices below.

"That's your brother singing," Warren said.

"I think it is," Ada said. Though it sounded to her like someone she barely knew. "You'll be off early," she said.

"First thing," he said. "Yes."

They heard the men below start in on *Here's to the Maiden of Bashful Fifteen* and they were quiet while it lasted.

"You never mentioned," Ada said then. "What was your daughter's name?"

"Sarah we called her."

Ada put a hand to her mouth.

"What?" Warren said. "What have I said?"

"Sarah was Mother's name," she told him.

"Well," he said.

Ada could see he relished the weight that bit of happenstance carried between himself and the orphan girl who was the same age as his vanished daughter.

"I wish," he said, "when I gave my Bible to Nance that I'd written Sarah's name beside her mother's and mine. It seems a terrible oversight not to have done."

"Yes," Ada agreed quietly. "So it do."

Before they douted the lamp she went to the shelf to retrieve the necklaces she'd fashioned with the bear's teeth and she made a gift of one to Warren. He bowed his head to allow her to set it around his neck. And she handed him the second necklace and bowed her head to allow him to do the same for her.

The cove was awake before light and the crewmen busied themselves packing the boat with the riveted copper pot and tarpaulins and the assorted gear they'd hauled ashore for one reason or other in the previous days. Setting about the work with a regimented ease so practised and complete it felt to Ada and Evered they had been left behind even before the boat cast off.

The sailors set their oars when the sun stood a hand above the water and as they rowed for the skerries they sang out their goodbyes to brother and sister watching from the stage. The boat rounded the eastern arm and the youngsters ran the path to the Downs where they had a view of the ocean beyond the cove. Ada had her telescope and they passed the glass back and forth until the vessel and its crew were beyond the horizon and crossed to the other side of the earth. They were standing close enough to touch and eventually they did, leaning into the other's weight.

Ada said, "You wishes you was going off with them I imagine."

"Only half so much as yourself," he said.

They were heartbroken to see their visitors leave, as they expected. The heartbreak was an old familiar they'd long since learned to accommodate, making up a bed in the same corner where their mother and father did not sleep, placing an extra chair at the table next to Martha's empty seat. But there was another blade at work that had never before touched them. It barely registered in the morning's glaring loss but that sting would grow sharper and more distinct as the season passed.

They had all their lives been the one thing the other looked to first and last, the one article needed to feel complete whatever else was taken from them or mislaid in the dark. But each in their own way was beginning to doubt their pairing was requisite to what they might want from life.

The Hope. A Marauding Army.

They fell into the heart of the season with the same regimented enterprise the sailors displayed as they readied to leave the cove. They rose in the dark and strapped themselves to the day as it lurched into motion, Evered on the water in all weather, Ada beetling through the interminable bog of shore work. They stood opposite each other at the splitting table through the middle of each day and through much of the long evenings as well, gutting and salting the endless parade of cod by the orange light of the slutlamp, nursing their fatigue and loneliness in the last hours with a mug of callibogus at their elbows.

They were newly attentive to one another even as they were furiously treading water to keep ahead of the fish, burnishing their losses by recounting the antics of Josephus Rex, by walking through Warren's journeys to the four corners of the earth. It was as if they had been away on separate trips and were trading stories of what they'd seen and heard while they were travelling. When they flagged too far for conversation Evered picked his way through a handful of the drinking songs he'd learned at the fire above the landwash.

Once they'd cleared the last of the day's catch they climbed the rise in the pitch black and the cold rain and the faffering wind, the little glow set alight in their chests by the rum all that kept them upright. They left the blanket that separated the beds in place and bunked on opposite sides of the room though they spoke a few minutes across that barrier before they fell into the void. The first to wake in the morning set the fire and boiled water for tea before disturbing the other's rest to begin the next iteration of the season's droning round.

The only reprieve in those devouring days was weather too foul to chance the water, rain drifting sideways in a gale, foam clipping off the lip of whitecaps on the ocean. If it was too fierce even to be out at the garden or on the landwash or in the woods they turned to indoor tasks, tending the fishing gear, mending clothes or treating their leather boots with cod-liver oil, razoring the splitting knives on a sharpening stone.

They both gave in to sleep through those rare sedentary days, drifting off in their seats with their hands still holding the materials they were working on. It was the only time through the season that they dreamt or remembered their dreams which were most often reflections of the labour that choked their conscious lives. The heavy chain of fish cranked across the splitting table one link at a time, the creak and smack of the boat's milling oars. Ada hauling water from the brook in her sleep, the weight of the buckets growing with each step and her feet sinking into the beaten path up to her knees, calling to Evered for help and waking herself with that throttled effort.

Evered dreaming himself with two lines down on the shoal ground and raising the fish the way his father had, watching the swarming school drift upward with an eerie uniformity, languid but purposeful as it came out of the black into shadowy light. No wind, the ocean dead calm. And a fear rising in him at the same steady rate, a panic to draw in the lines though he stood paralyzed at the gunwales. The fish coming clear in the blue light and the corpses he'd seen aboard the *Ark* borne up on that writhing platter like an offering from the deep, the flayed limbs animate and reaching for the surface.

He twitched and moaned in his chair, Ada calling his name and pinching his earlobes to bring him back to the world.

"You was lost in the dawnies again," she said. "What was it you was dreaming about?"

"I don't know," he said. "Some old foolishness."

"You're an awful liar, Brother."

He shrugged. "It idn't for lack of practice," he said.

They clawed their way toward September.

There was a week of prime drying weather in late August and they packed the cured fish into the bulkheads on the stage. *The Hope* sailed into view before the first of September, earlier than they could remember seeing it. They loaded the boat to ferry out the salt cod and when Evered climbed aboard he repeated his ritual greetings with the crewmen and they passed around a bottle of rum as they reacquainted themselves. Evered grown nearly the height of the crewmen now, despite the years of deprivation. They asked after the season's luck and how the young maid was and whether it wasn't time to find a man to marry her.

"Lots of fellows down in Mockbeggar lacking a woman," one of them said. "She could just about write her own ticket if she've a mind to."

"What about meself then?" Evered asked. "You got anyone for the likes of me?"

"You'd only be put to the back of the line," another man told him and they laughed together.

The bottle made a second round and Evered asked, "How's Mary Oram? Still wild as a goat, is she?"

The men looked at their feet suddenly.

"Mary Oram been dead this two months now," one of them said.

He would have thought they were making a joke but for the sombre look of them. "What become of her?"

"Went to bed one night and never woke up is what it looks like," the man said. "Was a day or two before anyone missed her gone."

"How old was she?"

"Idn't nobody knows the rights of it."

"It don't hardly seem possible," Evered said.

"Every way's likely," the man said.

They heard the voice of the Beadle calling from below decks and they drank another round in memory of Mary Oram before Evered went down.

As well as the winter supplies he left *The Hope* with yeast and hops for brewing and two demijohns of rum, with powder and shot and a dozen iron traps to use once the snow settled in. The cost of the traps put them further in debt than they'd ever been. But the furs would go a long way toward digging them clear if the winter went well. If they held their nerve. If a bit of luck ran their way.

Ada was on the stage when he came in and they carted the

works up to the store but for a demijohn of rum which they brought into the tilt and poured two fingers to each, drinking the liquor straight. Ada made a pea soup with salt meat and flour doughboys and they both had more rum after they'd eaten. There was a celebratory air to the evening though neither was quite able to set aside the pervading sense of drift.

"They wants to get you married off, Sister," Evered said.

"Who?"

"The works of them. Talking about how hard up the crowd is over to Mockbeggar. And never a thought to how I'd fare with you gone."

"You'd get on best kind I imagine."

"Might be I would." He shrugged. They were both a little drunk. He said, "I half expected old Bungs to ask after your hand before he went off the spring."

Ada could feel the heat coming into her face. "It wouldn't like that, Brother," she said.

Evered almost asked what it was like then, if not like that. But he held his tongue. "You think you might want to someday?" he said. "Get married?"

"I never give it much thought," she said, which was a lie. She hadn't come to a conclusion on the matter though it wasn't for lack of consideration. *Don't be beholden to a man* Mrs. Bruce had told her and she still couldn't say if it was meant to warn her away from marriage or if it was referring to something of another order altogether.

They were lying on opposite sides of the blanket before it occurred to Evered to mention Mary Oram.

"You are Josephus Rex," Ada said.

"Died in her bed they says."

She lay with that news a few minutes. "It don't hardly seem possible," she said.

She thought of the woman in her knitted cap and her child's hands without fingernails at work between her mother's legs with the razor. Kneeling beside Sarah Best with the string of knots, chanting the one line over and over, what was it? May earth bear on you with all its something something. She drifted off still reaching for the words.

Evered was out at the fall fish every day for two weeks after *The Hope*'s visit. He struck in handlining on the Wester Shoals late one morning, bringing the cod aboard hand over fist, as fast as he could shake one from the hook and drop the baited line overside. They were pooling thirty-five fathoms down and he was trying to raise them off the shoal ground, bringing them toward the surface a fathom at a time. He had the full of the fish pound and was loading the forward cuddy with more, the cod less than ten fathom then and still rising to his line. "Now Father," he said aloud. He could hardly quiet his breath to have finally got the knack of it and he was lost in the medieval alchemy of the process. The day turning while he had his back to the weather.

The waters darkened as the light left the sky, the schooling fish below him fading to black, and that warning sign finally forced him to lift his head. He turned to look east where a squall of billowing cloud and rain was stampeding across the bay. He brought up his line and set to the oars, the boat riding low and leaden with the cod he'd hauled aboard. He'd drifted to the far edge of the Wester Shoals and had to row directly into the streaming wind to reach the harbour mouth. Whenever he looked over his shoulder he could see the barrelling lop crossing open water, driving for him at a clip.

Ada was at the farm garden when a steady breeze coming off the water stood her upright. The wind so implausibly warm it might have been blowing over a bed of hot coals. She looked to the ocean and saw banks of dark cloud on the eastern horizon bearing down on the cove. She scanned for the boat away out on the Wester Shoals, drifting with the current as Evered worked the ground. She waved her arms and shouted to him though he was miles off. She saw him draw in his lines finally and turn for the cove and she watched him make for shelter as the storm-edge sucked the last of the light from the sky, pushing whitecaps in a jagged line ahead of it. A few minutes later the wind turned suddenly cold against her skin, a sharp arctic edge to it.

Evered's only hope was to slip through the skerries into the cove ahead of the squall but he was rowing straight for the weather and Ada could see he would not make it. Evered seemed to have reached the same conclusion, letting go the oars and forking his catch overside to raise the gunwales high enough he might stay afloat when the worst of the storm collapsed on him.

It was like watching a pantomime play out on the boards of the ocean's monumental theatre, Evered alone upon it as the tempest's slow-motion calamity crossed the surface like a marauding army advancing on a field. And nothing to be done but wait for the collision and stand witness. The crippling truth of it coming over her as the first heavy drops struck her face and her shoulders and seconds later the cold downpour whipped at her head and her clothes and she was soaked to the skin.

Evered was still half a mile shy of the harbour when the rain fell in sheets and the wind shook the little boat like a bit of rag. He had managed to clear most of the fish from the pound and he took up the oars again, trying to keep head-on to the weather, waves breaking over the gunwale as he smashed through. The bilge was awash with sea water running forward and aft like a pendulum as he climbed each crest and careened into the trough, the suck of it sloshing past his calves. The boat lay low with that rolling weight but Evered couldn't let go the oars to bail. He couldn't look over his shoulder to watch for the harbour, blinded by the rain and the spume whipping off the white-caps. He rowed for his life without making headway, managing only to hold his spot on the water as the endless string of waves lifted and cratered beneath him. He expected any second to be tipped face-first into the ocean with the boat crashing down on his back or the bow to drive under a crest and not shake clear. But each passing moment was so fraught with tumult, with his own feverish effort and the rain and the lethal wind ravaging his head that he didn't feel anything as obvious or simple as fear until the storm tailed past him.

The waves didn't diminish through the rest of the day but the wind settled and the clouds skated over as suddenly as they'd arrived, the incongruous sun scouring the sky clean behind it. Evered was able to make his slow way to the harbour mouth then, steering the logy vessel past the skerries into the relative calm of the cove. He sat the oars, staring down at his boots under the knee-deep water in the bilge. He was dazed and wrung out, every muscle in his body trembling with exhaustion and with the rolling wake of terror that washed through him now that he was safe and sitting still. There were three codfish that hadn't been forked overside or washed away by the storm and he watched them swim slow figure eights around his ankles for a time before it struck him how odd a circumstance it was. He reached for the wooden bailer tied to the taut and began methodically emptying the boat a pint of ocean at a time.

Ada ran down to the stage after Evered came through the sker-ries. She watched him bailing the boat, scooping and flinging with a distracted, mechanical repetition. He was close enough she could yell across to him but he seemed not to hear her. She was wet through from the pummelling rain and the steady wind blew cold across her and she started to shake in the open air. But she wouldn't turn for the tilt before Evered was ashore.

"Come in out of it," she called.

"I'll be in directly," he said without looking up from the bailing.

"Brother," she said. "Come in I wants you."

He swung his head toward her then and he glanced down at the bailer in his hand, considering. And after a time he set it down and took up the oars to row in to the stage. He climbed out of the boat and passed by his sister as if he wasn't sure who she was. The same look on his face as the day he'd buried his father at sea when he was eleven years old.

She followed him up to the tilt and she stripped him of his clothes, Evered raising his arms and turning and sitting and lifting his feet as she directed. Once he was stark she wrapped him in a blanket beside the hearth. She set the fire then and took off her own soaked outfit, wringing water from the material into a bucket as she stood naked in the chill, shaking helplessly.

"You'll catch your death so," Evered said.

She added more wood to the fire and spread their clothes on a line strung over the hearth and then took a chair beside him, wrapped in a blanket of her own. She'd set a demijohn of rum between them and she poured a generous shot into two mugs and they drank them back in a single mouthful. Ada doled out another round and the youngsters sat raw and shivering, waiting for the alcohol to hit their blood.

"Some day out there," Evered said finally.

"I thought you was gone," Ada said. "I thought you was as good as drownded."

"I thought the same," he said and he half smiled at her.

The heat of the rum brought him back to himself. He pictured his sister on the stagehead while he sat bailing the boat in the cove, as if recognizing her there for the first time. And it struck him that Ada would be standing on the stage even now, alone for good, if his luck had run an inch right or left of its course. Watching the sea for something that would never be delivered to her. That sense so strong in him it seemed almost a premonition and the same shrouding dread he felt in the worst days of her illness came over him.

"Sister," he said.

Ada saw that darkness seep into his features and she stared at the half-starved look of desperation on his face. Asking after some reassurance or succour she felt helpless to offer. She'd had a thought to pray to Martha as she watched him row into the maw of the storm, to ask she keep Evered safe. But it seemed a vain bit of foolishness to think the child had any sway over the brawling forces at work out there.

"Sister," Evered said again and Ada went to him, taking his face into her hands.

She said, "May earth bear on you with all its might and main." Not knowing why those words came to her or even what they signified exactly. He started crying as she chanted them quietly. She kissed his forehead and his cheeks, crying herself by then, and he reached to put his arms around her. She straddled his lap in the chair, the blanket sliding off her shoulders as he bawled into her neck.

They sat like that a few minutes, feeling beggared and solitary, each wanting back inside the other's skin. Evered hefted Ada aloft and laid her on the ground in front of the fire, rocking against the naked sling of her hips. Ada rising up to the motion, a quiver running through her that she felt to her very toes. There was a sudden piercing nick then, a tearing at the fabric she was made of, and she closed her eyes against the stinging shock until the pain rolled unexpectedly, the submerged weight of pleasure breaking into the light.

"Oh Jesus, Brother," she said.

She was just turned fifteen and she felt split open at the root of herself.

"Oh Jesus," she said.

A Dirty Puzzle.

They drifted off in each other's arms and dozed until the creeping chill woke them. Evered spent but still inside her and they both felt queered by the cold clabbered uncoupling as he pulled away. They went to their separate bunks without eating any supper and they slept through the night without waking. None of their clothes was near to dry come morning but they dressed in the clammy material regardless to be covered in the other's company.

They were inward and quiet, moving as if there were others asleep in the narrow confines of the tilt, barely speaking for fear of blundering into the place where they were both feeling nish. Delicate and uncertain. And they chose to spend their day outside at separate tasks.

Ada walked to the Downs, digging the last beets and cabbages and turnip from the farm garden. Sitting a vigil at Martha's grave when she took a spell from the work, talking aloud to her sister as she always had. Though it felt now like listening to the ocean in an empty shell. Years believing the dead infant inclined to Ada's every word from her heavenly anchorage. She couldn't quite credit the notion now. But she had no one else to turn to.

She described the marching storm and the terror of watching Evered rowing to stand still in the teeth of it, repeating the same horrific inconclusive moment for the length of the squall. The certain knowledge he was lost to her and how she surrendered to that conviction finally, wanting the boat to tip or swamp or founder and spare her the crushing wait, to get it over with. The sickening relief that followed on that betrayal as the weather passed over and he rowed safe into the cove. Calling Evered to shore and stripping his sodden clothes, sitting him naked before the fire with two fingers of rum. And she paused there on the cusp of what next had passed between herself and her brother.

She heard a rifle shot in the woods above the brook, the echo of it billowing over the cove. Evered had mentioned taking the boat out but when she stood to scan the coastline there was no sign of him. Off hunting some creature instead, she guessed.

"Some day out there it was, Martha," she said. And she went back to the garden work without saying anything more.

Hours later she sat beside the little grave and retold the story from the beginning and she faltered at the same place. "Now Martha," she said. She turned her reticence in the light as if it was a creature she'd just drawn up from the ocean depths on a hook, razor-scaled and whiskered and loathsome. And it struck her she hadn't revealed the first article of this one particular in all the years of talking to her sister, of presenting the freight and furnishings of her days in their mundane and gory detail. Her and Evered. Never once mentioned their wordless nighttime encounters, how she felt taken apart by them in the most unsettling, most provoking way. How nothing afterward seemed to fit in its proper order, as if she'd mislaid some essential element. All of it held behind a door that never opened a crack in Martha's imaginary presence.

And she had to turn away from her sister's grave.

Evered went down to the stagehead after Ada left for the farm garden. The boat sitting half-full of water and he untied the painter and led it along the side of the stage like an animal on a leash. When the keel brought up in the shallows he hauled it onto the landwash and tipped the water from the bilge. He'd planned to take it out to try for a few fish but the thought of being on the open ocean was making him feel qualmy and he left the boat lying face down on the rocks. He considered walking up to help Ada with the garden instead. But it seemed an imposition on her privacy to present himself unannounced. A thought so foolish and infuriating it made him want to go off into the woods and shoot something.

He collected the flintlock and powder horn from the tilt and headed toward the brook, following the bank into the trees. He walked three hours through the country without crossing the path of a living creature but for a lone grey jay he'd shot at early on and missed. He went as far as Second Pond and lit a fire in a shallow clearing, licked out and more distracted than when he'd started. His wet gear had chafed him raw and he took off his shirt and trousers and propped them up on birch sticks near the heat to dry the damp from the seams and creases. And sitting in his small clothes he tried to mollify the seethe in his head by bashing the Bishop, as Josephus Rex would have put it. Imagining Mrs. Brace naked among the sailors on the landwash, to avoid thinking of something other, each man taking a turn between the woman's legs. He rose up on his knees when he was ready and he came into the fire, his mettle spitting onto the coals. Falling to one side then like something shot, breathing hard, his legs quivering.

The fire was still burning high when he woke. He couldn't have drifted off more than a few minutes despite the dazed feeling he'd been asleep for hours. A sudden ridiculous conviction Ada was watching from the trees came over him and he covered himself, then walked to the pond to rinse his sullied hands. Wanting to bury his head in the water and clear his thoughts the same.

He was at a loss to account for it. He'd no intentions as they sat in their blankets beside the fire or when she leaned in to kiss his face. An echo of himself in the boat with the squall breaking relentless came over him, the same sense of impending ruin. And that compulsion had risen up in him as he bawled into Ada's neck, she repeating an old witches' phrase Mary Oram had taught her, sounding vaguely like a curse to his ears. The earth bearing upon him with all its might and main as the girl sat herself naked in his lap and they hasped together, mortar and pestle.

She'd been talking endlessly about Bungs since the sailors left the cove. Master Warren she called him, repeating his stories of ole Itchland and the exotic countries and alien people he'd encountered while at sea, as if she had some proprietary claim to them. But he could never bring himself to ask how she made that purchase. A blanket hung between the bunks all that stood between her and the cooper in the tilt. *A dirty puzzle* was what she'd been called and Evered had jumped the sailor who said so, wanting to kill the man for the slur. Because he couldn't but suspect it was true of her. That she was the same in her way as his own beastly self.

Evered was late coming in from the woods. Ada waited for him and served up their meals and they ate in silence. They poured their tea in the same quiet and afterward they shared a quiet glass of spruce beer from the dregs of Warren's brew before bed. The liquor was skunky and almost too foul to swallow even cut with a generous shot of rum but they persevered for the relief of the alcohol.

Ada said, "You was going out after a few fish today you said."

"Me outfit was still sopping from yesterday," he said. "Figured I could give myself long enough to dry out proper."

"You had no luck up in the woods."

"I had bad luck. Do that count for something?"

"Not for anything much, Brother," she said. "No."

They both smiled then, to see how hard the other was trying to hold to the old rhythms.

Evered looked into his mug. "This stuff is almost enough to choke you," he said. "I expects I'll have to try me hand at a fresh brew."

"I was thinking I'd go up for a few berries the week if the weather holds half-decent," Ada said.

He nodded. The sun had long set and the only light in the room was from the fire and Evered watched his sister in that darkling. Just able to make out her features though he could have touched her without moving from his seat. Her ebony ponytail only visible in motion, when she turned her head or tipped her face back to drain her mug. And he thought it was a genuine picture of Ada, that it was as true a sight as a person could hope to take of another in this life. That anything more was gossip and fairy tale, umbrage, wishful thinking.

"Sister," he said.

She looked across the little distance between their chairs. Seeing the same vague silhouette of her brother there, he realized.

"Did you ever?" he said. "You and Bungs?"

She stared down into her lap.

"Like Josephus Rex was saying?" he said.

She turned to face him and seemed about to answer. But she only watched him, her face too indistinct to reveal what she was thinking. She got up from her chair and went to the back of the room. He could hear her moving about behind him and moments later the ringing stream as she pissed into the slop pail. As if to say *There's your answer and may it serve thee.* The unhurried rustle of her undressing then and settling into her bunk.

He sat until the fire burned back and he banked the livid coals under ash and went to bed himself.

Ada made the pilgrimage to the berry hills in the morning. There was work still to be done at the farm garden but she was avoiding Martha in her little grave. As if all her unconscious prevarications were buried there now and could be ignored anew by keeping clear.

The berries were prolific and falling from the stems, some already touched by the early frost. Ada's hands stained red and black among the bushes, the long hours of picking tactile and repetitive and just consuming enough to make her feel she was absent any other concern. Her mind at the oars without pause all the same and the tumult crossed into her line of sight now and then, like the bear's tooth around her neck swinging free as she bent to the berries.

It was Evered's question about Bungs she was mucking through. There was nothing between herself and Warren to hide and still she suspected she was hiding something. In all her talk about his travels she'd never mentioned the *Lady Julia* or Nance Phair to Evered. She was being protective of the man, she thought. Though there was something other than the charitable at work in that oversight.

She was about to tell Evered that Warren wanted nothing more from her than innocent affection. And the same was true for her as far as she could spy it. But the truth lately seemed to stretch past the point where she could make out details with any clarity.

She knew what lay at the root of his asking. And she couldn't settle with any satisfaction how to feel about what happened between she and Evered, about how it unfolded or if it was all her doing somehow. It was never her intention to offer anything but comfort. Leaving her chair and taking Evered's face in her hands. The blanket falling behind her as she settled into his lap, as Mrs. Brace had straddled the unfamiliar man. That fact was not lost on her.

"Piss and corruption," she said aloud without pausing at the work.

The entire episode was a changeling creature, its appearance altogether different according to how it caught the light. It seemed all for Evered one moment, for love and pity's sake. The next Evered hardly figured in the equation and it was just herself at work, wanting to hold what she felt slipping through her fingers and clutching at the nearest thing within reach.

It seemed impossible she might have done the same with Warren or the Duke of Limbs or any one of the sailors on the landwash if circumstances presented themselves so. But she couldn't help thinking it would be foolhardy to make that claim for certain.

She straightened from the bushes, her fists in the small of her back to work through the ache there. She had inched her way into the heart of the clearing, the hillside a knee-deep pond of berries she stood at the middle of. She could pick through here for a month on end and still most of that bounty would go to rot on the bush. It was a notion that crossed her mind every fall but the thought made her furious suddenly. As if she'd lost patience with the circumstances she was born into, with the cockeyed rules that governed all things.

She started for the cove when the sun ticked toward late afternoon and the bone pendant from the Indian burial rose out of the ferment in her head as she walked. It was never far from her mind in the months after she'd gifted it to Captain Truss. But she knew it was more than a chance thought in the moment. It had been her one act of deliberate dishonesty in those years talking to Martha, keeping the stolen object from the ears of the innocent child. Because she was mortified to have taken it. Because she regretted wanting it in the first place and loved it with all her heart still. She knew now it was only herself she'd been lying to. But that seemed worse by far in the end.

Pleasure and shame. Shame and pleasure. These were the world's currencies. And it paid out both in equal measure.

Evered waited until Ada was gone across the brook on her way to the berry hills before he went down to the stage. He'd suggested rowing her over but she shook her head and offered some evasion about the walk doing her good. Both of them unsure if he would be able to face going out, dry clothes or no.

He climbed down the rails and untied the painter, set the oars. His hands shaking as he cleared the cove and turned toward the Wester Shoals. On the feral ocean aboard the little boat his father built and he was surprised to feel almost at ease once he passed over the skerries. At the mercy. But not entirely without assets or advantage, not altogether helpless.

He played out his lines and settled into the work with the reckless calm of someone who expects he might very well die young and fair play should it come to that. Nothing below the ocean's surface lay still for long and nothing upon it was much above a shadow. Vanity to think different of himself or his concerns and there was an unexpected edge of relief to the thought. As if it absolved him of all but the worst a man could descend to.

The cod were rarely plentiful this late in the season but they were fattened on a summer's feeding and he came in with a decent haul. Feeling lighter than he'd felt in months. He cleaned the fish at the splitting table and washed and salted the meat but for the fresh fillets he carried up to cook for himself and Ada.

He sat out on the rise to wait for her as the afternoon passed over, lifting a hand when she finally appeared on the far side of the brook with her brin sack of berries. But she was lost in her own thoughts. Even from that distance he could see the grave look about her, as if she laboured under the weight of something more than the bag she was carting home. It was a bearing he couldn't avoid feeling implicated in, a sight that erased whatever pardon he'd granted himself on the water. And he made his way inside before she marked him there.

They sat to their meal and talked through their days with a civility that belied the guarded distance they kept. They ate nearly half the berries Ada had picked, pouring a splash of rum over each bowlful. Lying on opposite sides of the blanket then and groaning through the surfeit of that annual indulgence, too full to turn on their sides, sated almost to nausea. Both relieved to be occupied by an animal misery without the slightest nuance or subtlety.

They passed three more days at the same occupations, heading in opposite directions as they left the tilt and spending the balance of their time apart. All the while inching away from the cloying intimacy of what had happened between them, hoping they might find something of their old selves on the far side of that circle.

There was a steady spell of rain then and for two days running they worked together at the farm garden in the cold fall, lugging the last of the vegetables down to the root cellar. Sitting at the fire in the evenings with their wrinkled slug feet bared to the heat, their boots and stockings steaming on the hearth.

On the third day Ada set about making jam of the hoard of berries. Evered poured out the last skunky dregs in Warren's puncheon and he put a mash on the boil and steeped spruce tea to brew a fresh batch of beer. They couldn't but see themselves in their parents' places as they went about the familiar tasks in that tiny space and they were wistful and hesitantly affectionate with each other. They tried recalling their mother and father with the odds and ends they held of them, bits of conversation, a handful of interactions that were blurring at the edges, and they were astonished by how little of those people was still in their possession.

It wasn't until Evered tried to dip a finger into a fresh pot of jam and Ada slapped at him with the spoon that their lost parents came alive for them, briefly, indelibly. He smiled at his sister who was ignoring him with the same casual menace their mother displayed at the outset of that ritual.

"I'll have a taste if I wants," he said.

"You values having two hands to work with," she said, "you'll keep your daddles clear of that pot."

He tried to reach past her and she smacked him across the knuckles again. "God's nails," he said. He shoved his hand into his armpit to tamp down the smart of it.

"I warned you, Brother."

He shouldered her away from the table suddenly and she had to fight to keep her feet, reaching to tie up his arms before he could touch the jam. "Off it, you dirty shag-bag," she said.

They wrestled around the kitchen space then, laughing at their own foolishness. Evered almost a foot taller than the girl and three stones above her in weight and he bore on her with all his might and main. Ada levelling herself against that advantage, the effort sucking the wind from her lungs. And the laughter drained out of them as they knocked against the furniture and the walls in a hissing knot of limbs, the two of them in a roke and the struggle suddenly gone serious. As if a reckoning was at hand for every unspoken resentment and slight and small betrayal ever to worm its way between them.

Ada wrenched an arm free and slapped Evered full across the face. He shook his head and bulled her into the shipwreck's door, pinning her against the wood with his hips, her eyes lifted level with his. Ada pitched forward to bite into his shoulder, Evered growling against the shock of it. He levered one hand high enough to grab her hair, hauling her mouth clear of his flesh. Staring at her, their noses almost touching. The red mark of Ada's slap like a scald across his cheek. "Now my little blowsabella," he said. He leaned in an inch and licked her chin without ever taking his eyes from hers.

"Don't," she said. She angled her face as far from his as she could manage. "Stop it."

"I'll have a taste of that jam," he said and he licked at her cheek and her bared ear.

She shook and wriggled and kicked in his grip until she exhausted herself and she went limp against the door.

"Brother," she said. "Please," she said.

There was a forlorn quiver in her voice that made him relent a little, stepping back just enough to let her drop. The moment her feet touched the floor she pushed off with every ounce of strength left in her and Evered fell backward, clinging to her as he went down, hauling her over with him. One arm came free as she careened onto the hearth and her hand plunged into the pot of boiling mash trying to keep herself clear of the fire.

The Scarred Arm. His Cross Fox.

She knew she was pregnant before she knew it.

Her body was a neighbour she'd cultivated only a nodding acquaintance with over the years, a creature she knew well but not intimately. She hadn't had her visitor since late in the summer and she expected its arrival all through the fall. Her breasts so tender she couldn't abide Evered's arm lying across her when they began sleeping in the same bed against the cold. Plagued by the irritable sense of anticipation that always preceded the first sign of blood though it went on for weeks without relief.

She spent much of that dark season alone, Evered off running the new iron traps once the snow settled in. He was away two and three days at a time depending on the weather and his luck, home only a single night before setting off again. Ada talked aloud to Martha through those solitary months, the illusion of conversation so familiar it was a comfort even if she'd given up the fantasy some invisible ear was taking it in.

She talked about her arm and how it was healing. About the furious wrestling match with Evered, the look on his face as he pinned her to the door, his bony little gaff pressed against her.

An unfamiliar twitch troubling his mouth. "It was like there was something I had belonged to him and he was going to have it," she said. Licking at her face to show he could. It was the only time in her life she'd been afraid of her brother, of what else he might do just to show he could. A sailor like the rest. She described pushing him onto his arse and being thrown toward the fireplace and how all of it passed over in the panic and horror that followed.

She talked about the weather and the state of the food supplies and the long separations when Evered was on the trapline, about the absence of her visitor and the persistent soreness of her breasts and the ache in her lower back, and when she ran dry of daily detail she retold Warren's sailing stories. It was just idle diversion, the sound of her own voice making the space feel that much more human. But at some point early in the new year it struck her she was no longer talking to her dead sister or to the empty air. That she was addressing another entity altogether. Keeping company with an animate listening creature.

"Now Martha," she said, a hand cupping the little pot of her belly. And then she stopped talking altogether.

A week later she woke to a migrant flicker in her stomach, a rippling agitation that she harboured but did not own. And she knew something momentous was upon her. Something so life-altering and incalculable that she turned all her resources to not seeing it as it came.

She wore her trousers without fastening them at the waist, holding them up with a belt of rope, blaming a surfeit of beaver meat for the distending spread. She was bunged up for days at a time and the beaver served as the culprit again. She suffered searing heartburn and swore off the black rum.

She was months at that tricky game, pretending not to know what she knew for a fact. She wished it all away with a religious fervour without allowing herself to name the specific thing she was wishing away. She covered her belly under the long woollen gansey when Evered spent nights at the tilt and she wore the sweater to bed, sleeping with her back to him. She wouldn't let his arm circle around, not wanting to arouse suspicions that would complicate the delicate balance of her own denial.

Ada had no clear idea what lay at the root of the event. She knew from listening to Sarah Best and Mary Oram talk there was some connection between pregnancy and the monthly bleeding, the onset of one cancelling the other though the how and why of it was a mystery. In the days before her mother died, after she'd been told about the visitor she should expect down there, Ada had taken advantage of the woman's candid turn to ask where babies come from.

"Sure you seen it," Sarah Best said. "With your own eyes."

"But where do they come from?" she said again.

"From heaven above I spose," her mother said. Though the forlorn sound of her made it hard to think she believed that.

As far as Ada could tell a mother's role was incidental at best, her body a passive vessel for the passing wildflower that was a child. The Virgin Mary had gotten her feet wet out picking berries and so fell pregnant with Jesus. It was a condition women caught like a fever or a cold, something that resulted from their own weakness or imprudence. Something vaguely shameful.

When Ada glassed back over the fall it was impossible to settle on one incident or other as the obvious cause. There was surrendering to the sight of Evered adrift in the squall, the primitive terror of watching that loss play out in slow motion as the cold rain soaked her to the bone. There was lying with him on the sand floor afterward when she felt something in herself come asunder. There was the injury to her arm, the vital shock of that scald setting her insides alight, the limb pulsing with a sullen ache that she dulled with medicinal prescriptions of callibogus.

Each was as likely as the others if genesis was as random and erratic as it seemed, the product of some innate abiding intent at the heart of chaos and chance.

Evered had never encountered anything quite like the iron traps, cold appetite mechanized with springs and trigger pans. He set the larger contraptions among the beaver houses above Third Pond in the slips kept clear of ice by the animals' steady traffic. The smaller he laid out along Black Bear River after fox but for two that he placed below otter slides into runs of open water. They were leg-hold traps and he set them deep enough that the beavers and otter drowned once they were taken but the fox were usually alive and watching as he came up to them. Pulling back to the limit of the stake chain without taking their eyes from him. Hauling to get clear of the iron jaw as he inched in with a wooden club, killing them by hand to save on shot and powder, to avoid ruining the pelt.

He was on the move the length of the winter to check the sets, spending more nights at the halfway tilt on Black Bear River than in the cove. Staying with Ada long enough to skin the animals he'd carted home and leaving the pelts to be cleaned and stretched by his sister when he went back to the woods. By the end of December they had seven fox, three otter and five beaver cured and ready for trade. Evered thought they might cover more than half the cost of the traps in their first season if their luck held. It made the notion of someday pulling even in the Beadle's ledger seem more than an irrational wish and their life on the shore less of a tenuous proposition. But it didn't offer him the comfort he would have expected to think so.

At the tilt he was attentive where Ada's ruined arm was concerned, doting on her in those first weeks when the flesh broke out in blisters and scales and leaked yellow crests of pus. He made a bread plaster with molasses and rum and cod-liver oil and applied the concoction to her arm, wrapping it all in a strand of linen. Every evening he removed and washed the bandage and soaked the arm in cool water. The scald was too painful to touch and they let it dry in the open air before he bundled it up again.

But there was a ripping undercurrent to their time together that made it feel like a sentence he was serving. Her scarred arm reminding him of how he'd pinned the girl to the door, licking at her face as if it was all a lark. Though he'd shed lark for another plumage altogether by the time he'd reined her in. Pulling her head back after she took a morsel of his shoulder between her teeth. Rutting against her, making sure she felt the swollen measure of that convincer. Until she said Brother, with that disarming quiver in her voice. Please, she'd said with her face turned to one side. And the next moment he was on the floor with Ada falling over him toward the fire.

He'd hauled her off the hearth as soon as he found his feet, dragging her to the water barrel to shove her livid arm into the cool, holding her there as the shakes overtook her. Oh Jesus Brother, she'd said, her eyes wide but seeing nothing. Oh Jesus.

He was too panicked to see it in the moment but those words came back to him on the trapline. His bare hands in the murderous cold of a beaver pond, his flesh as numb as the black iron as he set the trap below the surface. Thinking suddenly of Ada's arm in the water barrel, the skin coming over a raging red. That same blank look on the girl's face, the same words whispered as when they lay naked beside the fire in the wake of the squall that nearly drowned him. Her legs snared around his hips, urging him into her. Oh Jesus Brother. Oh Jesus.

He'd stopped seeing what he was doing and something levered the trigger pan, the jaws of the trap snapping up out of the pond like a nightmare creature and he fell back onto the snow, his face soaking wet, his heart hammering.

"God's nails," he whispered.

They shared a bunk when he stayed in the cove, neither willing to aggravate the surface calm by breaking their winter custom. But Evered was overly protective of the injured hand in the bed's intimate quarters. He woke with a start at intervals, afraid he might roll onto it or maul it accidentally. Or he woke to Ada shifting away from the weight of his arm as if the intimacy was causing her physical pain. Eventually she slept back-on to him, guarding against his tucking into her. They were both on alert when they were together, two creatures listening for footsteps at the door. And as the winter maundered on there was something increasingly secretive about her.

He couldn't blame his sister for the show of indifference. Admired it almost, the heartless cold brass of her.

———

He went out to take up the traps for the season in the middle of March. There had been rain off and on for weeks and the snow in the woods was soft and rotten which made for miserable travel. There was still ice on the ponds but he didn't trust it with his weight and skirted the shoreline instead.

He went up past Third Pond and hauled the beaver traps from the water and he walked them home across his back, the scrape and clank of iron sounding like a line of prisoners travelling in chains along the brook. He and Ada spent the evening cleaning and greasing the works with cod-liver oil and Evered hung them in the store. The next day he went up Black Bear River and stayed a night at the halfway tilt, then climbed the falls and walked on as far as the lake where he'd laid the highest of the fox traps. He backtracked down the river then, taking up each set as he came to it.

There was a cross fox in the trap just above the falls, a young bitch taken by the right forefoot. She'd been caught since he passed the set that morning and done a wild dance to the length of the stake chain in all directions, trampling the wet snow flat. She went still as he approached and he stopped a dozen yards shy of the chain's perimeter, laying aside the two traps he was carting and his rifle and shot bag and powder horn. She had already started gnawing at the mud-black foreleg, a ring of raw flesh showing above the iron. He loosed the cudgel from where it was tied at his waist and stepped slowly toward her.

The leg was taken at the first joint and from its crooked angle looked to be broken. He thought she might slip clear yet and he didn't want to panic the animal more than necessary. She limped left and right before backing away from him, dragging the trap as far as the stake chain would allow. She stood still there, her flanks heaving. He crouched toward her with his arms spread wide and she turned her face away in an oddly human fashion, watching him with one yellow eye as he raised the club. She gave a single yip and hauled against the iron, wrenching the ruined paw clear as he swung. He lunged at her, grabbing uselessly at the tail as he fell, the fox gone as quick as that on her three good legs into the bush and Evered left on his hands and knees in the wet snow.

He knelt back on his haunches. "Fair play," he said aloud. "Fair play, Missus Fox." He stayed there a while collecting himself before he got to his feet. He took up the set and knocked it clear of snow and hauled the stake, feeling foolish in a way that was familiar to him though it had been years since it came over him so sharply. That he was just a youngster playing at being a man.

It was hours back to the tilt and past dark when he arrived but he hadn't quite outwalked that old doubt. It hissed and spit in his stomach as he ate his supper and as he sat with a glass of callibogus before the fire in the evening. He told his sister the story of coming upon the fox, its desperate hauling to break clear and his stupid lunge and fall into the snow as it disappeared into the bush. Laughing at himself, hoping he might dout that smoulder by pissing on it.

"She got the better of me," he said.

Ada seemed barely to be listening to him, hove off at an awkward angle in her chair. Lately fallen into flesh he thought, from all the fresh meat they'd become accustomed to eating.

"Missus Fox is having a grand laugh for herself now I'd say."

"Her leg is broke," Ada said.

"I expect so. She wouldn't have managed to slip free if it wouldn't."

"She'll starve to death then."

He looked across at Ada, surprised. He could see a play across her face in the dim light as if she was about to cry or laugh and trying all she could to keep it at bay. She pushed herself up from the chair and walked awkwardly by him toward the bunks. And she laid her scarred hand on his shoulder as she went past.

Whether she meant him to draw a connection he couldn't guess. But he saw her again pinned to the door and twisting in his grip. Her face turned to one side as he leaned in. Brother, she'd said. Please. The quiver in her voice setting him back an inch and Ada breaking wild for the open the second he relented.

And another thought dredged into the light behind it, a dark little facet he'd never set eyes on before. Ada sitting naked in his lap, kissing his face to comfort him. Evered bawling into her shoulder and the urge rising up out of that stew as unexpected and as feral as the storm he thought would be his end. Ada's hips rising to meet his. He never doubted her inclination, then or since. But he saw now that was too clean and simple to be the whole truth of a thing.

If he'd been mistaken when he lifted her from the chair and laid her naked on the floor? He would have relented, he was almost certain. But he'd lost sight of the girl in the moment. Ada. His sister.

If she'd said Brother Please with that self-same tremor in her voice, it would have brought him to his bearings. In all likelihood. Though everything thirty or forty paces ahead was suddenly shapeless and indistinct and he couldn't swear it was so without lying to himself. Ada was moving about behind him, settling into the bunk. And he sat there until the fire burned back and he was sure she was asleep. Less certain of himself with each passing moment. He went out the door and walked up to the store and he spent the rest of the night there, lying cold and comfortless on the dirt floor.

He came down to the tilt in the early morning and lit the fire and set the kettle to boil. Ada waking to the noise.

"You're up early," she said from the darkness at the back of the room.

"Ada," he said. He didn't turn his head from the fire. "I was thinking," he said. "Perhaps I might shift over to Mockbeggar with *The Hope* come the spring."

After a minute she said, "If you says so."

"It might be a better chance at things," he said. "For you and me both if it suits you to come. You might," he said. "I don't know. There's men galore over there looking to marry. You'd have your pick of the lot."

"If you says so," she said again.

And he set about making their breakfast with no idea what she thought of the notion.

The Last Hope. The Scarred Arm.

By the beginning of May Ada couldn't make her way into the trousers, her belly protuberant and riding so low she wasn't able to work the waist halfway up her behind.

She'd hidden her mother's dress under one of the wood-shaving mattresses after Mrs. Brace questioned her about it and she knelt at the bedside to retrieve the article. Stood holding it at arm's length. She'd expected it to be sizes too large and was surprised to see it a little small for her frame. She had a flash of her mother throwing the skirt down over her legs after Mary Oram removed her stitches, of her vow to drown herself in the cove to be clear of it all. How much like a stranger she'd seemed in that moment. Though it occurred to Ada now the stranger might have been Sarah Best stepping forward to speak her mind true. That the years of reticence while the world inflicted itself upon her might have been the false view. Even the woman's winded laughter as she tried to fight off their father at the hearth might have been a mask for all Ada knew.

She pulled the dress over her head and tugged the skirt down around the expanse of her stomach. She picked at the

shoulders to adjust the snug fit. Slid one hand into the front
pocket, her fingers closing around the knotted string Mary
Oram had given her mother those years ago. She turned the
relic over in her palm, thinking it was too late to do either of
them any good now. And she set it back where she'd found it.

She went to the window and opened the shingle far enough
she could see Evered on the landwash, picking at some incon-
sequential job. Killing time away from her. They hadn't spoken
of leaving the cove since that single conversation but her
brother was already gone, she thought, abandoning her to the
endless line of men waiting on a wife in Mockbeggar. He slept
on his own each night and made no move to rind longers for
the stage or mend nets or haul seaweed up to the farm garden.
Biding for *The Hope*'s arrival.

She didn't know what to blame for the sudden change
but the burgeoning evidence of the child she carried. Evered
wouldn't look at her directly or sit evenings in her company
and it was his turning away that forced Ada to acknowledge
the fact finally. She was pregnant and Evered was shunning her.
Her gravid profile like a bell rung by lepers in the Holy Lands
to warn away the unafflicted.

When the sight of her brother began filming over with tears
she pulled the shutter closed, took as deep a breath as she could
manage. Got on to making something for their dinner, talking
aloud to the child as she went about the work.

She'd found her way back to those one-sided conversations as
a last defence against the poisonous solitude of her life. She wondered if it was possible the baby might not come, if she might
carry it indefinitely and never suffer being alone again. She had
no way of knowing if choice played a role in such a thing. Her

mother had threatened to cut the child out with a fish knife if its arrival was delayed. Ada hadn't reached that level of distress but it was near enough she could make it out with her naked eye.

The baby seemed no more contented than she was and it rolled and shifted and kicked within its constricted domain. "Now Martha," she said as the child struggled for purchase, "settle in." She thought of the baby as a girl and thought of the girl as Martha. She had one hand always supporting some part of her weight and she could make out an elbow or a knee pushing against her, the crown of the head or a foot grazing her palm through that nebula of flesh.

She was standing at the hearth with one hand to her belly when Evered came through the door. He stopped still when he saw Ada there in their mother's dress, the skirt tented out by her stomach. His face going pale at the sight of that ghost from the last days of his childhood.

"Brother," she said.

They ate without speaking. Evered trying to come to grips with the fact of Ada's condition. She is with child, he thought. He had even less a notion than his sister as to how such a thing might come to pass, of what paternity entailed. He was Sennet Best's youngster in the same fashion that the boat he used was Sennet's boat. What fatherhood signified beyond a proprietary connection to the mother he'd never been told and he assumed the baby was John Warren's. Josephus Rex as much as said Bungs had taken Ada as a wife in some fashion. And that was as close as Evered could come to making sense of the staggering turn of events.

He tried not to look at Ada or at her belly but it was impossible to ignore now that he saw it for what it was. The thin material of the dress pulled taut over that full moon. And a figure passed across the face of it as he stared, the baby somersaulting languidly in the womb, Ada's stomach dipping and shifting as the hidden life turned beneath it. He looked up at his sister, her eyes likewise wide and terrified.

"If she comes before *The Hope*," Ada said, "you'll have to help me."

The hair stood up at the back of his neck. "Help you how?"

She started crying and shook her head. "I don't know," she said.

They waited then, marking the anxious interminate days of that plodding race. They had a vague notion of when they might expect *The Hope* but the time of the child's arrival was a riddle to them both and there were weeks still when that event could descend upon them while they were alone on the shore.

Ada slept only in snatches of two and three hours at a time, too uncomfortable to lay in one position longer. She dreamt often of Mary Oram, of sitting at the strange woman's deathbed while she spoke endlessly and aimlessly about the world. Her colourful knitted cap on her head and her childlike hands gripping the edge of the blanket.

Who is it was the father? the dream woman asked her. One of them sailors on the landwash, she said without waiting for an answer. Or that Labrador man who come through, she said, he was a randy old fecker, that one. Mary Oram pointed a nailless finger at Ada. You soaked your feet out picking berries, she said before drifting to some unrelated topic.

The substance of the woman's monologues was specific and clear while Ada slept but little remained of them when she woke beyond a vague feeling of blessing or unease. A word here or there. A finger pointed from the bed in a gesture that might have been accusatory or conspiratorial.

It idn't much, the woman announced from her imaginary deathbed. A life, she said. I put more into it than twas worth in the end. Mary Oram nodded across at Ada. She said, I expect mine was much like everyone else's in that particular.

Evered worked outside as much as he could through the month of May, stringing out one job or another to pass the days, packing up the few materials in the store that would accompany them when they left the cove. Though he never strayed further than a shout from the tilt. As they crept up on time for the caplin scull he started to think they might make it through to *The Hope*, that he would be spared delivering Ada's child. He remembered raking out the sand floor of the tilt after Martha was born, the miry dregs of it, the astonishing volume of gore, and he had little desire to stand at the centre of whatever gruesome operation had produced that mess.

But it was the intimacy of the process he had no stomach for. He couldn't bring himself to revisit the questions that came up the day he lost the cross fox for fear the answers would be less ambiguous and more damning. Just being in Ada's company stirred up the boggy shame that had picked at him ever since. The thought of facing his sister as the baby came into the world through whatever unlikely entrance was available made Evered feel lightheaded and faint. Deliverance was what he wished for and it was only *The Hope* that promised it.

It fell on them suddenly in the first week of June, Ada waking to cramps and her water breaking as she hauled herself up ungainly and breathless from the bunk.

"Brother," she said. She shook him by the shoulder. "Evered."

"What is it?"

"I think it's time," she said.

He sat bolt upright. "Jesus, Sister," he said.

A contraction buckled through her and Ada leaned over Evered in the bed, pressing her forehead against his shoulder.

"Jesus, Sister," he said again.

Ada stood up straight and gulped buckets of air into her chest as the pain subsided, the relief so unexpected and complete she felt expansive, beneficent. She reached to touch Evered's face. It was dim enough they couldn't see but the barest outline of the other's features. As if they were children again, waking partway through the night and grateful for the other's company in that dark encircling wood. He nuzzled into her palm, into the foreign, familiar smell of her skin. He said, "You sure you can't hold out till *The Hope*?"

She laughed then as if he was making a joke of the desperate circumstances and he added his own panicked laugh to hers.

"We should light a fire," she said and Evered clambered past her to knock around at the hearth while Ada paced the tiny room.

"I was just dreaming about Mary Oram," she said to him.

"You was?"

"She was dead," Ada said. "Lying on her deathbed and gone," she said. "But still talking away to me."

"That sounds like Mary Oram all right," he said.

He set a handful of shovies over yesterday's coals and blew up a flame, set kindling crosswise over the new fire. He turned to look at his sister in that inky light. Surprised by the inhuman size of her belly showing through her small clothes. Terrified for the girl.

He said, "What did Mary Oram have to say for herself?"

"Just old foolishness," she said. "I don't remember a word of it. But for one thing she said the last going off."

"What was that then?"

Ada pointed her finger as the dead woman had in her dream. "A body must bear what can't be helped," she said.

Brother and sister watched each other then until Ada was crippled up by another contraction, leaning on a chair back to keep from falling where she stood. At the tail end of it she said, "You'll want to boil plenty of water." She had straightened from the chair but was talking through her teeth. "And you'll want a knife close to hand."

"Jesus, Sister," he said.

She walked her way into daylight, leaning on Evered's arm as they circled, stopping only to wait out the iron clamp of the contractions. It was a violence so ruthless that Evered stood the window open and looked out at the ocean while the pain worked at the girl, to avoid the sight of Ada in the throes, for the mindless relief of that expanse.

Mid-morning he spotted a vessel on the horizon as Ada dug her nails into his arm, the girl bent double at his side. The speck too distant to identify though he knew it could be nothing other.

"That's *The Hope* coming now," he said as Ada caught her breath.

And for a moment he thought he might be spared yet, that the ship might haul up to the holding ground before the baby announced itself and he could pass off the duty to the Beadle or some other unlucky soul on the crew.

He had a rag in his free hand and he wiped the sweat from Ada's neck.

"You think there might be someone," she said. "Over to Mockbeggar," she said. "Might teach me to read?"

"I couldn't say for certain," he said. He was confounded to see her occupied by such a trifle but desperate to ease her distress, to feel himself useful. "I expects they got whatever it is you wants over there," he said.

And she nodded without glancing up from the floor.

Evered had given no real thought to what would become of them in Mockbeggar other than escape from their present circumstances. It still seemed a kind of fairy-tale destination and he couldn't picture their lives transmogrified body and baggage into that improbable landscape. When it entered his head at all he was most concerned with what those strangers would make of them, brother and sister and the unborn child. How they would be talked about.

He was still rattled by the tale of the murderous brother who married the Irish servant girl somewhere on the shore. There was nothing to speak to its authenticity beyond the authority with which it was related. But when he picked through the few facts he knew of his parents' marriage and who was buried at the farm garden he was forced to admit one story served as well as the other. He had only his father's word on the drowned

sailor with the eyes eaten from their sockets. And there was
Ada's question about half-blind Sennet Best teaching his son
the distant catalogue of shore marks. Nothing conclusive enough
to sway the ambivalent and it seemed plainly impossible to
Evered still. Only his own feral instincts sowed a doubt about
what his father might have been capable of in the long-ago and
stopped him dismissing it altogether.

He couldn't decide whether it bothered him most to think
the sailors' tale might be true or to think it was specious in
every detail and passed around as God's word regardless. The
death of a horse is the life of a crow and a story was a rank scav-
enger from all he could tell, feeding on rumour and innuendo
and naked confabulation where the truth was too nimble to
chase down or too tough to chew. And making no distinction
between one meal and the other.

He couldn't know what fables had already attached themselves to he and Ada beyond the cove but he didn't doubt some
would be false in every particular. Even the credible few would
never manage to say the half of things, would never set them
down full and entire. And that lack would make little difference to how often they were told or how far they travelled in
the world. It reminded him of how it felt to see his family
splayed and picked over in the Beadle's book, names and dates
and fate. Helpless and oddly lonely. As if his life was not his
own somehow.

It was how he felt now, tracing a shuffling loop the length of
the tilt with Ada crippled and suffering on his arm. Evered
marked *The Hope*'s progress each time they turned near the open
window, though the vessel was still hours from the cove when
Ada stopped still to say, "I think it's time I lies down, Brother."

He looked into her face, not comprehending.

"On the bed," she said.

He nodded though his expression didn't change. "I don't know what to do," he said. "What do I do?"

"Just don't leave me," she said.

The last stretch yawed past in a breakneck slow-motion tumult. Evered lit the lamp against the gloom in the far end of the tilt and he laid out the rags he'd boiled and the splitting knife and he brought a pan of hot water from the hearth. Ada lay on her back with her shift pushed up over her massive belly, a ragged net of veins spidering across that pale distressed surface. He knelt between her naked thighs as she instructed, his eyes stinging with the cold sweat dripping from his forehead. Ada rising up off the bed with each contraction, one following on another without relief.

"Is anything happening?" she asked at intervals.

"I don't know, Sister," he said.

For the longest time it seemed nothing was. But eventually he could mark how she was being prised open like the jaws of a trap levered wide by a set screw. It was rupture he was witnessing, an uprooting, the unnatural sound of it in Ada's mouth so tormented that his head rang like he'd been beaten across the ears.

When the baby's crown finally appeared he nearly fainted, stars drifting across his sight. "There it is," he said. And the words weren't out of his mouth before it disappeared again.

"Is she coming?" Ada asked.

"Yes," he said. "No. I don't know."

That appalling dance went on a while, the top of the head showing a little ways into the open before it was swallowed up again as each contraction subsided. It seemed to Evered it might go on that way indefinitely, that it might kill his sister to carry on with the exertion. She was lying flat on her back and panting in shallow gasps like a creature shot and mortally wounded.

He stood up to lean over her face. "Ada," he said. "You got to get that youngster out."

She shook her head and started to weep. "I'm trying all I can."

"Sister," he said, a forlorn quiver in his voice. "Please," he said.

She looked at him above her and she rose up on her elbows as if hauled aloft by a rope and she bore down with what felt to her like the last grain of her earthly resources. And the baby's head came free of a sudden, eyes and ears and nose and chin, a ruffle of blood flowing around the tiny neck.

"Oh Jesus, Sister," he said.

The tiny shoulders canted clear one at a time and seconds later the darkly mucid infant was in his lap and bawling all she was worth.

Ada instructed him to cut the cord with the knife and when that was done she told him to tie it off but he hadn't left himself length enough to manage it. She asked him to hand up their mother's dress and she spent a long time picking at the material in her exhausted state, trying to find the front pocket and then to fish out the string she'd found there. She passed it along to Evered finally and he undid the line of knots and tied the cord off with that.

He set the infant in the pan and scooped handfuls of water over the pale skin to wash away the mire and blood with which she'd been anointed during her arrival. He said, "It's a girl, Sister."

"I knows it's a girl," Ada said. "Martha her name is."

Evered nodded over that without questioning how she knew what she knew. "Some set of lungs on her," he said.

"Is she all right?" Ada asked, too drained to lift her head or hold her eyes open. "Have she got everything? Fingers and toes?"

Evered took up the baby's feet and counted, and then each hand in turn.

"Evered," Ada said, a note of panic creeping into her voice.

"Yes, girl," he said, stalling. The left hand and arm was stunted, not half the size of the right, and there was a livid birthmark like a burn across the back. The hand had all its digits but there was a translucent web of skin between the fingers up to the second knuckle. For all their years in Mockbeggar the girl's disfigurement would be put down to Ada's accident at the hearth while she was in utero, the shock of the scald scarring her arm as it did her mother's. No one they encountered there ever doubted the plain fact and Martha would always be regarded with a mix of shy suspicion and awe because of it. Evered couldn't avoid seeing the blemished skin and webbed fingers as his unwitting mark upon the girl and the deformity bound him to the child from the moment he laid eyes on it.

"There's something wrong with her," Ada said and she tried to struggle up. "What is it?" she said.

Evered set a hand to her shoulder. "I'll look out to her," he said.

He laid the infant on a clean strip of cloth and wrapped her tight. Staring down into the child's face, her eyes open but adrift and looking through him, not quite anchored yet to the world she'd entered.

"Now Little Bungs," he whispered.

He would never call her by any other name and she would know him only as Uncle. He lifted the nearly weightless bundle and placed the girl on her mother's belly.

"There you are now," he said.

Ada looked down at her daughter. "She's all right then."

"She's handy about perfect," he said.

ACKNOWLEDGEMENTS

I'm grateful for the financial and moral support of the Canada Council for the Arts and the Writers' Trust of Canada.

Thanks to *The Innocents'* first readers/provocateurs/advocates—Martha Kanya-Forstner and Melanie Tutino @ Doubleday Canada; Lee Boudreaux @ Doubleday US; Shaun Oakey; Martha Webb @ CookeMcDermid; Julie Barer @ The Book Group; Holly Hogan @ sea.

*

A couple of characters in the novel bear a striking resemblance to historical figures. Most of the experiences and opinions of Captain Truss and John Warren were pilfered from *Captain Cartwright and his Labrador Journal* and *The Life and Adventures of John Nicol, Mariner* respectively. Some of their stories and conversation have been lifted more or less verbatim from those real-life antecedents. But I have changed more than just the names to suit the story.

Other incidents and notions were transmogrified from Bruce Whiffen's history of Bonavista, *Prime Berth*; Barbara Reiti's *Making Witches: Newfoundland Traditions of Spells and Counterspells*; and *Outrageous Seas: Shipwreck and Survival in the Waters off Newfoundland, 1583-1893*.

I was re-reading *The Selected Short Fiction of Lisa Moore* while writing this novel and Ms. Moore may find a moment or two here strangely familiar. Details from conversations with Mark Ferguson and Zita Cobb also made their way into the book. Francis Grose's 1785 *Dictionary of the Vulgar Tongue* helped with the flash lingo. *The Dictionary of Newfoundland English* has been a long-time source of inspiration and information. This book would be a different and lesser thing without it.

*

Thanks again and always to Holly Ann. To Arielle, Robin and Ben. And to Mike Basha. My life would be a different and far lesser thing without you crowd.

*

Mary Bridget Fitzgerald (1943-2018)